Praise for *This Far Isn't*

"It is not surprising that Lynn Sloan was a portrait photographer, nor that she has turned to fiction writing. Her bent is an exploration of the truths of the human heart, and this collection demonstrates her remarkable gift for it. Possessing hugely different personalities and backgrounds, the characters are compelling, even those with small roles in the stories. Sloan is inventive and fearless in the situations in which she places her protagonists, and the results are painful, sometimes funny, and always illuminating. In every story her continual flashes of insight, so precisely rendered, remind us again and again how heartbreaking in all its complexities is the human dilemma."

—Sharon Solwitz, author of *Once, in Lourdes: A Novel, Blood and Milk: Stories,* and *Bloody Mary: A Novel*

"…intelligent, beautiful storytelling. Lynn Sloan's stories exhibit a worldliness not often seen in fiction, focusing on characters who illuminate the complexities of modern life through brilliant allegory. She has a superb eye for detail and nuance…. Sloan's world is one of poverty and wealth, art and the quotidian, love and remorse, and in these apparent paradoxes she offers fascinating insights to the human soul. What a pleasure it is to read…"

—Joe Ponepinto, author of *Mr. Neutron*

"Sloan's characters are rendered with sensitive and realistic detail throughout.

—*Kirkus Reviews*

"The stories in Sloan's collection are tragedies that nearly break your heart, or often do…Though the underlying theme seem to be the same across stories, Sloan does a superb job of diversifying her characters and setting each scene on a new and fresh stage....Every one of Sloan's characters is a monument to "what if" and "if only" . . .[and] remind us to...live fully in what you have, and to cherish everything without the "if.""

—*Centered on Books*

"...engaging.... Reflecting Sloan's acute attention to humanity, her characters are varied and have depths that make them individuals I can care about.... The book leaves a flavor that lingers—not sweetness, but the mineral clarity of a deep well. It's a satisfying swig of human longing and learning."

—*Story Circle Book Reviews*

"... exceptional stories by a talented writer who understands that emotions are sometimes indefinable and conflicting, that facing adversity can require more than just courage, and that human feeling is complex and intricate. ... a layered exploration of both human weakness and strength. ..."

—*Windy City Reviews*

Praise for *Principles of Navigation*

"…a tender, thoughtful story of a couple whose once happy marriage dissolves amidst the stress of infertility and infidelity—and unmet expectations…quietly compelling. It is by no means a heart-pounding page-turner, but it is a page-turner nonetheless, a subtle story that gnaws and needles long after the cover is closed."
—*Chicago Book Review*

"… moving and vivid….unforgettable."
—Sharon Darrow, author of *The Painters of Lexieville* and *Trash*

"…fascinating and gripping."
—*Centered on Books*

"[A]n absorbing, poignant novel that artfully distills the many ways in which love can fail us—yet also take us by surprise when we need it most."
—Katherine Shonk, author of *Happy Now?* and *The Red Passport*

"…an annunciation, a miracle,…this novel of generation, of stasis, and of transformation."
—*Newcity*

"I wanted to turn the page—no, I needed to turn the page. The payoff at the end made me glad that I did."
—*The Collagist*

"…a hauntingly beautiful tale…"
—*Booksie's Blog*

"...this is a book which reeled me in slowly.... Any writer who can keep me thinking of their characters even after I have finished reading their story, is an author I can highly recommend. If you love literary fiction, do yourself a favor and pick up a copy of *Principles of Navigation* – I promise you won't be disappointed."
—*Caribou's Mom*

"Beneath their outwardly conventional surfaces, both wife and husband reckon with realities darker and deeper and wilder than they had grown up to expect. For its psychological acuity and for its narrative grace, *Principles of Navigation* is at once deeply satisfying and unsettling."
—Richard Hawley, author of *The Headmaster's Papers*, *The Headmaster's Wife*, and *The Other World*.

Sloan pushes back against stereotypes of gender and familial life, making a claim to a new and urgent sense of the domestic."
—*Necessary Fiction*

"Select this for your book club and enjoy discussing the unexpected twists and turns that lead to the evolving image of an unconventional family."
—*Hungry for Good Books*

Midstream

A Novel

Lynn Sloan

Fomite

Burlington, VT

ISBN-13: 978-1-953236-66-1
Library of Congress Control Number: 2022934402
Fomite
58 Peru Street
Burlington, VT 05401
08-16-2022

For Jeff, always

Acknowledgments

Everyone knows that writing is a solitary business, but a writer doesn't spring full blown into the world all by herself, doesn't learn what writing involves in isolation, or complete a manuscript without the help of others, and that manuscript doesn't appear on bookshelves and digital devices without the vision and commitment, craft and hard work of a publishing team.

To the team at Fomite, Marc Estrin and Donna Bister, a remarkable, talented duo, dedicated to producing books that reflect on what it means to be human, thank you. For your support of my work, your sharp eye, insights, wit, and kindness, and for the high level of standards you set for the press and for your authors, I am grateful.

Thanks to my parents who loved reading and started me off by handing me the funny papers on Sunday mornings. Thanks to my grandmothers, great storytellers all, who believed that the everyday doings of friends and family, what some might call gossip, were as full of drama and import as the doings of the "great gods on high," as my Southern Baptist grandmother would say. Thanks for teaching me that the small and the large in life are not just interconnected, they are often the same.

Thanks to Fred Shafer, who long ago taught me the rudiments of story writing, and who continues to inspire me. For Fred as my teacher, mentor, and friend, I am grateful.

Thanks to my wonderful writing group, Writers Bridge. Julie Justicz, Jan English Leary, Arlene Brimer Mailing, and Mary Beth Shaffer—your patience reading draft after draft, your probing questions, and your marvelous laughter mean more than I can say. Where would I be without you?

To Jeff, my husband, for his willingness to keep reading, and for his sustaining love, I am thankful beyond words.

1

May, 1974

IT DIDN'T FEEL LIKE TUESDAY. Tuesdays were the worst. Terrible Tuesday they called them in private, TT for short. First thing on Tuesday morning their boss would gather them all, "her staff," "her minions" as they joked, for their weekly meeting where corporate standards of performance were enforced and eager submissiveness was the only allowable response. The doublespeak, the layers of subtext, the pretend enthusiasm, the barely concealed jockeying for advantage, Polly still wasn't used to it. But none of this mattered today. After work, she would meet Eugenia—it had been more than a year—and Polly was happy as she stepped from the Michigan Avenue bus and lifted her face to the May sun. The Technicolor sky was dotted with whipped cream clouds, the air was soft, light sparked off the surrounding high rises, and later she was going to meet her oldest and best friend. She maneuvered into the swarming crowd on the Plaza and was caught up in a scene that could be the jazzy opening of a movie directed by Godard or Claude Chabrol. If she were directing, high on top of the Tribune Tower, a pigeon with a tiny camera strapped to its chest, not one of the nuisance Plaza pests, but one of those legendary, early twentieth century homing pigeons, would pick her out of the hordes streaming toward the skyscrapers and swoop down to film her as she dodged around the man shouldering out of his trench coat, past the tourists grappling with a map, excuse-me-ed by the wall of sign-waving war protesters, and follow her as she swerved into the slipstream flowing toward the Mandel Building. She was on a mission and she was surrounded by extras, everyone smelling nice from their morning showers, the men clean-shaven, the women crisply dressed, like her, high heels clicking, skirts swishing, everything fresh and full of possibilities, a breeze fluttering the leaves of the planter trees, the rush of street traffic, horns tooting.

In front of her the mob parted for some ragtag feminists who waved hand-painted signs as they shouted for the women heading into the office towers to cast off the shackles of employment and join them. "Equal Pay for Equal Work," "69¢ on the $," "A Woman needs a Man like a Fish needs a Bicycle." The camera stayed on Polly. She framed a cool, but sympathetic smile. Maybe, her smile said, if she were younger, just out of college, not thirty-four. With invisible per-istaltic action, the crowd pushed the libbers through, then surged forward. Clanging rang out. Everyone stopped. The pigeon's camera tipped up to discover a window-washing scaffold rising up the concrete and glass honeycombed façade of her building, then jarring to a stop. The scaffold tilted. She gasped, the crowd gasped, the men onboard struggled. The crowd held its collective breath as the platform tipped and banged against the building. When it was righted and resumed its climb, the crowd's breath eased, Polly exhaled, and everyone funneled toward the revolving doors. She tucked close her bag holding her new, pretty blouse for the evening, and Eugenia's letter. Earlier a closeup of her bag should have been inserted somewhere along the way, maybe when she got off the bus, maybe as a cutaway when the feminists slowed things down, or now, as she clamped it secure. The crowd pushed her forward. When the revolving door caught her and spun her into the lobby, the long take ended. She was no longer the heroine, director, and camera-operator, but one of many late workers pressing toward the elevators. From the boy passing out freebies of the *Chicago Tribune*, she grabbed a copy.

Getting off on fourteen, she faced the expanse of gray carpet, the immense reception counter made of some rare Brazilian wood, and the imperial logo of Encyclopaedia Britannica, and felt her usual ping of disbelief—this was where she'd ended up.

"Good morning, Milly," she said to the receptionist.

"Aren't you late?"

"Not intentionally."

The smooth elevators, the fancy décor, the hush—even after two years, this still felt surprising. Before, she had worked for industrial film production houses on the seedy west side, in offices with worn linoleum, grimy walls, and beat-up furniture—any extra funds went for new equipment, not thick carpet and expensive wood—and the pay, or at least her pay, had been miserable. Now she was a picture editor in the Illustrations Department of Encyclopaedia Britannica, a position that sounded more elevated than it was, and it paid well. She nodded to the new old guy in the mailroom—suspenders?—and rounded the corner into her department. Only the British would call "pictures" "illustrations."

She was lucky to have this job. *Damn straight lucky*, Bob said.

The other picture editors were already wending their way through the common area of worktables to the boss's office. Next to Polly's cubicle stood Janine Costain, senior picture editor, cartoonishly tapping her watch.

"I need to find my list," Polly said.

"The Queen will hand you your head on a platter, if she starts without you."

To Janine retreating, Polly called out, "I'll be there in a minute," and dropped the newspaper on her desk. Later she would see if Bob had a front page story. And she was lucky to have a cool reporter boyfriend, even if he was a million miles away in Saigon covering the endgame of the losing war.

She changed into flats, kicked her heels under her desk, opened her lower drawer to stow her purse, and paused to pull out Eugenia's envelope and the stained coaster from O'Toole's, their hangout in their post-college years. Why had Eugenia sent this? Or saved it? On the border, Polly had written, *I will be a filmmaker, making important documentaries about the film Greats.* On the reverse, *I will not be a fertile protozoon in the slumbering gene pool.* She had been drunk, *slumbering gene pool* her clever way of saying she wouldn't give up her ambitions to have kids. She hadn't become a filmmaker, not come close. She flipped the coaster across her desk blotter, arranged her agreeable work face, and found her Active folder.

When she arrived, the others had taken their seats on the velvet couch and chairs gathered around the coffee table that held a jiggly porcelain tea set, and the Queen, Vanessa Bartholomew, Chief of Illustrations—the same dark, stiff hairdo as the real HRH, but without her warmth—was at her desk talking on the phone, so Polly was not officially late.

Janine had saved her a place on the couch. Whispering thanks, Polly squeezed in, careful not to knock the coffee table. The Queen's tea set was a test: if you rattled it, you failed. Outside the floor-to-ceiling windows behind the empty chair that Vanessa would take, thick metal cables silently slapped the glass as the window washers rose into view, their blue jumpsuits puffy with wind. The platform stopped level with the window frame, and the men began swabbing their soapy brushes over the glass, apparently not terrified.

The Queen rose and everyone, the eight women and Hank Edmonds, said good morning in almost unison, like in first grade. Vanessa sat in the wingback chair and smoothed her tweed skirt that was too hot for this May day. In her impeccable British accent, she thanked everyone for coming. As if they had a choice. Janine nudged Polly's foot.

"Now, Janine," Vanessa cleared her throat, "if you will, give us an update."

"I have excellent photos for Butterflies of South America, a Blue Morpho and a Cloudless Sulphur, both in outstanding color, and I'm waiting for South Kensington's packet, promised three days ago, for African Butterflies. Everything else is at early stages."

Janine was always prepared, always modest, always smug.

"Hank?" Vanessa's voice went soft when she addressed Hank.

"Lift bridges will be on your desk by end of day. I'm collecting for Pendulum Action. Art sent back the photo for Colonial Williamsburg. They want a historic street plan instead."

Vanessa raised an eyebrow. She did not approve of Art sending back an illustration she'd okayed. "Ellen?"

Ellen detailed where she was with Geography of South Asia, almost complete, then Irene, who could never look directly at Vanessa, muttered that she was still hoping to find line drawings for Minting Money. Tina reported on her biographies. Vanessa called on each editor in turn. Polly would be last. Even with more than two years at EB, she was the most junior, the "most minion-y," as Tina said, so she got the worst assignments, which meant each Tuesday, she had the most incompletes to report. When Polly was up, Hank would blink extra-slow to express his disdain, and those not in the Queen's line of sight would mouth, "TT." Polly didn't bother to complain their jibes were getting old. Tonight she would ask Eugenia why poems about May featured flowering buds, lovers, and youth's evanescence, but never corporate meetings?

When Polly had interviewed for this job after being unemployed for more than a year during her mother's recovery, what she knew about Encyclopaedia Britannica was based on the leather-bound books from which she'd plagiarized many middle school reports. When Vanessa hired her, she learned she would be working on its replacement. Glad though she was to have landed a decent job, she was disappointed. She had prized those crackly volumes filled with all the world's information, too much for a girl to remember, but preserved forever on tissue-thin paper that fluttered with each breath. She had loved ruffling those pages, loved trying to memorize facts that had no bearing on what she was studying, but that would, someday, unlock what she needed to know as an adult. After a few months at EB, she'd figured out that Plan B would be the dimwit descendent of a historic and esteemed institution.

"Polly, I hope you've made progress with Mecca."

A wave of amused sympathy billowed from the others. They knew she had found one blurry, too dark, aerial photograph of what looked like a bathtub drain.

"I'm waiting to hear from Rapho-Guillumette."

Behind Vanessa, the window washers swiped their squeegees back and forth, oblivious to Polly's humiliation.

"Near completion then." Vanessa handed her a new folder. "I trust you can handle another assignment."

The History of Barbed Wire. "Thank you," Polly said.

Janine drew a frowny face on her notepad, then wrote, "Lunch? My treat."

Vanessa cleared her throat commanding attention. "As you know, Headquarters has been unhappy about the progress made in this office. Not the progress of Illustrations. Our work, your work, has been exemplary, but Editorial has had problems, of which you are not unaware. Yes, they've had more turnover than might have been hoped, and a few key writers have left. This has impinged on us, too, but we have risen to the challenge. Editorial's problems notwithstanding, Headquarters is determined that Plan B will wrap by December. That has not changed. The most recent communiqué from HQ clarifies what will happen between now and the conclusion of Plan B."

Polly stiffened. The room stilled.

"Production will remain the same, no staff cuts. Editorial must pick up the pace with no new hires. Staff reductions in this department will phase in after Labor Day. By the end of the year, Illustrations will be closed."

Closed? Polly would be out of a job?

Hank dropped his folders on the coffee table, rattling the tea set. "Fired? Everyone?"

"Let go," Vanessa corrected. "Your contracts state that your employment ends with the conclusion of the project. This can't come as a surprise."

But it did. Polly had almost paid off her debts, but she had nothing in savings. She had assumed that the paragraph about employment terminating was simple legalese, that EB, which employed God knew how many people and occupied three floors of this massive building, would begin another project. Half the staff in Illustrations had worked for EB for twenty years or more on projects before Plan B. Surely other projects would come along and she would transition to the next.

"Everyone will be *let go*?" someone asked.

"I have told you what I know. If you have any questions, take them to Personnel. For now, we all have jobs to do."

In the strained silence, Polly looked at the others. She had worked with these people for two years, they'd trained her at the beginning, and she knew them as well as she knew anyone she knew nothing personal about. They shared research tips, broke up the day with coffee from downstairs, joked together, covered for each other, signed birthday cards that someone remembered to circulate. Soon they would scatter and she might never see them again. Everyone would get jobs in offices doing something similar to what they were doing now, maybe in publishing, maybe insurance or business, and their lives would unfurl in crushing sameness, for all of them, for her, too.

From outside the window came soft knocking, cables dangling from the window washers' platform that was no longer in sight. Had the men sensing the disaster inside this room timed their exit to be discreet?

Vanessa stood and crossed to her desk, the meeting over. Everyone filed out.

In the common area, Hank growled, "fucking Terrible Tuesday," as he strode toward his cubicle, Ellen saying, at least some of them would stay on until the end of the year, meaning he had no reason to act the way he was acting. Everyone knew he would not be the first to go.

Polly said, "I'll be gone by Labor Day, less than four months from now." Last hired, first fired.

"Aren't you getting married?" snapped Tina. "Some of us don't have a safety net."

"What has that got to do with anything?" Polly said. Marrying Bob wasn't a sure thing. Janine must have blabbed.

"TT to the tenth power," Irene muttered, and everyone started talking at once.

Janine nudged Polly, nodding to Milly, who stood at the edge of the common area waving pink While-You-Were-Out notes. Walking toward her, Janine said, "Seriously, would you like a ten o'clock martini?"

"Aren't you upset?" Polly asked, frustrated by Janine's calm. "How long have you been here?"

"Seventeen years, but I'm in no better position than you. Okay, better than you, but I haven't heard about any new projects in the pipeline." Janine smiled her complacent smile. "How about that drink at lunch or after work?"

Milly interrupted, handing Polly a stack of messages. "How do you pronounce this name? I asked her to spell it, but I don't get it."

"It's U-Jean-ee-ah. Eugenia. It's a Greek name." The note said she would be in the Drake Hotel lobby at six thirty. To Janine, Polly said, "Not tonight. I'm meeting a friend."

"Friend, as in man?" She made a mock lecherous face.

Polly shouldn't have told her anything about Bob. "My college roommate."

Janine wiggled her eyebrows, pretending to believe the room-mate was a ruse, and headed toward her cubicle.

Polly surveyed the common area, the worktables piled with lay-outs and papers, trying to imagine all this vacant by the end of the year. Where would she be?

In her cubicle, she tossed her folders on her desk—barbed wire?— knocking Eugenia's coaster onto the floor.

I will be a filmmaker, making important documentaries about the film Greats.

Instead, she would be looking for another job. She slipped the coaster into her purse. Why had Eugenia kept this pathetic reminder of Polly's drunken swagger? And sent it now? Not to make her feel bad. Eugenia wasn't like that. She consistently played down that she had achieved what she'd set out for, while Polly hadn't. Eugenia had become a published poet, and after a string of crummy jobs, jobs not quite as dead-end as Polly's, she had a great day job, translator at the United Nations. *Getting paid to use words with precision, what could be better?* In New York City, better still. She'd left for New York right before Polly returned from her time in Peoria during her moth-er's convalescence. When Polly landed the job at EB, she'd phoned Eugenia and popped open a bottle of champagne when she picked up. They had laughed together, both of them finally launched as adults with health insurance and pension plans.

●　●　●

When Janine and the others left for lunch, Polly stayed behind in her cubicle, waiting for the department to empty—she didn't want to talk to anyone—then she slipped on her shoes, grabbed the news-paper, and in the lobby coffee shop, picked up a sandwich. Outside on the Plaza, she took the stairs down to the riverside where no one from the office ever came.

Sitting on a ledge, she unfolded the *Trib* hoping Bob had a story. Seeing his name in print reassured her that on the other side of the world, he was safe, but there was no Bob Kitchener byline, only an unattributed AP story filed from Da Nang, which wouldn't be his. She wasn't to worry he'd said before he left, and after he arrived, he signed off his first letter in February with *reporting safely from a barstool*. She pictured a sleazy bar, him hunched over a crowded table trading war stories with other Western reporters, like in Chicago, only in Saigon. Setting the paper aside, she unwrapped her sandwich.

She would have to find a new job. There were plenty of publishing houses in Chicago, but with all nine picture editors vying for work—not Irene, she was pregnant—what were the odds Polly, the least experienced of them, who previously had held a string of entry-level jobs in an unrelated field, that she would end up with a good one? Her stomach folded on itself as she thought about facing questions like: why did she think she was qualified? how fast could she type? why did she have an almost two-year-long break after a string of short-term jobs? what were her marriage plans? Watching the guy with the MIA/POW flag march along the river's embankment then back again, she formulated answers. She had experience with all forms of office work. She could type a barely respectable ninety words a minute. About her employment lapse, she would explain about her mother being injured in a bad car accident and needing Polly at home. About changing jobs so often before that, she would say, "Looking for new opportunities," not that she couldn't advance. Why was she leaving her current job? Her "project was ending," she would say, not "I was laid off," not "I didn't read the small print."

About marriage, she didn't know what she would say. Why should her marital status have anything to do with her ability to work? This she wouldn't say, either. No one wanted to hear that. And besides, she deplored women who used marriage as a safety net. "I have no plans" would be her answer.

When Bob got the assignment to cover what came after the troop withdrawal, he had proposed. Let's wait until he returned, she'd said. We'll plan something nice, nothing big, her mother, his parents, a few friends. She didn't say she wasn't sure about him—he'd been married twice before—and she wasn't sure about marriage. She leaned back against the concrete planter and closed her eyes, the sun beating down on her face. She missed him. She missed his lovely, strong, heavy body, his chest so vast that she could barely reach around him. She missed his assurance that there was nothing ever to worry about.

She stuffed her uneaten sandwich back in the sack. Tonight she would talk to Eugenia about her job ending, but she wouldn't bring up Bob. When Polly started dating him, Eugenia had already moved to New York City. On the phone Eugenia had said, *Cute, yes, fun, yes, interesting, yes, but long term?* She remembered him from the O'Toole's days. In college, Eugenia and Polly had decided that a man should not be the primary focus of a woman's life, not a safe harbor to avoid the responsibilities of the world. Was this from reading de Beauvoir? A man as equal, yes, but not a master. On this they agreed with the feminists, but having a man was nice. Men embellished the good life. Eugenia had several non-serious boyfriends when she and Polly shared an apartment, Polly did too. Now Eugenia was involved with a diplomat from Belgium, Mathias, who had a wife and family in Brussels. Eugenia said she didn't mind, she didn't want to be asked what's for dinner, or be expected to pick up his dry cleaning, or dovetail her work around his. Marriage was not something she wanted, maybe ever. When Bob suggested moving in with Polly a month before he signed on for Saigon, Eugenia's only comment was that Polly's apartment was perfect for one and the occasional guest. Polly agreed. What Eugenia hadn't said was, "Don't turn into his servant." Polly had agreed with this too. Now her extra bedroom was filled with Bob's stuff, so no guest room was available for Eugenia. When she called to say she would be passing through Chicago, Polly had offered it, but Eugenia said no.

●   ●   ●

At the end of the day, the department emptied earlier than usual, everyone eager to get away from the fallout of Vanessa's bombshell, but Polly stayed at her desk, having almost two hours to kill before meeting Eugenia. She added Barbed Wire to her assignment list, sorted through the transparencies that had come in with the afternoon mail, then packaged up the rejected submissions for her Ethiopian church article for which she'd had too many good choices. Returning from the mailroom, she looked across her cubicle at the few personal pictures she kept on top of her file cabinet at the one Bob sent from Vietnam, him looking glamorous in aviators, his beard bristling with sunlight, his long shirt sleeves rolled up to show off his beautiful hairy arms. She wished he weren't nine thousand miles away.

At this moment in Saigon, it would be early morning, too early for him to be in the AP office. She pictured him there, *think frat house basement, cramped, peeling paint, lazy-ass cockroaches, but we're on the second floor, two desks shared by five guys, four phones, the wires, next door, a smelly darkroom,* and she imagined his size

13

eleven cowboy boots propped on a battered metal desk with an old-fashioned black phone pressed to his ear. *Not possible*, he had written about phoning. *Spotty connections. We use the wire to communicate with headquarters. Even that is for shit.* Four months it had been since she'd heard his voice, during his layover in Tokyo, static in the background, and one day longer since they'd held each other saying goodbye. She missed him.

She changed into her high heels and new blouse, even though it was too early to meet Eugenia. The Plaza was nearly empty, and the breeze off the Lake soft and moist. She strolled up Michigan Avenue among excited out-of-towners laden with shopping bags, dawdling with them at the fancy store windows displaying nothing she could afford, feeling lucky to live in a mecca for tourists who lived in less interesting places, who marveled at the shops, the skyscrapers, and the Lake that was as big as an inland ocean. Eugenia loved New York, but Polly loved Chicago. She might ask Eugenia if she could find out about job possibilities at International Dynamics, where she used to work before she moved to New York, but Polly would keep it light. Tonight was about being together. She and Eugenia talked every week, but that wasn't the same as being together. Afterward she knew she would feel as she always did, as though she'd drunk from a fountain after a long parched spell, connected, satisfied, replete.

● ● ●

On the far side of the Drake's hushed lobby, Eugenia sat in an overstuffed chair, her hands folded in her lap, her long-sleeve blouse dropping from her shoulders as if there was no body inside. Even in the rosy dimness, her face looked chalky. Polly walked toward her, her approach muffled by the thick carpet, and waited for Eugenia to look up, recognize her and toss off her frightening disguise and smile her big smile. Something was wrong. On the phone, she hadn't sounded sick. She said she would be passing through Chicago on her way to her parents in St. Louis, nothing about being sick. No hint in their weekly phone calls, and not four days ago on Saturday when she'd confirmed her visit.

"I'm so glad to see you," Polly said, hiding her dismay. Eugenia's lovely, lush shiny shoulder-length black hair was a wig.

Eugenia smiled her big grin. Her teeth looked old.

"What happened to you?"

Eugenia made a rueful face. "I'm better than I look." She fluttered her hands above her purse, then stood slowly. "I made a reservation at the swanky restaurant downstairs."

When they were seated in a booth, Polly focused on Eugenia's too-big brown eyes, trying to avoid the hollows beneath and asked about her train trip, knowing Eugenia wouldn't talk until after the waitress had come and gone. A nice trip, she said. She'd slept most of the time. Tomorrow she would take an early train to St. Louis. She could have gone straight through, but she wanted to see Polly. Polly said she was glad. After the waitress left with their drink order, Eugenia rushed into the news story about the society girl kidnapped by a wacko militant group in California. Staged or real? Had she joined voluntarily? Had she been brainwashed? Polly said something about the impossibility of knowing what was in someone's mind. Why had Eugenia not told her she was sick?

The din from the other tables washed to the edge of their booth and died, leaving them in an island of silence. After the waitress brought their drinks, Eugenia wrapped hers in her napkin and Polly sipped her Southern Comfort. She had forgotten how tongue-coating sweet it was. When she and Eugenia lived together, they drank Southern Comfort in honor of Janis Joplin, who'd sipped from a bottle in her wild performances, so they'd heard, even before seeing her on the gold-leafed stage of the Auditorium Theatre stake her claim to drink and roar like the big boys. Janis was not going to be boxed in.

Polly lifted her glass. "To Janis."

"To Janis." Eugenia picked up her swaddled glass, then set it down without taking a sip. "On the phone I couldn't say 'Hey, I have cancer.' "

Polly reached across the table to touch her hands.

"It's not as bad as I look. I'm going home to my parents for this treatment that will knock out the cancer, that's what they say, but I shouldn't be on my own. I'll be weak. They've made arrangements for me to start the next, hopefully the final, round of chemo in St. Louis. It's curable, what I have. I'm more likely to be hit by a bus than die of this cancer, they tell me. It's Hodgkin's lymphoma. The young person's cancer."

"I thought the young people's cancer was leukemia."

"I'm special. I got the rarer one."

"But leaving your life? What about Mathias? I would have come to take care of you."

"You have a job and a life. Mathias was recalled to Brussels. I'm glad. I would have to worry about him being upset, the way you look right now."

"I would have come."

"I know. Mathias said this too. But you couldn't and he couldn't. This thrills my parents, me coming home for them to take care of me. I'm on extended sick leave, getting paid half of my ample income, which is still more than you're earning. I'll be back in New York with a new head of short curly hair by the end of the year."

Polly stared at her stiff, shiny wig. Some people did get well. Her mother's co-worker survived breast cancer. "When you and I are old ladies, a bus will mow us down. We'll be doddering along somewhere and meander into the street and the bus from hell will barrel along and take us both out at the same time."

"Deal."

Polly looked into her dark eyes, the hollows beneath as dark as plums. "What about your apartment?"

"I'm subletting it on a month-to-month."

Arranging a medical leave, renting out her apartment, all without letting Polly know. She wanted to ask when Eugenia was diagnosed, but couldn't. Eugenia should have told her, but Polly wasn't going to make her feel guilty by asking how long she'd gone through what she was going through without telling Polly, week-after-week not saying anything. Draining what remained of her drink, she slapped down her glass too hard, and flung her head sideways in a Janis-like twirl.

Eugenia smiled, her teeth too big. "To Janis," and squeezed Polly's fingertips. "I should have told you. It was January, January 8, a Tuesday. After that, I couldn't think about anyone else. I couldn't worry about telling you and how you would feel. I did what I was told, but nothing else. My life narrowed down to me and my treatment, nothing else."

She went on about how one thing led to the next, she caught in a downward-spiraling chute, and Polly thought about her own mother's car accident and afterward: Polly quitting her job, moving back to Peoria, her mother in a coma, her hellish long stay in the hospital, her slow recovery, rehab, not knowing what would come next, not knowing whether real life would ever resume. It had. Her mother had re-built her life, and Polly had returned to Chicago. Eugenia explained about how helpful and loving Mathias had been during the first days, before he was recalled to Belgium, and how her New York friends had helped—this hurt Polly, her New York friends had known, not she—meals delivered, magazines, flowers, prayer cards. "Imagine prayer cards."

"I can't imagine you and prayer cards." Eugenia made a funny face. "What can I do?"

"Don't forget me."

"What are you talking about?"

"I mean phone every week, the usual, and tell me funny things. Amuse me. Living with my parents—God, I am going to die in St. Louis."

Her eyes met Polly's and she guffawed, then Polly, knocking over a water glass, which made them laugh harder. Eugenia pounded the table, her body shaking, trying to take a sip of her drink, face reddening, seltzer spraying from her nose. People at the nearby tables turned to stare, then joined laughing. Polly grinned at Eugenia struggling to calm down, her long, flushed face streaked with laugh tears, as beautiful as ever.

The waitress appeared with a stack of napkins. As Polly wiped up the water they'd spilled, Eugenia, still hiccupping, ordered lobster for two. Seeing Polly's face, she said, "Don't worry. I'm buying."

After the waitress left, they smiled at each other, connected in the old way, and Eugenia launched into a story about her snooty subletter, a secretary with the British delegation, who had been dismayed by Eugenia's inadequately outfitted kitchen. Why would you cook with good takeout available? The woman had been persuaded by the one bedroom, with an actual door, the location, three blocks from the UN.

Waiters in white gloves placed silver domed platters in front of them and whisked them away. Stunned into silence by the ceremony, Polly stared at her fire-red lobster.

"You can't let them see you're scared," Eugenia said, and they both laughed, trying not to be scared of Eugenia's situation.

As they teased out clumps of flesh, Eugenia talked about Mathias, whom Polly hadn't met a year ago, about their favorite out-of-the-way restaurants, their late-night walks, the subterfuges they used to keep their affair private. Having a secret, mostly long-distance lover was liberating, she said, and yet, now that she had left New York, she missed him as she hadn't when he left for Brussels two months ago. On another night, this might have been the moment when Polly would bring up Bob and her uncertainties connected to marriage, and how she had the new pressure at her job, and this might affect her feelings about marriage, but everything about her future had become irrelevant. Eugenia described how she would keep Mathias a secret from her parents. He would send letters in business envelopes mailed from his office in New York, not Belgium. Belgium would invite her parents' curiosity. And no telephone calls, her parents might pick up. She couldn't phone him either. Long distance to Belgium would show up on her parents' phone bill, and at his end there was the wife, the children, the maid eavesdropping.

No phone calls—like Polly with Bob—but she didn't say this.

"You look sad," Eugenia said. "Don't be. I feel like a teenager, keeping a boy secret from my parents. But I'm tired now. I've got to go up to bed."

"I'll phone you every day."

"Not that. On Saturday, our usual." She waved for the check.

● ● ●

Outside the hotel, Polly stared at the decked-out carriage horses waiting to take drunks on rides around the Gold Coast, and hailed a cab she couldn't afford. She couldn't face the El with the late-night pan-handlers or the two-and-a-half block walk through dark streets to her apartment. As the cab headed west to the expressway and Polly's northwest side neighborhood, air rushed in the window, and she closed her eyes.

She shouldn't have brought up Janis, who died at twenty-seven. She and Eugenia were living together then—before Polly's mother's accident, before Eugenia left for New York—and they had mourned loudly, Janis-style, playing her albums, getting drunk on her trade-marked booze, spouting nonsense. *Live hard, die young.* A noble death. Not like cancer. But Eugenia's was curable. Polly fumbled in her purse for a mint to kill the disgusting taste in her mouth and touched the O'Toole's coaster. Eugenia must have sent it while clear-ing out her apartment for the sublet. If she meant it as a joke or a dig about arrogant youthful ambitions colliding with harsh reality, or something else, Polly couldn't ask now, just as she couldn't complain about how she had come to the brink of middle-age and had no idea what she was supposed to do with the rest of her life. Self-pity, this was the Southern Comfort.

● ● ●

First thing the next day, Polly descended to EB's chilly and sel-dom-used library where editions of the encyclopedia dating from

1901 were housed. Earlier editions were kept in deep storage. In the current edition, Polly found an entry on Hodgkin's disease. The text was dense and alarming and there were different kinds. The survival rate was better if diagnosed early—why state the obvious?—but worse if the patient was young. Eugenia was thirty-four, six months older than Polly, neither of them was young. Why should she trust a ten-year-old article over what Eugenia's doctors said? The treatment in St. Louis would knock it out. Her sick leave was temporary. She was subletting her apartment month-to-month. Polly shoved the book back in place, then pulled it out to line it up precisely with the other volumes, wanting to leave no sign that she had looked up Hodgkin's disease, in case of bad mojo.

In her cubicle, she opened the newspaper she'd picked up on her way in, and found another AP story about another Viet Cong victory, but nothing of Bob's. She wished they could talk. His rumbly voice had a way of making her worries seem small.

"Dear Bob" she scrawled across the top of a piece of paper. What should she say? The news about Eugenia was too raw and too private, and if she wrote about layoffs starting after Labor Day, he would write back, "Don't worry, you'll find something. Until then, you can count on me."

She pushed back from her desk and stood at her bulletin board staring at her movie cards that she'd pinned on every bulletin board at every job she'd had since her first, at Kino, Inc., and taken with her when she left. She and Eugenia had expected everything to fall into place. Not immediately, they understood you had to learn the ropes, pay your dues, wait your turn, live every stupid, threadbare cliché, but if you did, and if you had what it took, another cliché—Eugenia kept a list of career-related clichés—and if you had the talent—this they never doubted—you would make it. Another blitheringly stupid cliché.

She turned away, her eyes falling on the barbed wire folder Vanessa had given her. Back at her desk, she wrote:

While you are reporting on the devastation of war—please be safe—I have been given a new assignment, barbed wire.

2

July, 1962

POLLY TAPPED THE GRILL OF THE AIR CONDITIONER and held up her hand. Nothing, no breeze. Shelley, the cheapskate, didn't care that the public face of Kino, Inc. was a sweltering hellhole. Un-sticking her blouse from her waist, she turned and surveyed the tables stacked with old ledgers and cardboard boxes of miscellaneous stuff that should go somewhere else if Shelley ever got around to deciding where, her desk piled with mail she was supposed to sort, Eileen's nice reception-style desk near the door to the hall and the elevators: this could be any shabby office anywhere, small manufacturing, insurance, a booking agency, not a hub of creative filmmaking. The award plaques on the back wall were deceptive. Three months ago, when she came for her interview and pushed open the door with *Kino Inc.* spelled out in gold letters on the pebbled glass and saw the gigantic poster for De Sica's *The Bicycle Thief,* the award plaques, and a big wooden K, K for Kino, "cinema" in either German or Russian, she still didn't know which, she believed she had entered the antechamber to heaven.

She and Eugenia came to Chicago right after graduation, both of them intent on launching their brilliant careers. Right away Eugenia found her perfect job at International Dynamics, translating correspondence in five languages: perfect because it paid well, perfect because she loved working with words, and perfect because the precision required helped with her poetry. Weeks later, Polly had thought she had found her opening when she saw Kino's ad "Ass't/ film prod co-". On her resume she inflated her job mailing letters for the college's film department into an internship and added a line about studying film during her junior year in Paris. Why not call her immersion "studying"? Watching movies almost daily at the *Cinémathèque Française* with Vaughn had been a revelation, and a deeper learning experience than any she'd had in any classroom. She loved films, not the Hollywood movies she'd grown up with, but the complicated, personal, black and white *nouvelle vague* films she'd seen in Paris. She loved Godard, she loved Resnais' *Hiroshima mon amour*, and especially Agnès Varda's *La Pointe Courte*, even though she didn't want to make feature films. What she wanted was to become was a documentarian, a film documentarian. She like history and facts and digging into untold stories.

"Studied film, did you?" Shelley Shapiro had said that first day. With his slicked back hair, short-sleeved, almost transparent white shirt, suspenders holding up baggy trousers, he looked more like a mobster than a filmmaker. That should have alerted her. "You can type, right? What, sixty words a minute?" Another warning she had failed to grasp. "I need a gopher."

She thought "gopher" meant a hard-working, dig-in kind of girl who was unafraid of hard labor. She would lug equipment, adjust light stands, string electrical lines. A dream job.

"I'll do anything," she said. "I'll fill sandbags. I'll schlep the heaviest equipment. I only look small. I can carry my own weight and then some." This was a lie. Shelley's lie had been that he would teach her the film business.

What Shelley meant by "go-fer" was go for coffee, go to the stationery store, go to the post office, and do whatever Eileen, his office manager, didn't want to do. *Paying her dues,* Eugenia said, both sincerely and mocking. She'd begun to collect a list of working-life clichés.

Polly smacked the silent air conditioner again and returned to her desk. The mailman had delivered fall catalogues for studio supplies, a signed contract for a short promo for Copper-X, a check from International Harvester for a job completed last year, a request for additional prints of an in-house training film Kino had produced for the gas company. Shelley claimed he specialized in documentaries, and the awards on the wall said that once he had and those documentaries had been good, but all she'd seen of Kino's production were slick corporate promotionals.

A sound from the back. Polly turned.

"What happened to the AC?" Eileen asked, emerging from the supply room with a gift bag sprouting pink tissue paper. Another lunchtime baby shower. Eileen had no children but a million nieces.

"It died. Should I call a repair guy?"

Eileen handed her a card from the Rolodex. "Call this guy, and don't forget to remind Shelley that Mitch Kaine will stop by around one o'clock. I'll be back by three."

Shelley was holed up in his private office with the one functioning air conditioner and not to be disturbed until Mitch arrived. He and Shelley had worked together at Pathé Films in New York before they set up their own shops, Shelley here and Mitch in Minnesota where he produced mostly science films for high schools. Polly hurried to open the front door for Eileen overloaded with bags, glad Mitch was coming. He was the one client who didn't treat Polly as if she were part of the furniture, and she had an idea for a project she wanted to try out on him.

After the office door swung shut, she sat at Eileen's desk to dial the AC guy, who couldn't come until tomorrow at the earliest. Yes, he understood that it was at least a hundred degrees out there. His phone was ringing off the hook. Polly hung up, not banging down the receiver—the jerk might never come—and stood next to the dead air conditioner, watching an El train disappear behind the skyscrapers to the southeast, then glanced at Shelley's awards. He had taught her nothing, hadn't let her hold a camera, did not let her into the editing rooms when they are at work, told her not to even open the equipment cases, but she had figured out what she wanted to do. Organizing his back issues of *Cahiers du Cinéma* and *Sight and Sound*, then pouring through his film catalogues, she had discovered that there were no films about the greats like René Clair or Vigo, Bresson or Melville, or even Jean Renoir. Some big American directors, like Howard Hawkes and John Ford, had given filmed interviews, but von Stroheim and Lubitsch, who had had big Hollywood careers after leaving Europe, no documentaries had been made about them either. What she wanted to understand was how the giants who created what was called "cinema" did what they did, and make documentaries about them before they all died: interview them, record their voices, probe how they made their discoveries and innovations, and learn about the early days of film. She would do it, once she knew how.

Down the hall, the elevator chains rattled. She straightened her sweaty blouse, wiped her face with a tissue, and squared her shoulders.

"Hi, Mitch."

"Jeez, it's an oven in here." His droopy-dog face gleamed with sweat. He was the same age as Shelley and wore his graying hair slicked back with too much Vitalis, but he was kind.

"I've got a call into the repair guy. Don't stand in the sunlight, or you'll catch fire."

He eased out of his suit jacket and flapped his tie at his face, as if it were a fan. "Shelley, the bum, he should close the office if you don't have air."

"It just died. Before you go back there—he's on the phone anyway—can I tell you about an idea I've got?

"It's too hot for ideas, sugar."

"Quickly, it's—"

"Not another bug idea."

"No. But I still think that would be a good project for you." Last time, she had showed him closeups of insects her friend Camilla Rose had shot in the park and suggested a film-strip series titled, "What's My Secret?" about bugs that morph into something else, like caterpillars into butterflies. "This new idea of mine is smaller and local." And connected to her idea about preserving the history of old creative men. "At a party this weekend, I met a guy who filmed these jazz musicians back in the forties and fifties. He lives right here in Chicago and he's got a garage full of footage that nobody's seen."

Mitch perched on Eileen's desk and smiled down at her. "Now why doesn't this sound promising? Let's see. If no one's seen this guy's footage, there's probably a good reason."

"But this could be important historical material. And—"

"That was reason number one. Now reason number two for why I'm not interested: this guy at a party might be talking to a pretty girl like you with other things on his mind than history."

Polly stiffened. Could he be right? Josephson had leaned in too close, like a lech, and he had acted weird when Eugenia and Claire came over to say that it was time to go. "Everyone was treating him like he was somebody."

"Okay, sugar, if I give the guy more credit than he's probably due, he's a jazz buff with an eight-millimeter camera he bought in a pawn shop way back when. Which brings up the question: does he have sound?"

"Of course, he has sound." But Josephson hadn't mentioned working with anyone. Could he have recorded sound without an assistant? Hiding her doubts, she said, "Think about it, Mitch, this could be an amazing opportunity. I'd introduce you. And you could put me on the crew, just as a go-fer. I could run errands. I could—"

"You're eager. I get that. I like that. But some two-bit amateur with a garage full of grainy club footage ain't going to turn out to be…Who was that guy who recorded those blues singers in the cotton fields?"

"Alan Lomax. But Chicago jazz clubs, isn't that worth a look? This could be big. That's why—"

"And number three." He held up three fingers. "Shelley's own Rule of Three."

He didn't bother to repeat Shelley's mantra: You need three things to make a film: one, an exceptional idea; two, talent, either a big-name director or writer; and three, money. Any two can attract the third. You need three legs, like a tripod, to have a solid project.

Pretending she wasn't annoyed with his condescension, she smiled.

"At best you've got one wobbly leg, an idea." He wiggled his fingers and pushed off her desk.

Polly stood. "Two legs. You would be the talent."

"Not for me, sugar. I've got a new project, which is why I'm here."

"The Forgotten Jazzmen of Chicago is a great topic. Think about it."

"Will do."

She held her face steady and reached for the phone. "I'll let Shelley know you're here."

"Don't bother, sugar. I'll announce myself and catch him *in flagrante.*"

She tried not to imagine Shelley half-undressed. Walking toward the back, Mitch stopped to point at *The Bicycle Thief* poster.

"He's your man, sugar. Start with De Sica. He won't be around much longer."

"Learn Italian. Learn film. Find a backer. Find De Sica's phone number in the phone book—I'll get right on it, Mitch."

Grinning, he flicked his hand at the brim of an imaginary fedora and disappeared down the hall.

He was probably right about Josephson being a windbag. She listened to Mitch and Shelley's old guy laughter as she went through the rest of the mail, trying not to be angry. When she heard Shelley's door open and Mitch's footsteps in the hall, she arranged her cheeriest smile to show she was a trouper. "Bye, Mitch."

"Next time." He clicked his tongue and again pretended to touch the brim of a pretend fedora.

She made a pistol with her fingers and clicked back.

"Polly, bring in your notepad," Shelley yelled.

His too-big desk was surprisingly immaculate in his otherwise chaotic office filled with filing cabinets and buckling shelves that overflowed with editing books, some in Russian, film catalogues, decades-worth of film periodicals, and shooting scripts for Kino's former projects. Shutting the door behind her, she lifted her arms from her sides to let the delicious cool dry her sweat. When she first started at Kino, she had felt light-headed and desperate each time she entered this sacred kingdom. She still felt that way. Sitting in the wobbly mesh chair—one of Shelley's many rules, this one unspoken, the comfy barrel chair was reserved for clients and friends, she waited, notebook in lap, the devoted employee, ready to do whatever it took. Sometime he was bound to notice how able she was.

"Mitch has brought us something new." He reached for his Tums, sighing as if already exhausted. "I want you to get in touch with Mongo, Jules, Sid, Ernie, and Ray. Tell them to clear their calendars for the first two weeks of September. Mitch will firm up the dates later." It would be a one-week location shoot in northern Wisconsin. Mongo was to service the van beforehand. Shelley did not want a repeat of that breakdown fiasco of last year.

"What's the project?" Polly asked.

Shelley's jowls churned as he pulverized the Tums. "A forty-five minute on some hotshot photographer who's pushing eighty. Cole Watkins."

"I've heard of him."

"Mitch said the family doesn't want him relegated to the dustbin of history. Somehow Mitch got funding for this schmegegge."

Polly stared at her notepad, as a sensation, something like sequins spangling tingled along her arms. She watched her hand holding the pencil on the notepad, surprised it wasn't shaking. She took a breath, then looked up at Shelley. "I have a question, I guess more of a request. Will you put me on the crew, please, as a go-fer?"

"No."

"Shelley, I'll do anything. This is the opportunity that I've wanted. Anything."

"No."

"Why not?"

"It's not the time." He pushed his glasses onto his forehead and rubbed his eyes.

"This is what you always say. No on that hotel promotional. No on that stop-action skyline shoot."

"I'm not sending a girl to Podunk, Wisconsin with a bunch of guys. Next thing local —"

"The skyline job was local. That hotel job was downtown. I've worked here for three months and you haven't given me a chance." She hated whining, but couldn't stop. "It's the least you can do."

"Least I can do?" He tipped his chair forward with a bang. "I pay you a weekly wage. That's what I owe you. Now, get out of here, get to work, and I'll forget you ever stepped over."

The main room seemed even hotter after Shelley's office. That he didn't care that she and Eileen had to work in sweatshop conditions was another example of his being an A-one, unfeeling jerk. She took Eileen's Rolodex to her own desk, pulled out the cards for Mongo, Jules, Sid, Ernie, and Ray, and set them under her calendar. She would make the calls later, when she felt like it. If one of the guys got booked before she called, that would be one of those unfortunate things that Shelley would have to deal with. She returned the Rolodex to Eileen's desk and retrieved the ledger she was supposed to update. Shelley yelled from his office for Polly to get him an ice tea from the coffee shop downstairs, and she bought one for herself, too. An hour later he left for the day, not asking if she'd contacted anyone yet, assuming she had, she guessed. When Eileen returned from her shower, later than she'd said, tipsy and in a forgiving mood, Polly asked if she could leave a few minutes early.

"Sure, it's hot as hell out there, buses are breaking down."

• • •

Eugenia wasn't home yet. Polly opened the windows of their stifling apartment, wanting to unload her grievances in private before Eugenia's annoying cousin, Melanie, got home from whatever she did all day. Polly showered and changed, and still Eugenia wasn't home. Being a go-fer on a film about Cole Watkins would be perfect for her. It was unfair, pig-headed, selfish and mean of Shelley not to give her a chance. It wouldn't cost him. She could tell him that, that she would work for free. In Eugenia's room, she found the coffee table book her parents had given her for Christmas: *Century at War*. She found Cole Watkins in the index, then flipped to his photographs: wounded soldiers on stretchers in a muddied field; skinny children standing by an unlit fireplace; a two-page spread of a Baroque church commandeered as a hospital with a picture of a white-sheeted medical operation taking place beneath an altar painting of Jesus floating to heaven. *The Spanish Civil War*, read the section's title. The thirties, before World War II, her father's war, Cole Watkins had been recording history. Watkins was a more important figure than she'd realized. It wasn't fair that she would be stuck in Chicago answering the phone while Mongo and the crew of louts would spend time with Cole Watkins. Shelley would sneer if she were to offer to work for free. He'd say if she felt that way, she could start right away. Why should he pay her?

In the kitchen she splashed cold water on her face, then flicked on the TV and watched a news story about a young man shot trying to scale the Berlin Wall, the grainy footage looking older than the Watkins' pictures of the Spanish Civil War.

Hearing keys in the door, she sat up.

Eugenia called from the front hall, "Did you hear about the boy they shot climbing—"

"Eighteen years old, that's what they said. It's horrible. Younger than us. Imagine wanting out that badly." She followed Eugenia into the kitchen. "Listen to my day. In the great scheme of things, including East Germany, my day isn't a tragedy, I know that, but Shelley is a fraud, a stogey-smoking beast, and a miserable cheat. He wants a college graduate to sit in his front office to add class to his bottom-feeder business—that dean's list college graduate with an English major would be me—but he is never going to make good on the promises he made." She told Eugenia about the Watkins' job.

Eugenia offered her a glass of water.

Polly shook her head. "If I did not have to pay rent, I would quit."

"You *do* have to pay rent." Eugenia eased out of her shoes and started for the back to take a shower.

All the TV channels were broadcasting the same story, the poor boy's ragdoll body flopping over the Wall again and again, each time the image became less shocking, his humanity leeched away, which was sickening and scary. At the front door she heard Melanie struggle with her keys, as always, and turned off the TV, not wanting to give the dimwit an opening to say something stupid about the news. Melanie continued to fumble. The basics of daily life, using keys, washing her own dishes, keeping the shower curtain inside the tub, were beyond the Southern Belle. Melanie and Eugenia shared familial Greek genes, but they were nothing alike. Eugenia was smart, and Melanie was a bimbo. Eugenia looked like a Byzantine icon, Melanie looked like a shipping heiress who hung out on yachts in a skimpy bathing suit and sparkly sunglasses.

She flopped into the bean bag chair, dropping her bags, and blew her bangs off her forehead. "Momma says if you scowl like that and the wind changes, your face will be like that forever."

"Thank you, Miss Scarlett, for the beauty tip. It's your turn to take us out to dinner, some place with air conditioning." Turn wasn't accurate. Polly and Eugenia had never taken Melanie out. Why should they? She was camping in their living room, rent-free for the summer, and driving them crazy.

Angling her head toward the sound of Eugenia's shower, Melanie made a show of smelling her armpits. "How much longer will she be?"

The water stopped.

"*Alors, vas-y.*"

• • •

At their nearby Italian restaurant that had excellent air conditioning and a mural of Mt. Vesuvius, Melanie yammered about another cousin's upcoming wedding in the fall. She and Eugenia would be among the eight bridesmaids. Pink gowns, Chantilly lace, flowers to be determined, the groomsmen unknown, except for bad Bobby Lowry who would be the best man, whom Melanie would not dance with, no matter what her mother said. Melanie hoped to have such a wedding, and soon. She did not want to be an old maid.

"Seriously?" Polly said, "You're hanging around waiting for Mr. Right?"

"You Yankees are so strange. I am not *hanging around*. Finding Mr. Right takes real work. Why the devil Daddy insisted I waste my summer up here, I do *not* know."

Polly rolled her eyes at Eugenia. They had heard this before, and they knew why. Melanie's parents used their house-remodeling as the excuse to send her north for "broadening," according to Eugenia's mother. They hoped Eugenia would be a good influence. Not so far. As the cousins discussed bridesmaid duties, Eugenia acting far more patient than need be, Polly thought how she might finagle her way onto the Watkins shoot. Maybe if she asked Mitch, he could persuade Shelley. Mitch liked her spunk, he always said that. Maybe if she called him tonight, he would intervene with Shelley.

They left the restaurant and headed for their favorite tavern, the streets quiet, the shop-keepers pausing as they lowered their security metal grates to say, "good evening" and smile at the three of them. Polly loved the city and she loved O'Toole's, which was edgy and rundown in a cool way, a hangout for their friends and for reporters. Most of the reporters were married or blowhards, but they were fun, and usually someone would buy the second round of whatever Polly and her friends were drinking, another reason they liked O'Toole's. They were all poor. Eugenia was doing better since her promotion, but Shelley paid next to nothing, and Polly couldn't afford to offer to work for free.

O'Toole's was disappointingly empty. Two wizened regulars sat at the bar and one table of guys in dirty streets and sanitation department vests looked up. Ignoring their leers, Polly and Eugenia aimed for the table farthest from them, while Melanie stopped at the bar to order a pitcher of Brandy Alexanders. They all enjoyed annoying the grizzled bartender, who hated having to make blender drinks. Polly smiled at Eugenia as the bartender slapped his damp towel against the sink and meandered to the blender at the far end, pausing to chat with the old lushes bent over their drinks. "Anything to avoid making Brandy Alexanders," Polly whispered to Eugenia, as Melanie joined them at the table. Claire and Judy walked in. Judy made a face—where are the men?—ignoring the cat calls from the streets and san guys.

"Do you believe this heat?" Judy said.

"Beach party on Friday night? What do you say?" Claire said, sitting down, and noticing the lack of drinks. To the bartender she called out, "I'll have what they're having."

"I'll bring the beach ball," said Melanie.

Polly didn't say, you haven't been invited, as Judy walked over the bar to give the bartender her order. Judy didn't like shouting across the bar. They mocked her about this.

Judy was the beauty and Claire, the intense one, and they were both a year older and more experienced in the city. Polly and Eugenia had met them at the Laundromat, trading dollar bills for quarters, and after the usual, Where're you from? Where'd you go to school? They introduced Polly and Eugenia to O'Toole's. They were all stuck in boring jobs, trying to figure out how to get where they wanted to be. Claire waited tables at a steakhouse while waiting to hear about her application to the brand-new Peace Corps. Judy looked like Veronica in the comics and hoped to become a book editor at a prestigious house, not some crummy text book publisher. Currently she served time as a typist at *Hoof Beats*, a magazine devoted to trotters, which they all thought was hysterical. Trotting, she had to explained to newcomers, was horse racing with those weird two-wheeled carts. All of them, except for Melanie, were ambitious. Eugenia wanted to be a famous poet and teach at a place like Yale, and Polly wanted to be a film documentarian.

A bunch of reporters slammed in bringing in a blast of hot, exhaust-filled air and took over the bar. Skip O'Reilly, a sports columnist at the *Sun Times*, angled toward Polly's table.

"Mind if I?" he said, pulling up a chair, as Jack-the-Sprat, transportation desk at the *Trib*, broke away from the crowd at the bar to join them too. He had the hots for Claire. Polly inched sideways to make room, glad to see a new guy, Bob Kitchener, follow Jack over. A few weeks ago, she'd noticed at him at party in Old Town. He was younger than the other guys, maybe in his mid-thirties, and a certifiable hunk. As Skip and Jack wedged in chairs between Judy and Eugenia, Bob Kitchener stood near Polly and reached across the table to shake with the other women, turning last to Polly.

"Pleased to meet you, Polly Wainwright." His hand was as calloused as a construction worker's.

"I read your byline," she said, enjoying the attractive-new-man sizzle.

"Glad to know there is one informed citizen at this table."

"Me, too," chimed in Judy and Melanie—in Melanie's case this had to be a lie—and Bob Kitchener bowed elaborately. He was tall and heavier than most men Polly found appealing, but she liked the easy way he carried his bulk. Melanie offered him a Brandy Alexander from the pitcher the waitress had just delivered. He recoiled, signaled the retreating waitress for a draft, and pulled a chair from the empty nearby table as Jack-the-Sprat held forth about his efforts to reach his East German source to find out more about the boy shot at the Wall, but so far, he had nothing. The conversation switched to what was next with the space program, France ceding colonies to India, more moaning about Marilyn Monroe's death—suicide or overdose?—and a pitcher of beer arrived. Skip filled and passed around glasses. The men, loud, knowledgeable, competitive, and witty, dominated the conversation, as usual, but Bob Kitchener's presence changed the usual dynamic. Even though he was as loud as the other men and ignored the women like the other men, he electrified a current among the women, each of them becoming alert as birds, tense, coy, contributing nothing, but acting interested. Polly glanced at Eugenia. How predictable we are around men. Eugenia blinked slowly, agreeing. Polly wondered if Bob Kitchener had a girlfriend.

More reporters Polly recognized but didn't know crowded around their table, the hubbub reaching shouting level. Polly noticed Bob Kitchener's fine golden-haired wrist, and his watch— nine o'clock, too early to call Mitch—and excused herself to go to the Ladies Room. She stopped at the pay phone to get the number for the Clark Hotel where Eileen had let slip Mitch always stayed. Luckily no one had broken the phone or stolen the phone book. She found the number, memorized it, and feeling fortified by taking this first step, returned to her friends. A waitress friend of Claire's had joined their table, and someone ordered a pitcher of Pink Ladies, and Polly switched to soda water. She needed be completely sober when she called Mitch. Claire's friend left, Jack-the-Sprat left, the crowd at the bar thinned, and the talk at Polly's table shifted to office politics and Polly kept an eye on Bob's watch. When it was almost eleven o'clock, she excused herself, saying she had to make a call. Bob pushed back his chair and brushed her arm, his touch suggestive. He was interested in her, too.

Hunching against the wall to fight the din from the bar, Polly dialed the hotel's number, dropped in her coins, and waited, eight rings, ten. Had she waited too long? Had the night clerk fallen asleep? Finally, she got through.

"Mitch, it's Polly, from Kino. I'm not disturbing you, am I? I know it's kind of late."

"Polly from Kino is the only Polly I know. What's happened?"

"Nothing's happened."

'So, what's going on?" Rustling. "God, it is late."

"About the job you brought in." Silence. "Shelley told me about it."

"And?"

"So, I'm calling to ask you to—" The waitress nudged past her. "Could you tell Shelley to put me on the crew?"

"What are you talking about?"

"The Cole Watkins' job. You've been saying you'd get me in on a production. This is the opportunity I've been hoping for. I would work like crazy, you know that. You say how you like my energy and spunk."

"Jeez, sugar. Not this conversation, not now. It's late."

"I would have called earlier." Calling this late was a mistake. "But I figured you'd be out. This can't wait. Shelley is scheduling the crew now. He'll do what you say."

"It's Shelley's crew. I'm not going to tell—"

"You're the producer, Mitch."

A pause. "This isn't how you do it, Sugar. You don't hound a guy when it's eleven o'clock at night. Jeezus."

"You said you'd help. Please."

A sigh. "I'll think about it."

"I mean really, please." The waitress slid past again, going the other way.

"I said I'll think about it, Sugar." He made that tongue pistol-clicking sound. "'Night."

I'll think about it. She gripped the phone book shelf, shaking with nerves. "Three's the charm," as Eileen would say, and this was her third pitch to Mitch. *I'll think about it.* Her shakes subsided, but she wasn't ready to return to her friends. She pushed open the door to the Ladies, and stared at her reflection in the mirror, glad Mitch hadn't seen her blotchy red neck. Vaughn was right, she did look like the governess in a B movie they saw in Paris: pale, high fore-head, prominent cheekbones, good cheekbones, her mother would say. Wetting a paper towel, she leaned over the sink, and pressed it against her throat, then straightened. She looked like herself, a mod-erately pretty twenty-two-year-old with brownish curls who used to look like Orphan Annie, when her hair was bright red, but looked now—she tightened her jaw and glared at her reflection—like some-one whose ambition and determination would obliterate all obsta-cles. She tucked in her blouse and pinched her cheeks.

The stragglers who'd been at the bar when she left had joined their table. Melanie, the idiot, was sitting on Jack-the-Sprat's lap, and Bob Kitchener and Judy were gone. Judy was one fast operator, and a conniving bitch. What Polly had was even better, *I'll think about it.*

Before she sat, Eugenia shot her a desperate look—where have you been? Can we go?

• • •

The next morning, Polly arrived at work early. Shelley was already holed up in his air-conditioned office, and Eileen wasn't in yet.

Intending to stay close to the phones to listen for Mitch, Polly chose to type the non-urgent letters Eileen had given her a few days ago instead of inventorying the supply room. Shelley's direct line blinked on and off as he made calls, but no calls came in.

When Eileen pushed open the front door looking hungover, she answered Polly's unasked a question, "No wisecracks from you, young lady. And what the hell are you doing sitting at my desk?"

"I thought I should stay by the phones until you got in."

"I'm here. Now get going on that inventory I need today. First, take out the trash. Shelley's corned beef from yesterday is stinking up the whole place. And get me a coffee from downstairs. Did you call the AC guy?"

When she returned with the coffee, Eileen said Shelley wanted to know where she was with rounding up the crew for Mitch's job.

"I've been waiting in case Mitch called. He told me last night he might ask Shelley to make some changes. I thought—"

"When did you talk to Mitch?" She put down her coffee and glared at Polly.

"Last night at a bar in Old Town."

"Jesus, Joseph, and Mary—"

"Just a quick conversation."

"You are not to go talking with clients, even if you know them, even if they are friendly, and absolutely not about—"

"Hello ladies." An AC repair man stood in the open door. "The sun has done a number on this place."

Polly used the moment to step away from Eileen's anger and drag away the table from under the air conditioner to give the guy room to work. As the guy laid out his tools, Shelley emerged from the back hall, nodded to him, " 'bout time," and told Polly to "get the hell to the lab and pick up the other half of the order they failed to send over."

Glad to escape, but sorry to leave the phones, she grabbed her purse.

By the time she returned, the office was cool, the AC guy was gone, and Shelley didn't say anything about Mitch calling when she delivered the film canisters to him in the editing suite. When she returned to the front room, Eileen said, "Mitch didn't call. Now get on the horn and call the crew before Shelley asks again."

I'll think about it. She was a fool to believe he would help her.

She phoned Mongo first. He was Shelley's director and first camera. He didn't answer his phone. Neither did Jules. Ernie was glad for the job and had nothing booked for the first two weeks of September. Sid had something lined up but he could re-arrange. Ray, the lunk, said count him in. Polly tapped on the door to the editing studio and told Shelley where things stood.

In mid-afternoon, Eileen was in the back with Shelley when Mongo came in to view the footage. From her first day, Mongo's cadaverous face and wolf-like teeth had intimidated her, but she stopped him.

"Can you wait a minute, please? I tried to reach you about a new job Mitch Kaine brought in. It's a bio doc of Cole Watkins, a photographer, with shooting in northern Wisconsin. Shelley wants you and the crew to keep open the first two weeks in September."

Mongo leaned against Polly's desk and took out his notebook. "Got it. Watkins lives in Wisconsin? Didn't know that."

She told him that she had called the others. Ernie and Ray were in, Sid was going to juggle things, Jules she hadn't reached, and he, Mongo, was supposed to get the van serviced. After he quit writing, she said, "One more thing. I know this isn't regular, but I was hoping …can you add me as an apprentice? I'll be an un-paid, not-in-your-way helper. Go-fer. I'll work for free. Shelley wouldn't have to pay me. I can carry my weight in—"

"The big guy said no, right?" He grinned his wolf-grin, and slapped shut his notebook, securing it with the rubber band. "Not for me to get in on this," and sauntered toward the back and the editing suite, obviously happy to deny her.

She stood at the window looking over the river toward the Loop. All the ant-size people on the streets below and across the river were busy working, striving, achieving what they wanted to achieve, while she was going nowhere.

3

June, 1974

GALE FORCE RAINS HAD EMPTIED THE PLAZA, except for one war protester holding an umbrella draped with a POW/MIA flag. Polly splashed past him toward her building's entrance. She had overslept, missed her usual El, and even though job cuts weren't to begin until after Labor Day, she did not want to be caught coming in late. Fighting with her own umbrella, she shoved through the revolving doors and asked Humberto to hold the elevator.

At the Illustration Department's reception desk, Milly made a sympathetic face and offered her a towel. "You look like a water-logged rag doll."

"It's like wearing clothes in a whirlpool to cross the plaza," which was how Bob had described Saigon in his last letter. "Is the Queen in?"

"She is, and I saw her coming out of your cubicle." Milly lowered her glasses to peer at Polly with comically dire implications.

"Probably dropping off an assignment," Polly said, which wasn't Vanessa's way. Was she checking to see if Polly was late?

Standing outside her cubicle, she shook her umbrella. On her typewriter sat a small white wedding invitation-like card.

Please come to my office.

Please, that was Vanessa's way, velvet glove on her iron hand. Polly knew what this was: last hired, first fired. She folded the card and dropped it in her wastebasket. She had assumed she would have a few more months. She hadn't even begun to look for a new job. Everyone said not to waste your time, the good jobs appeared at the end of summer. Only in February had she paid off her debts from her year of not working while she cared for her mother. As of last Friday, she had one month's rent in savings, and two hundred dollars in her checking account. She dried her ankles with the ratty cardigan she kept for cold days, and ran her fingers through her hair. None of the other picture editors said hi as she walked along the row of cubicles toward Vanessa's office. No one looked up, not even Janine who was half-turned away on her phone. Was this on purpose? Had they seen Vanessa snooping in Polly's cubicle and been buzzing since then?

Vanessa's door was open and seated in her visitor's chair was a girl. Polly's replacement? She was too young, eighteen- or twenty-years-old, and Vanessa wouldn't hire someone now. The girl was trendy in an electric blue mini-dress that barely reached her mid-thighs, white lipstick, sleek shoulder length blond hair, and ultra-high platform shoes. She looked cool and elegant. Stranger still, Vanessa was smiling.

"Polly, come in. I would like to introduce my niece, Phillipa Radcliff."

The girl stood to shake hands, hers fresh and cool, Polly's damp and hot. So, Polly wasn't being fired? As Vanessa explained that her niece was visiting the US on a short trip and would like to see where her aunt worked, the bits of Polly that had been torn apart by fear slowly knit back together.

She would be happy to take Phillipa on a tour of the office.

Outside Vanessa's office, Polly looked at the open field of work-tables flanked by cubicles where everyone was busy bent over their desk. This couldn't interest this British Vogue doll.

"Your aunt's domain, the Illustration Department, where we picture editors do our work." Was it 'we picture editors,' or 'us picture editors'? "If you like, I can take you to my office and show you what I do, we do."

Not trailing Polly but taking her own route, the girl floated through the tables as gracefully as a heron, joining Polly at her cubicle entrance. In three strides she was at the bulletin board scanning Polly's movie cards and tugging off the black and white still of Tom Courtenay from *The Loneliness of the Long Distance Runner*.

She sighed and kissed the card. "This man, he belongs to me."

Polly took the card from her, "And this belong to me," making a comic big deal of rubbing off the white lipstick smudge, pretending she was amused. "I charge a dollar per kiss. Pounds sterling are acceptable. Place your bills there." She nodded toward a non-existent tip jar and pinned the card back. Her movie card collection had traveled with her from job to job. Not her personal altar, as Janine had joked and Polly had denied, although this came close to the truth. She kept it in view as a reminder of what she cared about. "This is my desk, my phone, my light table, where I look at slides."

The girl's gaze slid over the file cabinets, the upended umbrella, the wadded-up sweater Polly had left on her light table. "Did you always want to be a picture editor?"

"It's where I ended up."

The girl wasn't listening. She turned to the file cabinet where Polly displayed a few photographs, and picked up the hinge-framed one. "Parents?"

"That's right." Her father in his uniform after he returned from the war, before he got fat, before he died, and her mother, young and happy, too.

The girl set it down and picked up the one of Bob. "Who's the dreamboat? Boyfriend or brother?" With the harsh sun bleaching his hair, his face half-hidden by his bad-boy aviators and his Castro beard, he looked like a movie star.

"Boyfriend. He's in Vietnam."

The girl's mouth hardened imagining bombed villages, napalm, children fleeing, burning monks. Polly and her boyfriend were typical, subhuman Americans.

"He's a reporter," Polly said, "with the AP, the Associated Press. He's covering the end of the war."

The girl's face smoothed, forgiving Polly and her boyfriend.

Annoyed, Polly mimicked Vanessa's polite smile. "Shall we move on to the Art Department?"

The girl perched on the edge of Polly's desk. "This is what I'm going to do."

"You want to be a picture editor?" Why had Vanessa not said this?

"No, cinema." The girl made big eyes at Polly's movie cards. "I'm going to work in cinema."

"You and everyone else," Polly said, sorry she'd said anything.

"I'm going to be a costume designer. Tony, he's a friend of the family." She tipped her head at the card she'd kissed. "Tony Richardson is the director of *The Loneliness of the Long Distance Runner*," as if Polly wouldn't know. "Even though he does not make the sort of films I'm interested in, he'll find me a position in the costume department of some studio."

Too good for Tony Richardson's films? Polly hoped she hid her scorn as the girl yammered about how she'd always loved costumes, how her family expected her to go to university, but she was determined to be a costume designer, on and on. Rich kid rebels against family's expectations—didn't she find it embarrassing to be the personification of a cliché? But as the girl talked, her cheeks glowing pink as she imagined her bright future, Polly remembered being that young, that sure of herself, that full of dreams. Behind her breastbone an old ache pulsed.

The phone rang. The girl jumped. Polly ignored the ringing. "We can skip the instructional portion of the tour, if you like. I can whisk you up to executive floor for the view of the Lake and all the way to Indiana, which you won't see because of the rain, but your aunt will ask if I took you up there, and then we'll get coffee."

"Fab."

Why had Polly suggested this?

In the coffee shop, the girl nattered about her ambitions and drew on her paper napkin, first a costume for a space odyssey, and asked the waitress for more napkins to sketch an Elizabethan court something or other, a beach romp, a funnel-neck coat. "For you. I see it in green to go with your lovely auburn curls and freckles. An office girl's coat." She handed Polly the napkin.

"Thank you. If I had the budget, I would hire a dressmaker." *Office girl* stung, but she was an office girl on the verge of middle age and soon to need a new job in another office.

Watching the girl hunch over her drawing with her hair falling over her face and her shoulders tense with concentration, Polly understood how the girl felt. She too had wanted to cast off the bonds of what others expected, her high school advisor's insistence that she take a typing course, her mother's hope that she would find a nice secretarial job in Peoria after college, her friends' expectations that she marry right after graduation, her friends now expecting her to marry Bob. She understood almost quivering with eagerness to escape. She folded the girl's drawing of the coat, and slipped it into her purse.

Outside Vanessa's office, Phillipa thanked her for skipping the boring bits.

Polly ignored the pile of envelopes the mail guy had delivered, and looked at her movie cards: the one with the slight white lipstick smudge, the black and white still from Maya Deren's weird short, *At Land*, a lobby card for *Midnight Cowboy*, and the postcard for Wiseman's *Titicut Follies*, which she wished she'd seen but hadn't. She pulled it loose to see who had sent it, postmarked nearly five years ago and addressed to the apartment she and Eugenia shared before she left to care for her mother, before Eugenia moved to New York.

What you up to, Pollyanna? Here's my new number. Mitch

She hadn't responded. A few months before the card arrived, she had run into him at a trade expo. Disco lights flashing, music blaring, Mitch stepped from the crowd, slicking back his hair, amused at her cheerleader outfit emblazoned with a fuzzy red A as she handed out flyers. *So, you survived that ruckus with Shelley. But what's with the scarlet A?* She said her boss at A-Line had never read a book. She was doing well, but no, she couldn't go for a drink. Too busy. No time off. Must work late. She couldn't face Mitch's happy patter, she couldn't face telling him about her dead ends since Kino, or explain her current lousy job with A-Line Productions, bookings and billings, and handing out flyers dressed in a humiliating tunic emblazoned with a big fat red A. She gave him her address, seeing no way out.

She returned the *Titicut Follies* card to the bulletin board. Her mother's accident had given her the excuse she needed to quit A-Line. At the time, nearly four years ago, she had believed she was making a big sacrifice, quitting her job, giving up the apartment she shared with Eugenia, moving away from her life, but the timing of her mother's accident couldn't have been better. It gave her a reason to run away from her so-called career in film. As the months in Peoria rolled by, as her mother began to heal in rehab, and later, when she came home to the new condo Polly bought after selling their house, Polly had reflected on what she would go back to when her mother no longer needed her. That she would return to Chicago she hadn't doubted, she loved the city, but she was never going to make it as a filmmaker. She did not have what it took. She did not have the kind of ability that could not be ignored or the drive or the luck of someone like Phillipa.

4

June, 1974

Rounding the corner, Polly saw her apartment building in the middle of the block and felt the lift she always felt. The crenellated roofline made the ordinary, red brick nine-flat look as if it had once had dreams of being a castle. This evening in spite of this pleasure, the thought of Vanessa's niece gnawed at her. Though she had softened to her by the end, the girl's taken-for-granted immense good luck offended her even more deeply now, but it was how the girl was so like she had been, her enthusiasm, her confidence that she would succeed, her certainty that the world was wide open and waiting for her, this was what wouldn't let Polly go. And this was humiliating and infuriating. She set down her grocery bags to unstick her dress from her sweaty back, reminding herself of her own privileges: she was healthy, she had a nice apartment, hunky foreign correspondent boyfriend, friends, Claire and Greg coming to dinner in an hour, the Chinese barbequed duck smelling delicious in the bag at her feet, and for now she had a decent job.

What she should focus on was that the Queen had chosen her to show her niece around, not one of the other editors, so Polly might not be first on the chopping block.

She walked past Mrs. Menendez's graystone two-flat, smiled at the sweet-faced concrete Madonna centered in the tidy plot of grass in front, and turned into her building's courtyard, then paused to look up at the third-floor rear windows with the bamboo shades she had lowered that morning. Home, hers alone, not a shared apartment, not her mother's condo, her first apartment with her name alone on the lease. In the two years since her time caring for her mother, the surprise and happiness of having her own home hadn't dimmed. If Vanessa's niece were plunked down on this block, she would find Polly's place pathetic, this whole working class neighborhood so far beyond her experience it might not even register, but for Polly this quiet neighborhood, this building, her own apartment, two bedrooms, kitchen with built-in dinette, big dining room, and bigger living room, was exactly what she wanted.

In the lobby she dug out her mailbox key. Bills and announcements, nothing from Bob. She didn't expect a letter, she'd gotten two last week, but she'd hoped. When he left at the end of January, he'd said six months max. Next week would be five months.

Juggling her bags and the mail, she trudged up the stairs. For all the obvious reasons, she had said no to his idea of moving in with her before he left, but yes to storing his stuff in her small second bedroom. His cardboard boxes filled the room, along with his old plaid suitcase, his winter clothes, a rocking chair, and his Italian typewriter in its oddly stylish green case. At least he had sold his ugly furniture, all post-divorce junk. Judy had gotten the condo in Cleveland, the furniture, the car, too.

Polly dropped the grocery bags inside her front door and walked to the shelf where she kept the Greek prayer beads that Eugenia had given her, a gift in their college days that was both ironic and not ironic. She wished she could talk to Eugenia about Bob, and about the new, ugly tension at EB, about needing to find a new job and how she kept skittering away from even starting, which she'd never done before, even skittering away from thinking through what she wanted with Bob. She wasn't someone who avoided what had to be done. Look how quickly she'd acted after her mother's accident, quit her job, no hesitation, leaving Eugenia to find another roommate. Eugenia had understood. For more than a year, Polly had dropped out of her life to take care of her mother. Polly knew how to launch into action.

She pressed the silvery beads to her throat. They were so cool. If she knew the words that went along with the beads, she would say them, not ironically. She would ask for Eugenia to be made well. She was doing fine. Fine? Polly had no idea what this meant. Polly was allowed to call only on Saturday, she couldn't come for a visit, and she was not to ask questions. Eugenia did not want to feel *obliged to file reports*. Polly resented that Eugenia found her concern invasive, but she did as she was asked, and kept silent, even though she did want reports. She wanted to know exactly what Eugenia was experiencing, exactly what the doctors said, and she wanted to visit, a brief visit, she wouldn't stay overnight. It bothered her that Eugenia joked about what her life was like. She joked about stalking the neighbors with binoculars, like Jimmy Stewart in *Rear Window*, but in the suburbs. She joked about the liquor deliveries to the old couple across the street, about wild pool bacchanals next door, about the beautiful lawn boy who did her parents' yard and their neighbors'. Polly went along. She told exaggerated stories about her job, about her weird assignments, Vanessa's posh mannerisms, Janine's AC/DC bossy/friendly bizarreness, about her downstairs neighbors trying to sell her their rusted beater, and about Bob's hair-raising anecdotes, dateline Saigon.

She dropped the prayer beads into their basket, peeled off her stockings, and carried the grocery bags into the kitchen to open the backdoor and let in a breeze. Standing at her porch railing she surveyed the view, the alley directly below that ran along the back of her building and the intersecting one that led to the cross street a long block away where the buses ran. Along the long alley, the flat garage rooftops gleamed in the slanting, late afternoon light, while shadows hid the tiny backyards between the garages and the two-flats. This view always brought her back to herself, her personal village, filled with immigrants and other families who'd lived here since forever, a small insular part of a huge and modern city. To the east, the heavy rains earlier in the day had left a blue fog surrounding the high-rises that blocked her sliver view of the Lake. The rumble of the El two blocks away shook the porch floor, the vibration full of energy and promise.

To set up for dinner with Claire and Greg, she pulled the picnic table away from the wall and flicked out leaves from the Guatemalan hammock that Claire had given her years ago. Claire was among the last of her friends still in Chicago from when she, Eugenia, they all first arrived fresh from college. Back then in their O'Toole's days, they all had shitty jobs and lots of ambition. Claire had been the envy of them all with her plan to join the Peace Corps their handsome, young President had just established and serve the nation by doing good in some poor, foreign country, before the Vietnam war made the idea of doing good in a poor, foreign country a mockery. When Claire left for Morocco, Polly was stuck at Advanced Media, the office manager in the three-person, barely-viable company, and Eugenia was still at International Dynamics, well-paid, but increasingly unhappy. Claire had an affair with a Moroccan man—the glamour of this!—but when he wouldn't introduce her to his family, she returned home heart-broken, but dark and sinewy as beef jerky. Eugenia and Polly had envied this too. Then Claire got a job in a downtown bank, met and married boring Greg Alexander, and had two kids, twins, now eight-years-old. The women libbers were wrong, she said, you couldn't have it all, but she had what she wanted. Most of their O'Toole's circle had married by then, Judy being the first, when she married Bob. Polly had felt snubbed and jealous, even though he had ignored her from the start. After Bob and Judy divorced, he returned to Chicago and Claire invited Polly to her Fourth of July party.

"You remember Bob Kitchener, don't you?"

He was taller than Polly remembered, and he had put on weight. With his middle-aged waist—he was forty-three then—and his curly beard, he looked even more like a Roman general than he had last time she saw him, which had been almost ten years. When he stood to shake her hand, she had felt the same hum of attraction she'd felt ten years before. He had had courtly manners back then too.

She plucked dried leaves from her potted geraniums and placed the prettiest one in the center of the picnic table, wishing he were here and not half a world away. The phone rang. Hoping it was he, even though he never called, she hid her disappointment hearing Vaughn's voice.

"Are you coming to town?" She asked. He only phoned when he planned to visit.

"Polly, friend of my youth, I am calling with bad news," his voice mock-somber.

"Your horse came in second? You're going bald?"

"This is terrible. Jean Pierre Melville died."

She reached for a tea towel to wipe the sticky tang of geranium leaves from her fingers. "He died a year ago." When they were in their junior-year abroad in Paris, Vaughn had dragged her to see Melville's *Bob le flambeur*, claiming it wasn't just a gangster movie, it was a stylish gangster movie.

"I just heard."

"A year ago, he died a year ago. You're always saying that Kansas City is behind the times."

"Seriously, he's dead? When I read this, I thought of your filming the greats, and thought, poor Polly, there goes another one."

"Melville wouldn't have been high on my list."

"You would have turned up your nose at the inventor of the jump cut?"

"I would not, you're right, and you're right again, another film great has gone to his grave without revealing all to Polly Wainwright."

"Are you annoyed with me?"

"Remember Claire and her square husband? They're coming for dinner in a few minutes."

"Poor Polly."

"I'll say hi for you. I've got to go."

When she introduced Vaughn to Bob last October at the Chicago Film Festival, he called Bob *le flambeur*, and Bob had been flattered, thinking it meant "flame." She had explained it meant "gambler." He liked that too. He and Vaughn didn't like one another. That night, they'd gone to the screening of Truffaut's *Day for Night*, which they all found silly. Vaughn pretended to be jealous of Bob's career, his pretend-jealousy masking his genuine jealousy, and Bob pretended not to be jealous of her *friend from the Paris year*, his arch italics audible. Later, she'd explained that she and Vaughn hadn't been lovers, and he hadn't believed her. If she'd told him the truth, that she and Vaughn had had sex once and decided never again, he wouldn't have believed that either.

She turned on the news, the story about the Viet Cong launching an attack from Cambodia, the story that had run yesterday in the *Trib*, under Bob's byline. He was mining pure career gold; he'd written in one of his first letters. The war was supposed to be winding down, but there was still plenty of killing to do, and plenty of stories for him to cover, he'd also written. Nothing for her to worry about. He wasn't one to risk his neck. She pictured his neck edged by his thick bronze sexy unkempt curls.

Her doorbell rang.

Claire wrapped her in a hug, no longer skinny and dark, but bosomy and freckled, which still came as a surprise, and behind her Greg smiling stiffly. Polly's neighborhood made him uncomfortable, too many rusted cars, too many fat women on porch stoops, too many kids who might steal hubcaps. He held out a bottle of wine she was sure was expensive.

"In the kitchen, left of the sink you'll find the corkscrew, but I've made sangria."

He turned down the hall toward the kitchen. His bald spot had expanded to the size of a monk's tonsure since she had last seen him at Bob's going-away party five months ago. Bob would be amused to learn this.

"You look great," Claire said, running her hands up and down Polly's arms, not saying as she usually did, that single woman had an unfair advantage in the weight department, since they did not have children whose meals they felt compelled to finish.

"And you look terrific," Polly said, not lying. Claire did.

"It's the glow," Claire, said, touching her belly.

"You aren't?"

"I am, but don't let on that I've told you. Greg wants to wait until we've told his family. But you're like family."

This wasn't true, but it pleased Polly. "No sangria tonight?"

"Or white bread or white rice or vanilla ice cream or white anything."

Greg called from the kitchen, "What's this on the platter?"

"Barbequed pterodactyl. You'll love it," Polly answered, looping arms with Claire and explaining it was duck from the Chinese market.

Seated around the picnic table with drinks and plates piled high, Claire said, "So what fire-fight is Bob covering these days?"

"Still reporting from a barstool in Saigon. He had a byline in yesterday's *Trib*. Did you see it?"

"What I mean is what does he say in his letters?" Polly knew what she really meant: when were they getting married?

"He likes the sweet coffee. The Paris Accords aren't exactly working, and there's this Cambodia angle."

"When's he coming home?"

"Soon. He said six months."

"He's nuts," Greg interrupted.

Polly twirled her sangria glass. "Bob has worked hard to be where he is, and he's happy. Covering big stories, not City Hall and the mayor's cronies, his byline appears all over the world."

"He's reporting from a war zone where no one knows who's going to shoot at you next."

"Stop, Greg," Claire said. "Switching topics—this pterodactyl is very good. I have one story about the twins, that's all, I promise."

Polly pretended to listen. Candyass was what Bob called Greg. Showboating was what Claire called Bob's going to Vietnam, not to Polly but to Eugenia who reported back. Bob needed a steadying influence, and Polly was a fool to let him go.

"Have you heard from Eugenia recently?" Claire asked.

Was she a mind reader? "We talk once a week."

"Coming home to an empty apartment, no kids, no family. I would think that gets old."

Claire didn't know that Eugenia was sick. Polly pictured Eugenia's bedroom in her parents' home, the lily of the valley wallpaper, the eyelet curtains, unchanged since high school Eugenia had said in her first phone call. "Are you talking about me?"

"Please. I envy you." Claire smiled, patting Greg's knee. "I just think long term."

"I have a mother, Claire. It's her job to think long-term." Her mother asked about Bob, but she stayed away from asking about their plans.

"I just worry you'll miss out."

She meant kids. "I'll get the ice cream." Polly picked up the decimated platter of duck.

Last fall, driving back from Claire and Greg's, after an awful dinner with the quarreling twins who used the rock-hard profiteroles as weapons, she and Bob agreed that they did not want kids. Marriage was the unspoken question for every couple after a certain point, marriage, then children, although until that night, she and Bob hadn't spoken of either. She had never liked kids, beginning with her babysitting days in high school, which was the only way for girls to make money. Her aversion had fortified after college when her friends paired off and became parents. Bob had said forty-three-years was too old for a guy, and furthermore, the irregular hours of a journalist didn't jibe with domesticity. Polly had not said that neither did his being twice married and twice divorced. Bob never talked about Judy, his second wife and Polly's former friend, or his first wife. She admired his discretion. But when he was sleeping over at Polly's most weekends and they became exclusive, she had wondered if either his early, brief marriage to Lisa or his five-year marriage to Judy had left any mark on him. She enjoyed being with him, loved their sex, and was glad he was unburdened by the wild emotional swings of the other divorced men she had dated, but when he brought up living together and suggested marriage, his being so unmarked by his previous women troubled her. Wasn't that what life did, mark you? Wasn't that the definition of being an adult, being marked by life?

"Are you sure you don't want to take any of this duck home?"

After Claire and Greg left, she dropped into the hammock. Against the dark sky fireworks exploded. She had wanted them gone an hour earlier, had even withheld the offer of the French brandy she kept for the last stage of fun dinners with friends, but with them gone, she felt lonely and abandoned. Everyone she loved was far away, Bob, Eugenia, her mother, even Vaughn in Kansas City, all of them were out of reach. If Bob were here beside her, not on the other side of the world, she would rest her head on his chest and feel his voice rumble through her while they dissected the evening. He would say Claire had reverted to type, and Greg had always been a wimp. Polly would counter that they had all become middle-aged, she and he, too, which he would deny, saying, not you, babe, you've not lost it, which was what she wanted to hear. She wished it were true.

5

September, 1962

A FLUKE AND POLLY GOT HER CHANCE. A week after Mongo and the Kino team went north to film Cole Watkins, Ray, the crew's tattooed muscle, broke his ankle in the woods. Ernie, Kino's gaffer, drove him home to Chicago and he needed to return to Wisconsin with another pair of hands. Shelley, "against my better judgment," put Polly on the crew. She was the cheapest option and she was standing right in front of him when he got the call.

It was still dark when Ernie picked her up, his beat-up Datsun smelling of his cloying aftershave and White Castle sliders. Pulling away from the curb, he announced they weren't going to stop for breakfast. Conversation was out, too, he didn't have to say, as he turned up the volume on the crooner channel. Bottling up her questions—Who was at Starlight Lodge, besides the crew? How was the shoot going? Who handled the electrical with him gone for two days? What would her job be?—she leaned back into the uncomfortable passenger seat, trying to ignore the schmaltzy songs on the radio, excited to be on her way, not headed to the office, but on a road trip, her future starting.

She was surprised to wake in Wisconsin. "Where are we?"

"North of Milwaukee. You won't be sleeping in when we get there, Princess."

"How much longer?"

"Geez, you are a kid. Maybe eight hours, depending."

"What's it like up there? What am I supposed to do?"

"What you'd expect, Princess." He tapped a cigarette from the pack he'd left on the dashboard and again set his face to do-not-disturb.

If she knew what to expect, she wouldn't have asked. Rolling down her window, she let the wind whip her hair across her face, glad the buffeting noise threw a barrier between them. Ernie was trying to make it hard for her, but she would be such an asset to the Kino crew, so quick at everything, even Mongo would be grateful that she had replaced Ray, even if she couldn't lift heavy equipment. With her can-do attitude she would wow them. She would be everywhere, eager to please, jumping to every request, no complaints, a whirlwind of assistance, no job too daunting, but if she could, she would try to find a way to tag along with Jules on second camera and lighting, although she'd be happy to take on anything.

They stopped for lunch at a roadside café surrounded by forest, and Ernie softened. He had ice-fished around here when he was a boy, he said, before telling her the shoot at Starlight Lodge was going as expected, except for dumbass Ray breaking his ankle. That put them back. And Mongo being Mongo had made an enemy of the housekeeper, Mrs. Boris Karloff, who was no longer feeding them, which was a drag, now it was box lunches from a dump in town someone had to waste their time getting, and the sons, Watkins' sons, were royal pains in the ass. Did Polly ice-fish? No, too bad. Neil, the older one, he was a largemouth bass, going for the bright lure, making trouble, seeing money coming out of this. Who would want to watch an old geezer blather about the bygone glory days? Ernie would like to know. Back when Ernie was a kid fishing with his uncles, they'd throw back crap fish. Watkins' younger son, Cyrus, he was a crap fish.

"What about Mr. Watkins?"

"Half out if it." Ernie dug into his sandwich.

"What do you mean?"

"Can't light a cigarette hisself without shaking. I hope we get the hell outta there before he sets the place afire, but he's all right. Makes no fuss about nothing"

Mr. Watkins, his two sons, the Kino crew of four, that would make seven men to her one at Starlight Lodge. "Is Mitch there?" Cold water sluiced along her spine as she remembered begging him to make Shelley put her on the crew.

"Mitch the Man, he's come, he's gone, he'll be back at the end to take a victory lap."

She exhaled a breath she hadn't realized she was holding. All she could do was pretend her humiliating groveling hadn't happened and neither had his rejection.

When they left the café, Ernie paused before unlocking the car doors. "Smell those Northwoods."

It smelled like Vicks VapoRub. As they drove north, the villages became sparser and the forest crowded both sides of the narrow, two-lane road. Ernie talked about fishing, learning to tie jigs, his cousins, the tragedy of the cabin being sold, and she thought about what it would be like to be sequestered in the middle of nowhere with a bunch of men. Ernie was benign, dull and stupid, but not a worry. Mongo had a string of ex-wives, and he was a fulltime jerk personally as well as professionally. Sid and Jules were married, so they would be somewhat civilized, and both of them were nice to her. Mitch—she didn't want to think about him—but he was married. And the two sons, and the great man himself.

• • •

The sun slid down the western sky, and Ernie switched on the headlamps. "We're a few miles out now. Start looking for a sign for Echo Lake."

"Can we stop at the motel first so I can clean up?"

"No can do."

"Why not?"

"Because we're headed straight to the Lodge is why."

Was it because they were getting close to the rest of the crew that he'd fallen back into his usual jerk-ness?

Ten minutes later, he swung the Datsun into a break in the forest on the right, and the headlamps carved a tunnel through the thickets of boughs and brush. A ghostly moth hit the windshield. In a scary movie this would be the moment before things got bad. She wished she were at home, with Eugenia, talking over cups of cocoa, or maybe getting ready for a date with Harris, who had possibilities. What was she doing here? She hated the woods. She had hated Girl Scout camp. She was scared of snakes and bears. She didn't belong here. She shouldn't have been so eager. Shelley was right. She should have waited for a project in the city.

The car's lights broke through the brush and swept into a clearing unrolling a carpet of mown grass against the dark. Far ahead in the murky haze, barely visible, hunkered a sprawling building, about two stories high, at its center a glowing dome above a glass entrance that shone with the same faint yellow. On either side extended silhouetted wings. Starlight Lodge. She had arrived. Smoky meadow, mysterious building with a glowing heart, ragged black woods on all sides, dark sky above: this was an image she would fix forever in her mind. Someday, when she was a famous filmmaker, an interviewer would ask her where she got her start, and she would say Starlight Lodge, letting resonate the fitness of the name—starlight, light against the dark, the very definition of film. This would go in her journal.

Ernie pulled alongside Mongo's van, which she hadn't noticed, and cut the engine. She saw a wide wedge-shaped courtyard that narrowed toward a wall with a blue door. Light fell from a window on the right.

"How many wings does this house have?"

"Five."

"So it's star-shaped?"

"You're a quick one, Princess. The master designed it himself." He nodded toward the crates in the backseat, "leave that," and groaned out of the car. Watching him hobble through the courtyard toward the door, she was washed with excitement, inadequacy, eagerness, and fear. She was in the middle of nowhere and it was dark, but Shelley wouldn't have sent her if he didn't think she would be safe. Ernie passed through light streaming from the window, while she climbed out of the car, and took a deep breath.

"I'm not holding the door for you, Princess."

"Stop with the Princess." In the window, she saw Mongo, Jules, and Sid sitting at a table in a cloud of cigarette smoke, and beyond, a wide, old woman lifting plates into a cabinet. Her hair was dyed the color of root beer. She didn't look like Boris Karloff.

Polly grabbed the knob before the door shut and stepped into a softly-lit white circular space, wider than her whole apartment. The high-vaulted ceiling, capped by a glass dome, glowed from a ring of dim lamps that were reflected in the shining white marble floor. Everything quivered with soft light. The space wasn't quite circular, but angled with five flat walls centered with wide double doors, set between four narrower walls, and the glass entryway on her left—ten sides, an irregular decagon. Opposite the entrance a curving staircase rose to a gallery on the second level, with three closed doors. Beneath the gallery were two sets of double doors, and between them, Kino's cases.

"Get the hell in here." Ernie stood holding an open door on her right. From behind him came Mongo's rumble.

"It's like an antechamber to heaven in a nineteen-forties movie."

"Would ya think there was so much money to be made in still photography? Bedrooms and bath above—we're not shooting up there. His highness's studio over there doesn't have a room above. Same with the wing behind you, the library. Cathedral ceilings. Perfecto lighting. Come on. You can gawk later."

She glanced at the three doors on the second floor. "The bathroom's upstairs?"

"Off limits, Princess. It's the great outdoors."

"You're not serious."

"We don't use their facilities, Princess. I recommend you take the long way around that barn and go out a-ways. And watch out for poison ivy."

"Oh, come on."

"Hurry back." He let the kitchen door slam shut behind him.

He might not be teasing about poison ivy. She wondered if she should try to hold it. Wishing she had a flashlight, but she wasn't going to go back in and face their laughter, thinking about Ray breaking his ankle, she walked slowly over the patchy ground away from the Lodge and into the dark. She could take whatever they dished out. *Leaves of three, let them be.* What good would be her Girl Scout poison ivy identification skills if she couldn't see the leaves?

When she entered the kitchen, she waited by the door as Mongo talked about the schedule, the others taking notes. No one greeted her, but after a few moments, Sid lifted an eyebrow toward the empty chair at the far end. When she eased behind Mongo, he broke off.

"Ernie give you an idea of what you're supposed to do?"

"I should do whatever you guys ask."

Mongo laughed. "That's about right." He rocked forward, banging his chair legs on the floor. "Well then, we're through here. And you," he said to Polly, "you be ready at eight-thirty sharp, waiting, out there, with the equipment." He jerked his thumb toward the door to the atrium.

"Wouldn't I be with you?"

"You thought you'd be staying at the motel with us? No missy. Special treatment for you, Shelley's orders. Mrs. Borus, the soul of kindness, will put you up in her cottage."

Shelley had made her a pariah. She hid her anger as Mongo flashed his wolf-grin and the men stubbed out their cigarettes and gathered papers. Mrs. Whatever-her-name held a glass at the sink, taking a sip and giving no sign she had heard herself mocked.

In the silence left behind after the door closed behind the men, the woman said, "Get your things and come back in here. I'll walk you over. It's Borus, Mrs. Borus."

Ernie had left Polly's bag on the ground near where his Datsun had been parked.

The cottage was bigger than it looked: a good-size pine-paneled room with a wood-burning stove and a lounger patched with duct tape parked on a braided rug; on opposite sides of the room, doors to two bedrooms; in the back, a barebones kitchen and a tiny bathroom.

"You'll take the second shower. The water tank's small." The woman handed Polly some clean sheets.

The bedroom had a single bed with a flat, pin-striped mattress with a blanket folded at its foot, an old washstand, and a high-backed chair. Except for the bedside lamp with a rawhide shade painted with cowboys, the room was spartan enough to serve a circuit preacher who seldom visited. And it was cold. The window beside the bed had been left cracked open—Mrs. Borus had planned for Polly's arrival. She lifted the curtain and saw the Lodge's dome, like a beckoning lighthouse. There, that was where her future would begin.

She made the bed, unpacked, and put her journal on the bedside table. She was too tired to even brush her teeth. Later she would write what she saw as they drove up, and Ernie's threat about poison ivy. She listened to worrying night sounds from outside, exhausted from being tugged in so many different directions, and fell asleep.

Running water woke her. Mrs. Borus taking a shower and it was almost eight o'clock. Mongo said eight-thirty. She threw back the covers, gathered her best shirt and her new jeans, and waited for Mrs. Borus to finish.

• • •

Fifteen minutes later, Polly closed the cabin door behind her and saw in the dewy grass Mrs. Borus' footprints leading to the Lodge. The sky was clear and blue, with a few puff ball clouds to the east above the forest that circled the sunlit meadow that was as big as two city blocks. The Lodge was off to one side, near the forest, and behind her, beyond Mrs. Borus' cabin were two sheds, a broken-down pump-house, and the barn she'd walked around last night. In the bright light of day, she could see that the Lodge was all black, black roof, black-stained wood siding.

High-stepping through the wet grass, she hurried toward the Lodge's entrance and peered inside. The atrium was as beautiful as last night, but different, dancing with wands of daylight from the entrance and the skylight. She stood back to look at the two black wings on both sides converging on where she stood. The proportions were not exactly overwhelming or grand, but solid and steadying, which wasn't something she'd ever thought about in connection to a building. Dark and heavy, weighted to this place, but not part of this nature, Starlight Lodge was emphatic and obviously created by a singular mind, Cole Watkins himself, according to Ernie.

Wondering if she had time to take a quick tour, she turned to look at where the car tracks entered the forest. No sound of cars, no sound except the wind. She took off, loping through the tangly grass that bordered the wing Ernie said housed Mr. Watkins' studio. High up ran a band of windows. Rounding the pointed corner, she came to a wide, wedge-shaped space between the studio wing and the next wing. The open space was the same size and shape of the courtyard she'd passed through last night and filled with yellowing weeds and crickets. Hurrying on, listening for the crew, she strode past the next wing and came to another weedy space, with the forest not ten feet away, and another wing, another space, until she arrived at the paved courtyard with the blue door. She looked up into the brilliant sky. From a bird's-eye view, the Lodge would look like five triangular barns, if there was such a thing, each with a pitched roof, the wide bases of the triangles converging in a circle, like a gigantic silo topped with a glass dome.

Mr. Watkins had his vision of what he wanted and he sure disregarded the conventions of what makes a good house or even an impressive one. It was weird and impractical, with wasted space at each wing's tip, and the construction had to be all custom. Was this what creative meant—ignore the norms? What she called creative was how the film giants pushed beyond what had been done before. They pushed forward by ignoring the norms, or maybe they simply experimented until something clicked. *It just seems right*, what her mother said about positioning the paper roses on her decoupage wastebaskets, but what her mother called creative wasn't what Polly called creative. Creative wasn't willy-nilly messing around, of that she was sure. Creative, or what she had accepted as creative, was what the experts declared to be great. Creative equaled great. Could someone be creative and produce bad work? Could someone be creative and design an ugly house? Was creativity, the practice of it, something different from making great things?

Mrs. Borus' face appeared in the kitchen window. She signaled for Polly to come in. Mongo and the crew must be late. Wishing she could stay where she was until they arrived, she wiped her damp, grass-flecked sneakers on the doormat, and went inside.

Mrs. Borus pointed to the coffee pot. "There's muffins if you like cherry."

"Isn't anyone up?" Polly asked, choosing the biggest muffin.

"Mr. Watkins sleeps in." Mrs. Borus tucked a napkin under a juice glass on the tray.

Polly waited for more as Mrs. Borus filled a coffee carafe and put it on the tray. "The sons, they sleep in, too?"

"They don't stay here."

From her tone, Mrs. Borus didn't like them any more than the crew did. The sons were behind this film, but they didn't stay in their father's house. Odd. How had this film idea come together? Did Mitch say it was the sons' idea? And who was putting up the money? The business behind this was what she needed to learn. Hearing the rumble of Mongo's muffler, she swallowed the last of her muffin and hurried into the atrium. She would be waiting exactly where Mongo told her to be.

He stomped in the glass entryway trailing the rest of the team and the smell of cigarettes and coffee. No one greeted her as they headed toward the equipment. She stood aside, waiting to be told what to do, as bins clattered open and were dragged out on the marble floor. Mongo looked up from his clipboard to scowl at her.

"You standing there doing nothing, you're with Sid. Help him with the equipment."

While the rest of them laid dolly tracks for the camera to approach the house from across the meadow, Sid would record sound in the woods. She was to do exactly what Sid said and keep his notes.

"Got that Sid? She's yours. No fuck ups."

Sid nodded, he wasn't worried.

Mrs. Borus pushed open the kitchen door and they all fell silent watching her carry the breakfast tray upstairs. When she opened the door to what Polly assumed was Mr. Watkins' bedroom, Mongo looked at Polly. "Just to be crystal clear, you do not talk to any of the

Watkins, sons or the old man. When they're around, you are a piece of furniture. No one talks to the Watkins but me."

"Got it."

Sid handed her a bag. "Get the small generator and the hand cart, and don't worry about Mongo."

Dragging the cart, she followed him out the back door and across the cobblestones, fighting the tippy cart, and over a mown stretch of grass before they entered the woods. Sid was the kindest of the guys. She was glad her first assignment was assisting him, but she was sorry to miss what the others were doing. What did laying track involve? How carefully was every shot planned beforehand? Did Mongo scope out other options as they went along? When the sons arrived, what would happen? She wanted to be everywhere, taking in everything.

After they unload the bins, Sid unfolded a tarp for the Nagra, the sound recorder, "state of the art, costs an arm, don't touch," gently lifting it from its case and connecting the cables, she memorizing every move. He aimed a microphone at a clump of leaves, then pointed to the Nagra. When the leaves fluttered, the needle jumped. She laughed and he did too. He showed her where to write the scene description in his notebook, read off numbers from the counter, then he pulled out a tiny microphone, no bigger than a watch battery, and placed it under a pile of leaves half a dozen yards away.

"Quit breathing."

She stared at the spot where the microphone's cable dove under the leaves, and tried to match Sid's Buddha-stillness while small critters scurried through the underbrush. Overhead, a bird cawed. The Nagra's needle jumped, then stitched a zigzag line as she slowed her breath and drew around her the happiness of being part of the crew, a part of this busy world of beetles and squirrels and rustling leaves, of recording all this life.

Except for when she stepped on a twist in a cable and almost broke it, things went well for the rest of the morning. By the time she and Sid returned the equipment to the atrium, the others were eating lunch on the grass in front of the Lodge near what looked like narrow-gauge railroad tracks that curved over the meadow toward the woods. They had already filmed the approach to the Lodge, and camera and the dolly were already packed away. She was sorry to have missed all that, but she was glad they'd saved a box lunch for her. It was as bad as Ernie had said, but that didn't stop her from devouring the stale sandwich and bruised apple. With the sun on her shoulders, listening to the men banter, she was right in the center of her dreamed-of life.

When Mongo stood and shook out his bad knee, she gathered up the lunch remains without being told, while he gave out the afternoon assignments. Jules and Sid would take Ernie's Datsun to scout locations in the nearest town, for filler; Ernie would stay at the Lodge to build a new box. Mongo was leaving them on their own, and he would meet up with the guys at the motel in the morning.

"And me?" Polly asked.

"Doesn't matter. Join the location scouting. Tomorrow's a big day. Pissant son interviews loco dad. But right now, with me." He limped toward the Lodge.

Maybe Sid had ratted on her about the twenty-five-dollar cable he'd had to repair. Maybe Mongo wanted her to separate from the pack before pouncing, like the lion she'd seen in a documentary. She followed him into the atrium, trying to hide her alarm.

From the top of an unopened crate, he picked up the logbook, not the cable. "Know what this is?"

Was this a trick question? "The logbook." Logbooks were the Bible, Shelley said. Every scene shot, all technical details were recorded in the logbook. The logbooks of every film Kino had ever worked on, even the ones that died along the way, were stored in the editing suites. If any were pulled out for consultation, it was her job to make sure they were returned to the right place.

"This baby is essential, got that, essential, and I am entrusting you with it. Here's the drill—at the end of each day, after I fill in the last of my notes, Sid too, I hand it to you and you take it somewhere safe. Me and the boys go out at night, the motel's not secure, so this baby stays here on this property with you. You keep it overnight. When I hand it to you, you keep it as safe as if your life depended on it, which it does. Right this minute, before you head out with Sid and Jules, you take it to your room. Tomorrow you give this back to me in the AM."

She clasped the logbook to her chest, hiding her elation. Outside sun sparked off the meadow, dots of green and gold, crowning her happiness.

• • •

The next morning as the crew pulled out the equipment bins, Mongo said they would film in the studio, the maestro leafing through old tear sheets from *Life* magazine and jawing on about the good old days. Polly was to assist Jules, but first she was to put the logbook in Watkins' studio, on the cabinet near the closet door where the walls narrowed.

Lighting with Jules, sound with Sid, this was better than she'd hoped for. She pressed open the studio's doors and took in the blinding white space. Everything was white, white walls, the floor, worktables, deep flat-file cabinets, lockers, white light streaming down from the row of high windows. Mr. Watkins' photographs were pinned on the long wall opposite the windows and spread out on tables. Some of the pictures she had seen in Eugenia's book: the interior of bombed-out church, soldiers crouched by sand dunes, tiny planes overhead releasing bombs, the close-up of an exhausted GI, his eyes crazed.

"Quit gaping," Mongo said, coming up behind her, "and put the logbook there." He pointed to the cabinet. "Then get your ass in gear and help Jules mask the windows."

Nothing from outside would be visible, the windows were too high, but the daylight flooding in was too intense. She held the ladder steady for Jules, and together they juggled rolls of gray acetate, the box cutter, and tape until all the windows were covered, and the room dimmed to a soft glow. While she and Jules were busy, Sid had set up his Nagra and was testing a microphone near where Ernie sat on a stool as a stand-in for Mr. Watkins. After Mongo had set up his camera on a tripod in front of Ernie, Jules raised the light stands and checked the angles with Mongo. Her job was to move the stands.

"Small moves, go slow. Don't tip anything over," Jules said, standing beside Mongo.

"This one?" She moved it three inches closer. It was alarmingly top-heavy.

"Now the left lamp, back six inches, no, a foot. Ten degrees off midnight." Jules held his light meter to Ernie's face as Mongo switched lenses.

Inching the stands back and forth, as instructed, adjusting the barn doors and reflectors, she watched the effects on Ernie's face. Some moves created caverns below his brow ridge, some flattened the planes of his forehead and cheeks, others softened every contour until his face looked air-brushed. Ernie went from kindly to clown, from threatening to magisterial. It was magic. Sculptural lighting she'd first noticed in Orson Welles' *Lady from Shanghai*, and been wonder-struck, not knowing but wanting to know how he achieved such effects. Maybe he wasn't the lighting genius, maybe his cinematographer was, but interviewing Orson Welles would be a great start for her Greats of Film.

Something banged. Mongo slamming his fist on the table. He growled, "What the fuck?"

Everyone went still. Ernie's face slackened and he swiveled in her direction. Jules, too, and Sid, they all stared at her.

She turned to Mongo. "Me? What did I do?"

He pounded his fist on the table again. "You fucking wandered into the frame. This isn't a fucking field of daisies here. Get the hell out!"

Was he kidding? All she'd done was move a few inches. The camera wasn't running. She'd lost track for one minute, that was all. Nothing happened. Mongo glared at her. Trying to hide her rage and confusion—a little mistake, that was all—she walked jerkily past Jules and Ernie, who kept their eyes down. Her face flamed, she could feel it.

In the atrium, she was startled—two men on the staircase stared at her, one pudgy and middle-aged, the other, tall with crazy white hair, had to be Mr. Watkins. They stared at her.

"Where are you going?" Mr. Watkins said.

"Nowhere." She kept walking to the kitchen door.

"Come back."

"I can't."

She slammed shut the door behind her. Mrs. Borus looked up, then away as Polly pushed aside a chair to stand at the window, trying not to cry. Mr. Watkins had spoken to her and she had brushed him off. She couldn't do anything right. The pudgy one must be a son taking him to the studio where he would be interviewed and she would miss it. She hoped it was a disaster. She could hear nothing, the studio doors must be closed. Mrs. Borus gave her a mug of coffee.

Sometime later, Ernie came in to say she was needed for breakdown. She pretended nothing had happened.

In the studio, the atmosphere was grim. Mr. Watkins was gone, the son too. The light stands had been folded flat, Jules was boxing them, Sid was disconnecting his cable, and Mongo scowled, strapping shut his camera case, not looking in her direction.

"Get a handcart," Ernie said. "We're moving to the barn." They would film Mr. Watkins' car collection.

Six cars under loose covers were lined up in a row in a barn too immaculate to have ever housed livestock. Jules flicked back the canvas on the one nearest the door.

"Oh my God, an XK 140," he moaned, ogling a sleek black sports car. Jaguar, spelled out in chrome, a perfect name.

"Polly, get something soft to dust this beauty, then shine up the chrome." Jules pointed to a shelf of rags and a rusted tin of wax.

Without Mongo, the atmosphere was relaxed as they set up for a low tracking shot. Mongo had remained at the house with Watkins' sons, intent on not letting them near the barn because they'd fucked up the morning shoot. Apparently the elder one, not the one Polly had seen, had screwed up the interview with Mr. Watkins. He had interrupted the old man's answers, twisted the questions, and veered from the script agreed to with Mitch.

When she'd finished polishing the chrome and the men laid the dolly tracks, Mongo appeared at the barn's entrance alone, his face red with annoyance. Polly kept her eyes on the car and they all fell silent as Mongo inspected the tracks, and stayed silent as he set up the camera.

Her job was to flick the tarp off the front of the Jaguar as the camera approached without snagging the cloth on any part of the car's body or letting it appear in the frame. She was precise and careful with every movement, determined not to have a repeat of the morning's fiasco, and soon the air thickened with dust from the flicking on and off. Even when the canvas got caught or failed to puff in the right way, Mongo didn't yell at her. His fury with Watkins' sons must have eclipsed his anger with her.

After they packed up and returned the equipment to the atrium, Sid invited her to join them for dinner, and Mongo didn't object. Not believing her luck, she squeezed into the back seat of Ernie's Datsun next to a carton of reflectors and C-clamps and listened to Ernie and Sid complain about Mongo, the hothead, Neil, the bigmouth bass, whom she had not seen, and the shaky old man. What she had done wrong didn't even merit a mention.

Near a T in the road, they pulled alongside a log tavern with "The Woodcutter" spelled out in loopy neon on the roof. By the entrance standing guard stood four-foot high trolls hacked from tree trunks.

"You got ID," Ernie asked.

"I'm twenty-two, and yes."

The low-ceiling dim space smelled of BO and stale beer and was half-filled, mostly with guys who might be lumberjacks and a bunch of families. Kids? Who takes kids drinking? Behind the bar a long picture window overlooked a menagerie of gnomes and clumps of spot-lit trees hung with birdfeeders. To attract bears, the bartender said, winking at Polly, adding the bears ate the birds that came for the seed. When she returned to the table with the first of many pitchers of beer, Ernie said the bartender wasn't teasing. They'd seen a bear their first night. Mongo ordered pizzas, not asking what anyone wanted. The pizza was tasteless, but she was ravenous, they all were. They finished off four large ones, ordered two more, and the men talked about the inconvenience of not having a film processing lab nearby, whether Mongo should have used a wider lens in the barn, and how Mitch's coming in the morning would make everything that much slower, while Polly said nothing, happy not to be singled out or mocked or teased, happy to be one of the gang.

6

July, 1974

IN THE SIX WEEKS SINCE VANESSA ANNOUNCED LAYOFFS would
begin by the end of the summer, a stilted courtesy had descended
over the Illustrations Department. No more seeking advice about
picture sources, no more jokes about HQ's Brit-style directives or
the guy with suspenders in the mailroom or Lowry in Art who
might or might not wear nipple rings. The old editors, the knitting
circle as Polly thought of them, took lunch together on the Plaza
on nice days, but for her set, the under-forty, everyone ate alone at
their desks, giving the impression that they were diligent workers,
and no more companionable complaining about work or men or
diets over drinks at Riccardo's. No one wanted to invest in office
friendships that would end in a few months, or maybe each of
them saw the others the way she did, competition in the soon-to-
be-entered job market, a job market made worse by the economic
recession. Except for staff meetings, they kept apart. Which was
why she was surprised to look up from her slide viewing table to

see Janine standing in her cubicle entrance holding a package and grinning in her old, usual way.

"Saw this in the mail room. It's for you." Janine shook the package that was wrapped in re-used grocery bags and held together with twine. She'd been away on vacation for a couple of weeks, unaccountably unworried that vacationing before the layoffs began might not be the best policy. "It rattles, and it's from Idaho." She cackled manically.

Ignoring how Janine irritated her, Polly waved her in, glad for any distraction from worrying about what was ahead. "Could it be Christmas in July?" She reached for her scissors. "How was your vacation?"

Inside was a shirt box wadded with crumbled tissue paper nestling lengths of rusted barbed wire, each about twelve inches long and braided with barbs. One had toothed metal discs, another sharply-pointed stars, another had tiny fierce triangles, all looked like they could rip open your skin.

Janine picked up the one with crescent moons. "Cut from old fences, I bet."

Polly read aloud the handwritten note.

> Dear Sir or Madam,
> My friend Bethune Miller of the history
> society in Boise told me about your search. I
> hope these pieces will be of inerest to you.
> Yours very truly,
> Herbert P. Smith

Examining the wrapping, Polly said, "Return address missing and no information. Thank you, Mr. Herbert P. Smith, but I need facts."

"You need a photograph, not this junk."

"I'll ask Lowry for help."

"Good luck with that."

They both turned at the sound of someone tapping. The summer intern, The Lurker, crossed to hand Polly a stack of phone messages. "You weren't picking up."

"I was here." She glanced at her phone. "Must have knocked it off the hook." She replaced the handset as Janine shot her an amused look and followed the girl out, ducking back to ask if Polly wanted to go out for dinner after work.

"Can't," she said, glad to have an excuse. "My old friend, Vaughn, is in town. Don't make that face. He's married. Bob is fine, thriving in chaos. I got a letter yesterday."

Janine twiddled "too-da-loo" in her annoying way, and Polly turned to her phone messages. Nothing urgent, and one surprise, from Mitch Klein. How had he tracked her down at EB? Eileen must have told him.

Call. It's important, what he'd said when he phoned after Shelley died. He called to tell her that and urge her to go to the funeral. She was at Advanced Media then, so five years ago, months before her mother's accident, and she already knew about Shelley's death. Eileen had told her. Eileen had also said that Shelley and Mitch had been on the outs and at each other's throats about money. Polly hadn't gone to the funeral. It was a relief to know that she would never have to see Shelley again. In the twelve years since her fiasco at Starlight Lodge, her only contact with Mitch had been that one phone call, and the time when he appeared at the trade show and caught her wearing a cheerleading outfit as she handed out brochures for A-Line Productions. He'd given her his card. As soon as he was out of sight, she had thrown it away.

Under Mitch's name was his company, Wingspan, which The Lurker had adorned with a pair of wings. *Call. It's important.* Not to Polly, it wasn't. She wadded up the note and lobbed it at her wastebasket, then re-packed the barbed wire. Important was a matter of who you were and where you stood at any particular moment in the world, and right now, hanging onto her job as long as possible was important to her, even though there was nothing important about what she actually did in this job, today or any other day. No one would claim that attaching pictures to dumbed-down articles was important to any one, except the bosses.

Leaving the messy grocery bag wrappings on her desk, she carried the flimsy box holding the barbed wire to Lowry, head of Art. He spun his chair to face her, his belligerent expression unchanging when she said hi and entered, nipple rings not evident under his tight Oxford cloth shirt. Smiling, not looking at his chest, she asked if his photographer could take a picture for her. He held up his hand, Stop, like a crossing guard as she laid the box on his desk and opened it, hoping that the prickly lengths of wire would be weird enough to interest him. They were. He was delighted. Could he keep these marvelous examples of Americana after his guy took the photos? Sure. He smiled at her. He would get his guy to jump on it today. Polly would have the photo on her desk in the AM. He could keep these samples? He might mount them on board, make a piece of wall art, but she was not to tell the other picture editors that he'd done her a favor.

Wishing the days of joking around with the other editors weren't over, wondering if she could brag to Janine about wresting a favor out of Lowry, she pounded down the stairs to the library. If she had a photo by the next day, she needed caption information. Vanessa insisted on full and detailed captions.

The last time she'd visited the library was seven weeks ago, and as always, she was alone. She might be the only editor who used the place. In the first aisle with the most recent edition of the encyclopedia, the volume she'd consulted on Hodgkin's disease was aligned perfectly, as she'd left it, compressed in the middle of the shelf, giving no sign that she'd read about blood chemistry, symptoms, and prognoses. Eugenia was doing well, she said, her doctors said. She was weak. Polly could hear that in her voice, but their conversations would last more than an hour, so she wasn't too weak, but she didn't want Polly to visit, not yet. If Polly asked too many questions, Eugenia would push her away saying, *tell me something I haven't heard before.* Eugenia could be as private as a cat.

Polly turned into the aisle with reference books on American history, and for an hour, read about the settling of the American West, land management, herding and grazing rights, corralling techniques, and the Bessemer technique of steel production. Learning new things was what she enjoyed most about this job. Bob said she had a magpie mind. She found almost everything interesting, random facts, the look of the world, how people in different places and cultures did things, the objects they made. Finding illustrations so good that reading the actual encyclopedia article wasn't necessary was her secret goal. Let the visuals do all the work. That was her private challenge. This and the paycheck were what she liked about this job. When this job ended, she had nothing to fall back on. If Bob were here, he'd croon, "You've got me, Babe."

She pushed away the thought and turned back to the book.... *barbed wire, invented and patented in 1867 by Lucien B. Smith of Ohio.* Nothing else. Could Lucien B. be related to the Herbert P. Smith who'd sent her the old samples? Did the Smiths have a lock on the early days of barbed wire? This would make a good story for Eugenia—the old coot in Idaho, the Smith of Ohio, far flung members of a barbed wire clan, the ineptly-wrapped package, Lowry wanting to make wall art. But she had no facts for a caption. Polly returned her books to the shelves.

"Assorted examples of old barbed wire." Vanessa might kill the illustration instead of letting it run with such a caption.

Even if Polly bombed on the caption, she had a great photo, so she might not be the first editor Vanessa would let go. Irene had to be cajoled to turn in completed assignments, and Tina spent so much time in the Ladies Room with her morning sickness, she might voluntarily quit, which would take off some of the pressure for Vanessa to thin the ranks. Still, Polly needed to start looking. The kinds of jobs she'd once hoped for didn't exist and the recession was bad, but she would find something that would pay her bills. What was making her procrastinate was the nauseating process of making herself into a pert, eager, hard worker who was malleable, a peg to be fit in whatever hole they had. She couldn't delay much longer. In a couple of weeks, by the end of July, she would start looking through the want ads and calling the employment agencies. If she were lucky, she would find a place before Vanessa fired her.

After the office had emptied, she changed into her Givenchy knockoff mini dress and good heels. She wasn't going to tell Vaughn that she was broke at the end of every month and she'd soon be looking for a new job.

Waiting at the usual spot, she waved at his cab as it U-turned to halt in front of her.

She climbed in and kissed his cheek, liking his manly, prosperous smell. The Vaughn who had been so broke he swiped food off other people's plates and bummed cigarettes off strangers now wore tightly-cut suits and white-collared blue shirts, like the wealthy Parisians he once mocked, *reverting to type*, as Bob had said about Claire, what she could say of most of her friends. *Early onset middle age*, Eugenia would say.

Vaughn muttered something to the driver who swung the cab into the Michigan Avenue traffic, horns blaring, then turned to Polly. "Have to say, I'm surprised you almost missed this Wiseman screening." She'd told him this when he suggested they see Wiseman's latest documentary at Doc Films. "Glad to save the day, but what's happened to my favorite cinéaste?"

"What happened to the guy who was going to roam the world writing for travel magazines?"

He grinned. "I married the boss's daughter and got fat and happy. You look great, by the way. Am I allowed to say that, or have you become one of those feminists?"

"What's wrong with feminism? And, no, I shave my legs." She extended a leg, showing off her fancy purple pump. Vaughn expected her to show off well, and she liked dressing up, and she liked him. "You look good too."

He radiated pleasure. Settling his arm over her shoulders, he talked about his flight, problems with his hotel room, the tense business meeting that afternoon, how glad he was to get away for an evening with her, and she relaxed with his arm on her shoulder, his weight pressing into her thigh. Bob had been gone six months and she missed sitting close to a man. He asked about Bob, she asked about his sons, six and three, the six-year-old now in T-ball, and after they dispensed with what neither of them cared about, they switched to movies, their common ground. He approved of *The Sting* winning the Oscar for Best Picture, and Polly insisted Bergman's *Cries and Whispers* should have won. They agreed that *Last Tango in Paris* got Paris right. He said Marlon Brando was amazing, she said he was revolting. Neither of them had seen the best documentary, a rodeo film. No places ever screened documentaries in Kansas City, and only a few in Chicago, like Doc Films.

The University of Chicago's auditorium was packed by the time they arrived, but they found two seats far off to the side as the room dimmed. Circus-style letters appeared on the screen, *Titicut Follies*, followed by a mid-shot of a men's chorus, the men in bow ties and too-small party hats singing, "Strike up the Band." The New Year's Eve show in a prison. The warden with big teeth congratulated a ter-rified-looking man. Cut to a cinder block corridor and a guard prod-ding a withered, naked man into a cell. Polly felt sick.

Afterward, the silent crowd streamed out of the auditorium.

"How did he do that?" Vaughn asked as they made their way out.

"Without one word of narration. It's amazing."

"I mean how did he get permission? You'd think they'd wouldn't let a camera into that hellhole."

"What's really astonishing was that he told the story by letting the camera record what was going on, no voice-over, no talking heads, no inter-titles, no explanations. We were simply dropped into each scene. Where they stripped those guys down, can you believe they let them shoot that? And the lobotomy. And that lunatic shrink interviewing the sex offender. All the while, no one is acting as if strangers were present. Imagine Wiseman's bulky camera strapped on his, or his cameraman's, shoulder, sometimes a tripod, always bulky sound equipment, and no one seems aware. Wiseman got access, that is amazing, but what knocks me over is how he took us there with him. His approach, his style, that's what's groundbreaking."

Vaughn stood at the curb of the quiet street looking up and down the dark looking for a cab, then turned to her. "You're still my little cinéaste."

"Stop it, Vaughn. I don't like it when you call me that."

"You didn't used to mind."

"I do now."

She wished the evening were over. She wanted to be alone. She wanted him and his presumptions about her gone. "Paris is over. We're not kids anymore."

"Is that a hungry woman talking? We're not going to get a cab around here. Let's hoof it a few blocks north. I remember a dive with good burgers and a decent juke box. Then we can call a cab."

● ● ●

Lowry left her a phone message saying her barbed wire photographs were ready for pick up at Art's front desk. When she returned to her cubicle, an envelope that looked like a wedding invitation was propped on her typewriter. She set down the pack of photos and reached for the luxe envelope.

> *Dear Polly,*
>
> *I must thank you for your kindness when my aunt dragooned you into giving me a tour of her office. You were very encourag-ing. Because of your interest, I want you to know that in September I will begin working at the BBC as a general runner in their stu-dios based in Ealing. While this job is not in*

the design department, it is a beginning.
Thank you for your interest.
Sincerely,
Phillipa Radcliff.

Encouraging? Had she been encouraging to the privileged brat? What she recalled was being dumbstruck by the girl's naïve confidence. Surely, she had thought, the girl would not succeed, but of course she had. The BBC, that was scalding. General runner was probably no better than Polly's go-fer jobs. She dropped the note and stalked into the Women's Room. The social forces were either with you or against you. Phillipa had all the forces aligned with her: one, she was Tony Richardson's neighbor; two, Mummy and Daddy supported her; three, she was young and beautiful. Phillipa had a trifecta. Polly leaned close to the mirror and bared her teeth. The BBC? Once she had been certain she would be a shooting star into the firmament the way Phillipa must see herself. She, Polly Wainwright from Peoria, Illinois would make a contribution to the world. She, Polly, would preserve the wisdom of the elders that was slipping away in the film world. She, Polly Wainwright, would make a difference. She, Polly, would not be just like everyone else.

• • •

As she washed up after dinner, still upset about Phillipa's note, she argued with herself about calling Eugenia. Only on Saturday afternoon, Eugenia had asked, but Polly needed to hear her consoling voice. She dialed Eugenia's parents, then tugged the phone's stretched-out cord through the back door and sat on her picnic table. She wouldn't bring up Phillipa. She wouldn't bring up that Vaughn had become smug, that everything he had was based on his marrying the boss's daughter, even his personality. She wouldn't bring up being nowhere in her life. She listened to the phone ring in St. Louis picturing the Pappas' upstairs hall, the wall niche with the black phone, the ladder-back chair below, Mrs. Pappas picking up.

Eugenia answered.

"It's me," Polly said.

"Why are you calling on Thursday? I'm doing fine."

"I just wanted to talk." Polly heard a sliding sound. "Are you okay?"

"I wish I had a cigarette."

"You don't smoke."

"I want to. My mother, she threw away *her* cigarettes when the doctor said I shouldn't smoke. She hid her ashtrays. This is my mother. She thinks she's me."

"She doesn't want you to be tempted."

"Don't try to talk me out of being angry. If I want to be pissed, I get to be pissed."

"Don't be pissed with me, I'm just—"

"Concerned, worried, which is the standard condescending state of mind of the well when confronted with the un-well."

Polly pressed the phone against her ear. "I want you to be well." She heard another sliding sound. "Should I call back? If you don't want to talk…"

"All anyone wants to talk about is how I am. Some ignoramus once said, 'I don't have a body, I am my body.' Not me. My body is not me. I've had enough."

"I didn't call to ask how you are."

"Why did you call?"

Polly tugged a splinter from the rough top of her picnic table. "You said you were fine, but I'm not particularly fine. I've had an ordinary day, but I feel a little down, so I thought, why not talk to my oldest friend in the world? Sure, I said to myself, you're strong and healthy, you don't have poisons running through your veins, and you're living in a nice apartment without a mother watching your every move, you're going to and from your fairly okay job in an exciting city, so why not call Eugenia and have her cheer you up?"

Eugenia barked a laugh.

"You sound like you're a serious smoker."

"A side effect, like constant flu. I am, the doctors say, doing well. I'm weary, that's all and I would welcome a distraction. Tell me a movie."

Polly wedged the phone between her chin and her shoulder, grateful Eugenia wanted their old game. "Close up of a woman's lip-sticked mouth—"

"Color or black and white?"

"Black and white. Think *Lady from Shanghai*. But we know the lipstick is Revlon's, probably *Fire and Ice*—we'll have to check with Perc Westmore, the makeup guy, for verification—but the vibe is definitely espionage World War II. Think Orson Welles lighting."

"I won't keep interrupting."

"It's okay. You need your bearings. Luscious lips pucker on a long cigarette in a long cigarette holder, then her lips part to exhale a languorous plume that coils up along her pore-less perfect face, the camera tracking back to reveal that she's sitting in a nightclub—"

"In Morocco, at a table overlooking the moonlit dunes."

"Okay. A man's shadow falls across her table. She turns. 'Is that you, Roderick?' He says, 'I've come to take you away from all this.' "

Eugenia snorts. "No, Roderick says, 'I have a gun aimed at your head.'"

"It's my movie. Roderick says, 'You must tango with me, now.' Cut to closeup of his manly hand alighting on her womanly bare shoulder, a slow zoom out. She and Roderick dance on the night-club's crowded floor, in the background tiled archways—"

"Where bad guys with guns bulging in their tuxedo jackets wait for the music to end."

Polly hesitated. "Okay. Chaos erupts on the dance floor. Cut to a train station where—"

"Hey, how did they get past the bad guys?"

"Sssh. You can't keep talking during the movie. If you're tired, I'll quit."

"Don't treat me like an invalid."

"I'm not. I don't mean to. Back to the movie: Roderick and the woman in disguise enter a second-class train car." Sensing Eugenia withdraw, Polly raced through tropes from old movies—tunnels, snowy mountain passes, shady alleys. "In the final shot, the couple stands on the deck of an ocean liner, watching the dim coast of France recede."

"They do not say any of the stupid last lines you are thinking about quoting."

"What am I thinking?"

After a pause, Eugenia said, "I don't want an uplifting closure."

"A simple fade to black, and I call you on Saturday afternoon?"

"I'll be better on Saturday."

Standing alone on her porch again, Polly surveyed what she thought of as her village, although she knew no one who lived in the two-and three-flats that ran in parallel on both sides of the alley, their backyards plotted with grass and skinny beds of tomato plants, or in the big buildings at the end of the block. She loved the city, loved its energy and possibilities, but this evening it felt like a desert. Below, wind fluttered a row of white undershirts hanging on a clothesline. Eugenia was pulling away. Polly could feel it as clearly as she could see the undershirts waving good-bye. She felt abandoned, and ashamed for wanting Eugenia to care about her, even now, even when she barely had the energy for a phone conversation.

7

September, 1962

AFTER TWO DAYS AT STARLIGHT Lodge, Polly knew she had been accepted as a member of the crew. Best of all, Mongo entrusted her with the logbook for the film. There was the terrible moment when she was kicked out of Mr. Watkins' studio for daydreaming, but that was either forgotten or forgiven when they filmed a scene with his cars in the barn, and afterward, they invited her to join them for dinner at a Northwoods crossroads tavern, the kind of place, Ernie said, his uncles used to take him. Mongo got smashed and Jules had to half-carry him to the van. Ernie drove her back to Mrs. Borus', who'd left on a light for her. It was a wonderful night.

Flopping onto her bed, Polly reached for her journal and flipped past yesterday's pages describing sound recording with Sid in the woods, lunch in the meadow, Mongo giving her the logbook—the logbook, where was it?

You keep it safe as if your life depended on it.

She shut her journal, alarm unfurling in her stomach. It wasn't on the bedside table, or the bureau, not under the chair. She reached for her duffle. Not in there, she wouldn't put it in there, not under her pile of dirty clothes, not under the bed. Not in her bed. She slumped onto the floor and thought. She did not have it with her when she came into the room for a sweater before going to dinner. Mongo had not given it to her after they boxed up the equipment in the barn. But she had taken it to the Lodge in the morning. Mongo told her to take it into the studio, and she had, she'd set it on the cabinet, as instructed. Later, when Mongo kicked her out, she had carried nothing, thinking only of getting away, hadn't given it thought, hadn't had it in her hands when she raced past Mr. Watkins and his son and into the kitchen. She hadn't seen it with Mongo when he came into the barn. Mongo must have screwed up. He must have left it in Watkins' studio, but she would catch the flak since he had handed off to her in the morning. It was probably still in the studio where she'd left it. Mongo would not take the blame, that was for sure, she would, for not keeping track. She spun on the bed to glance out the window. The Lodge was dark, except for the faintly glowing dome, and the moon was high.

After quietly closing the cabin door behind her, she ran over the lumpy ground toward the kitchen wing courtyard, thinking about Ray breaking his ankle.

The blue door was unlocked. She tiptoed across the dimly lit atrium and eased open the studio doors. The acetate they'd hung to mask the windows had been taken down and moonlight washed through the shadowy room, enough to see that the tables had been cleared and the cabinet where she had put the logbook was stacked with print storage boxes that hadn't been there before. The logbook wasn't in sight. Feeling sick, she walked between the tables to the cabinet and shifted the boxes to the side. The logbook wasn't behind them. She snaked her arm into the narrow space between the back of the cabinet and the wall, her sleeve catching on something, then halfway down, she felt a hard edge, a book, and tugged it out. Shaking with relief, she flipped it open. The last two filled-out pages held the notes she'd copied from Sid's notebook. Mongo had added nothing since then. The logbook must have been overlooked after the disastrous studio interview with Mr. Watkins, and Mongo didn't think of it later, after the barn shoot.

The lights flashed. "What're you doing?"

She froze. Mr. Watkins stood in the doorway, his hand on the wall switch, a stretched-out, once-green sweater covered his pajama bottoms.

"I forgot this." She held up the logbook.

"What time is it?" Before she could respond, he turned away. "This way." He lurched across the dim atrium toward the library.

She wasn't supposed to talk with Mr. Watkins, but Mongo wasn't here. She had never met anyone famous before. She switched off the lights and closed the doors behind her.

Mr. Watkins had turned on a lamp by an armchair near the fireplace. Except for the floor-to-ceiling bookcases surrounding the fireplace, the other walls were covered with his photographs. A long table in the middle of the room held photo books, some laid open.

"You know how to light a fire?"

She nodded.

"Then light one."

She set the logbook on the table next to a stack of books, wishing she'd left it where she found it. Mongo had failed to keep track of it, not her. It was his responsibility during the day. Later she would slip it back behind the cabinet. Let Mongo panic. Even if he yelled at her, he would realize it was his fault, not hers. Liking this plan, she knelt on the hearth and looked at Mr. Watkins, who'd settled into one of the armchairs flanking the fireplace. In the faint illumination from the lamp, his face seemed to be whittled from a chunk of wood. Once he had been handsome, she'd seen the pictures. He still was, in a ravaged way.

The logs and kindling were already arranged in the classic firebox she'd learned at Girl Scout camp. All she had to do was open the flue and strike a match. With his eyes on her, she reached for the box of matches, struck one that fizzled, another, the same, and another, and another, as if she didn't know how to strike a match.

"Bourbon?"

"Sure." She didn't like alcohol except for Southern Comfort, that was for Janis, and silly girl drinks to annoy the bartenders.

Finally, a match caught and she touched it to newspaper between the logs. Rocking back on her heels, she watched the tiny flames lick the logs, grateful to have succeeded and afraid to look at Mr. Watkins, afraid of what might come next, afraid of being a girl who shouldn't be where she was, afraid of not being interesting enough. She wanted to impress him, but she couldn't think of how. She stood, accepting the glass from his spotted, brown hand.

"What are you doing here?"

"I'm with the film…"

"Not your old games, Maureen, please."

"I'm Polly Wainwright. I came two nights ago, with the film crew." She had never been this close to a famous person before.

"What's the point?" he growled.

"The point of the film?" She sat in the chair opposite his.

"The film," he sneered.

Should she have said documentary? "The point is to make a film about you."

He snorted. "It's all in the books." He waved toward the table. "And the prints, which are archived God knows where." He drained his glass and poured a refill, offering her a top-up.

She declined. She hadn't touched it. "You've had a huge career. Your pictures are part of history. World War II. My dad fought in that war. He was in the Army Air Corps, stationed in England."

"And he let you come up here with that pack of thieves?"

"He died when I was twelve. Long after the War."

He lifted his eyebrow in half-sympathy. She hated mentioning her father's death. She hated people's pity.

"And Kino is not a pack of thieves. They're, we're, a professional film company. Kino has won national and international awards. And …Don't you think history matters? You're part of history."

"Everyone's part of history." He winked at her.

Unsure what this meant, she took a sip of the bourbon, its sting a surprise, but nice. "I don't know exactly what's planned with this film—I'm nobody—but you're somebody and your work is important enough to preserve." She turned her head toward the pictures hanging on the wall opposite. "How you work, what you've done, you as a person, as an artist, that's worth saving."

His nostrils flared with disdain. He thought she was a fool.

"Actually, I'm more interested in film than photography," she said.

"You and everyone else." He saluted her with his re-filled glass.

"Film is for everyone. That's why it's so wonderful. It's the democratic medium. Everyone, Westerners, people in sub-Saharan Africa, India, Beverly Hills, we all watch movies. You don't even need to be literate to get movies."

"To 'get' photographs, you don't need to be literate either. Is an illiterate audience a defense of what some call an art form?" He waved his glass saluting his photo-covered walls, spilling bourbon on his hand. "You know Renoir?"

"Jean, the filmmaker? I saw *La Règle du Jeu* at the Cinémathèque Française when—"

"Did I tell you he likes music? Couperin, like me. You remember that time, don't you? At the Chateau St. something—Aubin?—before the War. Who was playing that night? That arrogant popinjay?"

"I wasn't alive."

"Maureen, don't be a goose."

"I've been to France once, in my junior year. 1959."

"Look at me," he commanded.

She did. His eyes were disturbing, an eerie light blue, too light, like glass, the whites around the irises marbled with red veins. She wanted to look away, to lift her glass and take another sip, but couldn't. His gaze pinned her in place, as if he were seeing through her, into her thoughts, seeing so deeply that he understood everything that had ever happened to her and what she felt at this moment, electrified and terrified. She couldn't move. Was this what it was like to be photographed by him? To be truly seen for who she was. But he wasn't like those men whose gaze undressed her. There was no sexual charge between them. He didn't find her attractive. He found her worth looking at. Her pulse beat in her temple. She knew he could see this. A log hissed in the fireplace between them. She was aware of her breath, the weight of her hands on her lap, her face hot on the side nearest the fire, her jaw heavy, her tongue like mud. She waited to be released. After a time, he blinked and leaned back, his chest deflating. "Your name, get a piece of paper and write it down."

She stood, her head barely attached to her body. He wanted to remember her. Beneath the big table, she saw a pen, but on top among the books, no loose paper, so she tore out a blank sheet from the back of the logbook, and wrote her name.

"Now get my diary." He waved toward the bookcase.

Was she about to become a diary entry? Or was he going to look up the musical evening at the Chateau? It didn't matter. She touched the row of bound notebooks.

"Not there." He waved toward the lower shelves.

"This?" She pulled out a leather volume with gold-tipped pages.

"Put it back." A woman's angry voice.

Polly jerked.

Mrs. Borus stood in the doorway, her radar eyes taking in the bourbon decanter and their two glasses before zeroing in on Polly. "What's going on?" Below her ratty robe, her bare legs looked like baseball bats stuck into her short rubber boots.

She marched past Polly, her cheeks quivering with rage, and wrestled the tumbler from Watkins's grasp. "You know you're not supposed to drink. And you," she turned to Polly, "out of here."

"I just came to…" She shoved the diary back.

"Get out." Mrs. Borus struggled Mr. Watkins to his feet, and Polly grabbed the logbook. She couldn't return it now. She would have to wait until morning.

Outside in the courtyard, she peered through the library window watching Mrs. Borus maneuver Mr. Watkins toward the door. He had seen deeply into her, he had wanted to remember her name, he was about to reveal something important in his diary, and she wanted to hold onto every detail of the scene, the fireplace, the tribal rug, the chairs where they sat, the table heaped with art books, the crowded shelves, the diary. Mr. Watkins and Mrs. Borus were gone. Polly looked up at the blue-black sky dotted with stars, thousands of them, bright and faint, more than she'd ever seen before, their invisible cosmic energy shimmering down on her. This was her night.

She started toward the cottage, clutching the logbook, careful with each step. In the morning she would hand it to Mitch, saying she figured it had been overlooked in the confusion in the studio and she'd gone in the night to retrieve it. The truth. If Mongo yelled at her, she could take it. And he might not. He would look like a fool.

• • •

In the morning when Polly woke up, Mrs. Borus had already left. Polly dressed quickly and hurried to the Lodge, wanting to apologize to Mrs. Borus before the crew arrived. Through the courtyard window, she saw her at the kitchen sideboard, preparing Mr. Watkins' breakfast tray. She opened the kitchen door quietly, realized she was carrying the logbook against her chest like a shield, and lowered it as she said good morning.

Mrs. Borus kept her back turned as she set a doily in a saucer and placed a cup on top.

"I'm sorry about last night," Polly said. "He came downstairs."

"See to the coffee."

"I didn't mean to disturb Mr. Watkins, but I couldn't get away. I know he's not okay." From outside she heard Mongo's van.

The woman spun around. "Who told you he's not okay?"

"I'm just…I'm really sorry."

Mrs. Borus' glared at her as if Polly was not recognizably human.

Noise erupted in the atrium, Mitch's big laugh and the tumble of other voices. Mitch was here already? Nervous after pressuring him to put her on the crew, him refusing, her succeeding, all of this embarrassing, and eager to get away from Mrs. Borus, Polly pushed open the door to the atrium.

"Hi, Mitch." Instead of his usual white shirt, necktie, sleek suit, he wore a plaid shirt and jeans. Feigning calm, she handed Mongo, who was standing beside him, the logbook.

Mitch gave her a mock salute. "You made it, Sugar. How's she doing, Mongo?"

Mongo's attention was on the logbook.

Polly said, "I found it in the studio last night. I wanted to keep it safe, like you said."

"Shit."

Outside, beyond the glass double doors, a silver sedan pulled up. The sons had arrived. Mitch hurried toward the doors to welcome them, all smiles, taking charge, and Mongo seeing what was happening, snapped shut the logbook, yelled at Mitch to get them to "follow your fucking script," and barked orders to everyone, telling Polly to help Ernie haul the stands into the library.

Grateful there was no big scene with Mitch or Mongo, she shouldered the sandbags and followed Ernie into the library. Mrs. Borus had tidied up. The books on the table were neatly stacked, none left open to display Mr. Watkins' pictures, the fizzled matches Polly had left on the hearth cleared away, the glasses she and Mr. Watkins had drunk from were gone, and the decanter. Without the pool of lamplight and dancing firelight, without Mr. Watkins' intensity, without their connection, the room seemed lifeless, which made her happy. What happened last night happened because of the two of them, and existed only for the two of them.

Jules and Sid pushed past her, studied the room, obviously not for the first time, and moved a small table to the left of where Mr. Watkins had sat last night and where he would sit for the interview today. She and Ernie were to assemble the light stands and organize the reflectors by the long table. When Jules and Sid returned to the atrium, she and Ernie got to work while the hubbub in the atrium grew louder, bins dragged across the noisy marble floor, Mongo angry, a son objecting, Jules chiming in, Mitch trying to calm everyone down. Then silence.

"Who the hell are all these people?" Mr. Watkins' voice.

Polly tiptoed to the library's open doors and peered out, seeing Mr. Watkins at the top of the stairs, his chubby son beside him, the Kino crew staring up at them. The other son pushed Mitch aside to stand at the base of the stairs.

"Dad, this is the film crew."

Mr. Watkins smoothed his wispy hair as his watery old man eyes traveled slowly around the atrium, taking everyone in. "Why so many?" Then his gaze shifted past the crowd below him to look across the atrium to Polly. His face lit up. "Maureen, you've come. I was afraid you wouldn't, not after..."

He smiled at Polly, wrenching out of his son's grip, and stepped forward seemingly suspended above the stairs, then he fell, legs crumbling, arms flailing, head, shoulders, hips banging the steps, the bannister, his torso twisting. The son beside Mitch caught him before he hit the marble floor.

"Maureen," Mr. Watkins wailed, his eyes searching for her.

Polly gripped the door.

Chubby son ran screaming down the stairs as the men clustered around Mr. Watkins, everyone shouting—"Take him to the library," "No, upstairs," "Don't move him," "Get a blanket"—as one son crooned, "Dad Dad Dad," and the other, "Dad, can you hear me? Can you hear me?" Mrs. Borus hurried for the phone.

"Dad, we're going to…" The sons lifted him. "You'll be okay, Dad." Between them they carried him up the stairs, Mr. Watkins whimpering.

When the bedroom door closed behind then, the Kino crew and Mitch turned to Polly.

Mongo, a vein throbbing in his forehead. "What the fuck just happened?"

"I have no idea," she whispered.

"Maureen?" he growled. The others moved forward like a pack of wolves.

"He thinks I'm someone he knew."

"Why the hell does he think this?"

She tried to explain, the logbook, he cornered her, she couldn't get away, she had tried. She didn't know who Maureen was. She didn't know why he confused her. She was sorry sorry sorry.

"A goddamn houseplant, you're supposed to be a goddamn houseplant. Have you forgotten? Not one fucking word to him. That's what I said." Mongo jerked his head. "Ernie, drive her to the nearest fucking Trailways." To Polly, "Get your things."

Mitch raised his hand and pistol-clicked.

She was dead.

8

July, 1974

"POLLY, A WORD, IF YOU HAVE A MOMENT."

Polly paused outside by Vanessa's door. The Queen's lifted eyebrow was as insistent as a sailor's semaphore, even at more than twenty feet. The rest of the staff had already left for the day, and Polly had been held up on a long-distance phone call to Vancouver. Was she about to get the ax? Shrewd of Vanessa to wait until no one else was around. Collect your things and your last check at Personnel, she could say, and Polly's assignments would be distributed among the other editors by noon tomorrow. Her movie card collection, the pictures of Bob and her parents, her old cardigan, the few personal things in her desk, her extra pair of heels, everything would fit in two totes. Polly crossed to the visitor's chair.

"Sit. Taking on Tina's work and the barbed wire assignment, you're doing well." She smiled. "I'm not keeping you, am I?"

"No. About the barbed wire picture, I wish the caption could have been more specific."

"Given the givens, I'm satisfied." She settled her reading glasses and pulled out a breath-mint green folder, the color only Personnel used. Polly squeezed her knees together, girding herself.

"How long have you been with us?"

Vanessa knew the answer. Polly said, "Two years, four months. I was hired in March, 1972."

"Which makes you the junior member of my staff."

Polly acknowledged this with a small nod, keeping her face relaxed.

"Two and a half years. The longest you've held at any job, is that right? Before starting at EB, you were unemployed for almost two years."

"Not quite that long. My mother was ill. I cared for her."

"Commendable. Before that, you had a string of jobs."

"I was never fired or laid off." Fired only from Kino, which she hadn't put on her resume. The four months after college wasn't a gap anyone had noticed. "Each job I left for a better opportunity." So it had seemed.

"I have a policy of never hiring anyone in their twenties. They simply do not know how to work for others. They are used to thinking they are clever, they believe they have been hired for their ideas. Expendable." She snapped her fingers. "Each and every one." She rested her hands on the Personnel folder. "But you are older. You have done very well, even though you are the youngest of my editors, and you came to the job with no experience."

"Thank you."

"But now I must make a hard decision."

Polly reasoned that with two-weeks' notice, plus her accumulated sick and vacation days, she wouldn't run dry until late August.

"Layoffs will be announced at the end of August, to begin after Labor Day, based on the premise that Plan B will wrap by

December. I doubt it will. Nevertheless, HQ has sent word that I may keep one editor until Plan B does wrap, someone who will most likely transition to a permanent position here in our Chicago office. This is confidential. As I weigh the options of whom we might ask to stay on, I would like to know if you want to be considered. I must emphasize at this point that nothing is definite. This is a purely exploratory conversation. With that clearly understood, would you be interested?"

In staying on? In keeping this pleasant, decently-paid job? To not have to go through the hell of scrambling for a new job, that probably wouldn't be as comfortable, well paid, prestigious? Polly expelled her breath. "I am interested."

"Good. To be clear: I am considering others, nothing is settled in my mind, but I would hate to cut you loose. Again, this conversation is confidential." She folded her hands on Polly's Personnel folder, the meeting over.

Polly stood and thought better of extending her hand. Phillipa's liking Polly had to be why she was included among the select. The others would be Janine and Hank. Janine had the seniority and was excellent at her job, but Vanessa favored Hank, who was barely adequate. The Queen liked bossing the man around.

• • •

Walking home from the El, the flat hand of reality pressed against her chest. The odds were not in her favor, she would still need to find a new job. When she'd complained to Janine that the only jobs advertised were for Gal Fridays and receptionists, Janine persuaded her it was a waste of time to look until after Labor Day, when want ads would be flooded after the summer lull. This would be cutting it close, but

Bob would be back soon and this would change what Polly could do or what she might want to do. If they married right after he returned, she wouldn't have to grab at the first decent opportunity. She could take her time, find something she enjoyed. She could rely on him. His income would always be more than hers, his job would come first, he had a real career, but she would work too. If he had to move to another city, she would follow. This was too much to think about now.

It had been six months since they had made love, twenty-five weeks, she had counted that morning, and he had said he didn't expect her to be a nun. You either, she had added. Her three dates since he left had all been busts: one with bad-breath Kowalski who worked the city news desk at the *Sun Times*; the back-booth petting session at the Earl with that guy Jake, whom she hoped never to see again; and a fixup with Janine's boring cousin after Janine's Fourth of July party at Oak Street Beach. Polly should not have accepted that invitation. When she tried to remember what making love with Bob felt like, all she had were images, his shoulder, round as a dolphin's and blue from the security lamp filtering through her bedroom blinds, the pebbled skin of his neck disappearing into his animal-dense beard, her hand on his chest, their pale skin a perfect match, but even these fragments were slipping away, as if she had dreamt, not lived, these moments.

She rounded the corner of her block and saw Mrs. Menendez wave frantically from the stoop of her two-flat next to Polly's building. As she got closer, Polly saw that in the middle of Mrs. Menendez's flowerbed, her three-foot high concrete Madonna had been festooned with a clunky necklace weighted by a peace symbol, the kind of junk sold at rock concerts. Bob had one, smaller and not so ugly, made of brass, which looked silly on him too.

"Who do such a thing?" Mrs. Menendez wailed.

"Kids."

Polly stepped over the knee-high iron fence bordering Mrs. Menendez's carefully-tended lawn and lifted off the necklace. Beneath the marigolds she spotted a reefer. Making a distracting fuss of straightening the little American flags, she slipped the joint into her pocket, then held out the necklace to Mrs. Menendez.

"In the garbage," she hissed, shooing Polly toward the passageway. "You get rid, in the garbage."

After dropping the necklace in the dumpster, she pulled out the joint, which was tightly rolled, barely bent, and never lit. Never before had she held a joint in her hand without some guy urging her to pass it along. Never before had she held a joint that she'd acquired on her own. She felt a silly grin take over her face. It was guys who controlled dope. They bought it, they sold it, they provided it at parties, the way the women provided the food. Bob always had a nickel bag. The teenage boys she saw in the alley around sunset, the scent of their weed drifting up to her third floor porch, it had to be them who hazed Mrs. Menendez. She was always threatening them with the police. Since spring Polly had watched the same five, six boys swagger down the alley, smoking joints, one of them dribbling a ball, then turn north at the street, heading toward the park, where girls in hot pants would be waiting for them to show up. Polly slipped the joint into her pocket and climbed the back stairs to her apartment. She was going to enjoy this sometime soon.

The phone rang as she unlocked her back door, her mother.

"I'm wondering if you're coming for Labor Day weekend." Her speech was still a little slow, not quite what it had been before the accident. She could drive, and she worked afternoons at the Chamber of Commerce, which was a miracle after the semi hit her car, crushing her leg, hip, arm, and breaking her neck.

"I just walked in and it's more than a month away. Can we talk about this later? If I come, I want to plan a one-day visit to see Eugenia sometime that weekend."

"You could spend the weekend here, either way. The Lindstroms are having a big party on Sunday, and there'll be the fireworks on the river, as always. You used to love that, but I don't know if you care for that kind of thing anymore."

"I love fireworks."

"Kate will be at the Lindstroms with her new baby."

Kate. In high school, Polly has babysat for her. "Oh, good."

Polly placed the joint in a saucer between Bob's blender and the vase he'd made for her—she should throw out the wilting snapdragons—while her mother talked about the house Polly had grown up in, the Dutch Colonial, once again changing hands, three times since they sold it, and that was only four years ago. "If it weren't for the stairs....I miss that house and the big lawn your dad hated mowing. I don't get why it keeps changing hands."

"Woo woo. Could it be that you and I are haunting our old house?"

"You know I didn't mean that."

"Kindly widow and middle-aged daughter—"

"You're not middle-aged."

"Not quite. I'll let you know about Labor Day weekend after I talk to Eugenia."

She changed into shorts and headed downstairs to collect the mail. Among the bills and junk was an envelope with exotic stamps, a letter from Bob. She bounded upstairs, raced through her apartment, tossing the rest of the mail on the kitchen counter, and paused at her open back door to smile at the bright July sky, wanting to hold onto this moment. She studied the illegible postmarks, trying to imagine the route this tan envelope had taken to reach her, thousands of miles of ocean and continent. Hoping to find some lingering trace of Bob or the fragrant world he inhabited in Vietnam, she lifted it to her nose. What she smelled was old paper and fake strawberry. She opened it. Two pages, typed, as always. She wished he wrote by hand.

> *Dear Pollyanna,*

Pollyanna?

> *The military is keeping a lid on us these*
> *days. What's left is sniffing down dubious*
> *leads picked up in the strip joints and bars.*
> *Stu and I bought a pre-war Vespa from an*
> *Italian staffer recalled from his embassy—*
> *the Italians are the first rats to leave this*
> *sinking ship. It's cheaper than paying for*
> *rides every time, but more often than not,*
> *we need a guide into the quagmire of neigh-*
> *borhoods, so there's no savings there.*

Why a motorbike now, after five months?

> *Saigon is a maze with sinkholes. Most of*
> *the overt political action has shifted to Paris*
> *and DC. What's left is speculation about*
> *the coming purges and the effects of the war*
> *on the people. No one in America wants*
> *to read these stories, which means that no*

one wants to pay for them, but these are the
stories I want to write. What this hell has
created, and what comes next.

Which leads me to—Frank, Stu and I are
setting up shop in Bangkok.

Bangkok? Setting up shop?

Cambodia is going up in flames. Burma's
next. Frank's in Bangkok now. He rented us
an office with a darkroom for him and he's
setting up the wires. My contract with AP is
good for now. If they pull the plug, I'll get by.
There's enough here to keep me happy. Every
week I get offers from the European agen-
cies. I like the life here. Bangkok will exist as
an earthly paradise long after Saigon sinks
into the Communist sewer. This isn't forever,
but for the foreseeable.

He wasn't coming back?

It will take Stu and me a week or more to
close up shop here . . .

She folded the two pages and returned them to the envelope, tucking in the flap she'd almost torn in her eagerness. If you looked at it from the front, you couldn't tell she had opened it, which was what she wished, that she hadn't opened it. She dropped it on the porch floor and turned in the opposite direction of Vietnam and Bangkok, or wherever the hell he was, and fixed her eyes on the dissolving line above the distant high-rises on Lake Michigan's edge she could barely make out, where the blue sky dissolved into white nothingness.

Below, on Mrs. Menendez's garage roof, pigeons quarreled.

...enough here to keep me happy.

Happier than with her? They had been together for eighteen months before he left. Add in the last six months, and they had been a couple for two years. *I'm serious. Let's go to city hall, today.* She had insisted they wait until he returned. She'd said let's wait whenever he brought up marriage, the first time driving to that party in Bridgeport, then during the Thanksgiving weekend when they ate at the pancake house—she had given him half her bacon—and at the lakefront, last December, watching windsurfers ride the treacherous waves. Waiting made sense, he agreed.

Had he mentioned their marriage plans? She pulled out the pages, then shoved them back.

I'm serious.

Serious was not dumping her with a typed letter. How had he signed off? She lifted the envelope's flap to see and stopped. She had spent the last two years of her life with a man who had probably typed "ciao". She focused her gaze on the shadow of her building inching across the garage roofs below, but missed the moment when it reached the edge and fell into the alley, missing the moment when pigeons fled.

...enough here to keep me happy.

She slid from the hammock and stomped into the kitchen where the joint rested safely in the saucer near Bob's damn blender. *You could use this for frozen daiquiris while I'm gone.* She hated daiquiris. That he hadn't remembered this should have tipped her off. That he had made an ugly green vase from a Riesling bottle should have tipped her off too. She didn't like Riesling, any white wine. He believed he was clever and arty because he made shitty junk out of stuff other people threw away. A functional object deserved to end its life intact, not sawed in half. She flung the decapitated thing with its stinky flowers at her wastebasket and hit the rim, spraying scummy yellow-green up the wall, like dog piss. Bob had marked every corner of her home, like a mongrel dog. His blender on her clean kitchen counter was an abomination. She yanked it from the counter, its plug snapping against her thigh, stinging, but she didn't stop, she carried it outside, stubbed her toe against the picnic bench, and hopped to the railing, holding the blender high for one long moment, before dropping it over, thrilling to the glass shattering, the housing splintering, parts blasting all over the asphalt. She waited for something to happen, shouts, sirens, police storming up the stairs to arrest her, but nothing. Silence. Two backyards away, the woman bent over her tomato plants didn't even look up.

She hobbled into the kitchen, holding her hurt toe, to call Eugenia, tell her about Bob's perfidy—Eugenia had never liked him—but she stopped. She couldn't lay this on Eugenia, but she had to tell someone. Not Claire who was to blame for bringing Bob back into Polly's life. Not anyone who knew Bob and not anyone would think that setting up shop in Bangkok was cool.

She pressed her forehead onto the reassuringly solid front of her refrigerator. When she pulled away, Janine's Fourth of July party invitation bloomed in her vision, RSVP and her phone number. Dialing, Polly stood on one foot cradling her swelling toe.

Janine picked up.

"I got a fucking Dear John letter."

"Polly?"

"I have been dumped." She shouldn't have said fucking.

"You've been dumped? By Bob?" In the background something rattled.

"Who the hell else would dump me? Not your cousin, Phil."

"Paul. His name is Paul." The rattling quieted. "Are you okay?"

"Long distance. An honest-to-God fucking classic Dear John. Out of nowhere."

When had he written it? Ten days ago? Two weeks? Around the Fourth of July, the date of Janine's stupid party with her dweeb cousin? The postmarks were too blurred to decipher. Whatever day Bob had dumped her, it was weeks ago, but before that—weeks? months?—their relationship had ended for him.

"Are you there, Polly?"

"We were getting married."

"I'll come over," Janine said.

Polly gripped the phone, her heart throbbing in her fingers. He had put her behind him. He had moved fucking on, but for her, the end was just beginning to unfurl. She wanted out of this moment. She wanted tomorrow. Tomorrow, this wouldn't hurt so much. She would go to work. She was good at her job, so good Vanessa might… Janine was her competition.

"Don't come. I just had to tell someone."

"I turned off the pasta water. Twenty minutes, I'll be there."

"You don't know where I live."

"I've got your address."

Her party invitation. "Come up the back way."

Small blinking airplane lights crossed the sky. She dug out the Southern Comfort and sat at her picnic table, wishing Eugenia were coming, not Janine.

Footsteps on the stairs. "Up here."

Janine appeared in a sleeveless blouse and jeans, her stiff page-boy mussed, not her usual prison matron look. Was nothing stable? Janine set a filled salad bowl on the table. "I made this before you called," and eyed the bottle of booze. "Glass for me?"

Polly told her which cabinet. When she returned with a glass, plates, and forks, Polly said, "You'll never guess. I found a joint. Is this my lucky day or what?"

"If you say so," Janine said, pouring an inch of booze into her glass.

"Except for the being dumped part. He wanted to get married. City hall, make it legal before he left, but I was the voice of reason." Polly hit her chest with her glass, splashing her hand. "I said, let's wait until you return. Did you know that? Did I tell you that?"

She sounded drunk, she was drunk, but Janine's face softened. She understood. She knew that Polly had been wise to refuse to marry him. But Polly had not been wise. She had been stupid. She slammed down her glass. She had been timid. She was timid. She should have said yes to City Hall, the white dress, the posies, her mother exultant, and Bob's parents, whose church directory photo she'd seen, they would come from Albany. Bob and her friends would be there, Claire bragging that she'd fixed them up, and Eugenia, her long, solemn, pale face would shine as she straightened Polly's shoulder-length veil. Polly should have married him. If she had, he would still love her.

She stood, head wobbling and lurched to the kitchen. "I'll get the joint. It's somewhere." After patting down the counters, she found it in the saucer next to the ring left by his ugly vase. He had promised to cut more wine bottles to make her a whole set of ugly drinking glasses, another fucking broken promise.

With the joint between her lips, she bent over the stove's gas flame, watching the end catch fire, and took a hit, then another, her throat scorching as the metal cage in her chest opened and released the angry thing banging against her ribs. Letting the glowing tip guide her outside and onto the porch, she passed the joint to Janine. "He's a journalist. You know that, right? His next headline should read: Kitchener Gone Kurtz."

Janine's fish lips sucked on the joint.

"Have you ever been seriously in love?" Polly said.

"Once," puff puff, "when I was a teenager. Frank Sinatra." Janine's nostrils quivered as she held onto a lungful. "I was sort-of engaged to a guy who went to Korea. But no ring. When he came back, he'd become, I don't know, less civilized. He expected stuff I didn't want to do."

"Like what?"

"And my mother had died while he was gone. That made it easier, breaking up. You know. You have a mother."

Polly dropped her forehead to the splintery tabletop. "Oh, God. What will I tell my mother?"

"Say he got syphilis…from a prostitute." Janine tapped Polly's shoulder to pass her the joint.

Polly took a hit. "Do you want to see the shit he left here?" She stood, her head not attached to her body, and crossed to her open back door. Clutching the doorjamb, she pirouetted into the kitchen and stumbled against the stool beneath the wall phone, then crept hand on wall toward the back bedroom where she flung open the door and flipped on the light. Stacked boxes filled with books and papers, a ludicrous plaid suitcase, his childhood rocking chair holding his precious Olivetti typewriter. *Don't touch this while I'm gone.*

Janine leaned over Polly's shoulder, her boozy breath hot and noxious. "You could have a garage sale."

"I would toss a match in here, but I don't want to torch my whole place."

Janine switched off the overhead light, and shut the door. "Come. Figure this out later."

9

August, 1974

SEVEN READ THE STOVE CLOCK. Seven in the evening said the pink-tinged sunset outside her kitchen window, and she had lost a day. She unlocked her back door and inched past the picnic table to stand at her porch railing, offended by how prettily the flat garage rooftops shone in the champagne light and how the late-day shadows hid the dirty plastic buckets, rusted barbeque grills, tilting clotheslines, unraveling lawn chairs, all the signs of entropy. The sanctuary she'd felt here in her village was a sham. She gripped the porch railing and lowered her head to rest her forehead on her fists. Three stories down, Bob's shattered blender sparkled on the asphalt under Mrs. Menendez's security lamp, which never went off, day or night. Why hadn't anyone shot it out on the Fourth of July, as a public service? That would have been a right thing to do. Tossing out the blender, that was one right thing Polly had done. Getting drunk was one thing she'd done wrong, inviting Janine another. Janine who encroached, who wanted to weasel into Polly's life because she didn't have enough going on in her own, who was a happy cog in a soul-crushing sys-tem, who was exactly the kind of woman Polly never ever wanted to become. Feeling woozy and sick of herself, she returned to the kitchen that Janine had cleaned with her typical punctilious thor-oughness. The washed ashtray was sitting on the window sill and Bob's envelope leaned against the knife-holder, not where Polly had tossed it. Janine had read it. Miss Nosey. Not that it mattered, not after Polly had stupidly revealed so much more than she should have, to anyone.

Six months, at most, he'd said and she'd believed. They would resume their life together. She had put him off, but she had never doubted they were a couple. They would live together eventually, find a bigger apartment, have friends over, take vacations, get a joint credit card. Whatever happened, he would be her backup. When Tina and the others at work implied she had nothing to worry about, she would be getting married, she hadn't bother to say that they were retro conventional boobs. She believed she was driving her own independent life, but without thinking about it, she had believed she could rely on him, as Tina and the chorus had assumed. She was a fool, no different from them. Behind this shaming recognition bloomed a frightening vacancy, her life without him.

She dropped his letter onto the limp remains of Janine's salad in the wastebasket. A damp stain that looked like an ancient map crept over the envelope and around the stamps. Wherever he was, Bangkok, Saigon, it was not today. He was a day ahead, doing what he loved, chasing down new stories, cutting deals for information, beating out the competition, looking forward to what would come next, while she was looking forward to nothing. She splashed water on her face at the sink and stared out the window. What she wanted was to get high. The stub of the joint she'd smoked with Janine wasn't in the mess in the garbage, she remembered flicking it over the porch railing last night. But the alley boys who'd dropped it in Mrs. Menendez's yard would be in the park, if not now, soon.

Dusk had fallen by the time she dressed in shorts, a fresh T-shirt, and put a ten dollar bill in her pocket. She'd been warned that the park was dangerous at night, but away from the street and beneath the trees, the air was cool and soft, and there were plenty of people out strolling. Near the empty bandstand, a girl in a fairy costume slept on a blanket while the daddy smoked and the sari-clad mother put foil-wrapped packets in their cooler. The scent of his clove cigarette mingled with the smell of curry, sun-heated dirt, and a ghost-whiff of marijuana. Beyond the next stand of trees and a fountain surrounded by preening girls, the basketball court was as brightly-lit as a used-car lot. Boys she didn't recognize passed the ball back and forth, while others watched on the sidelines beyond the bleachers. Polly steered clear of the wino on the bottom row and climbed to the third tier, sitting on the metal that was shock-ingly cold against her bare thighs. A few rows up teenage girls with frizzy perms giggled as the ball circled the rim and dropped in, then turned to glare at her. She looked away, toward the game, pretend-ing she hadn't been staring at them, and watched boys lunge and spin around one another, feeling as if a Klieg light had been turned on her. She was an outsider. What was she doing here? Had she really thought she could walk into the park and score a joint? Had she believed a kiosk would display little baggies with a price chart, or a bunch of teenagers puffing away would beckon her over and offer her a hit, she, a thirty-four-year old, square, boring woman? She had no idea how to get what she wanted.

More boys joined the game, girls at the fountain laughed, families pushed baby carriages along the path beyond the far side of the court. If this were a movie, the barely-heard score would play "Hot town, summer in the city" as the camera zoomed in on Polly, the spectator, always on the sidelines. Something flew at her. She jerked away as a basketball twanged the bench beside her, bounced high, then dropped to the tier below, and down. A gangly kid jogged over to grab it. He looked up at her through thick seductive eyelashes. "Want to play?" His friends on the court hooted. She shook her head, her heart thudding. Was she a target? His friends on the sidelines howled as he jogged backward and lobbed the ball over his shoulder toward the court.

Afraid to show her upset, she sat rigid as the girls several rows above her flounced past, their weight springing the bench she sat on. A guy she hadn't notice arrive sat a few feet to her right. Faded jeans, a Rolling Stones T-shirt, sleeves rolled up, a bicep tattoo of a skull beneath an Army helmet. A Vietnam vet. Probably not a threat. The right leg of his jeans hung loose over his too-thin thigh. An injured vet, who smelled of patchouli, motor oil, and sweat. From his T-shirt pocket he pulled a pack of Camels and shook free a cigarette, saying something that she didn't get.

"Are you talking to me?"

He lit his cigarette and took a long drag. "Nice night."

Was he hitting on her? "Yes," she said, cool, throwing up the usual invisible barriers.

He exhaled a long plume of smoke. "Haven't seen you around here before."

"No." She kept her face toward the game. No, she hadn't been here before and no, she wasn't interested.

He set his pack of Camels on the bench between them and appeared to be following the game, but she felt his attention on her. Listening to the overhead fluorescence lamps buzz, she wondered how long before she could leave without seeming afraid.

When the middle-aged couple from the top tier clambered down, Polly stood.

"Night," the vet said, keeping his eyes on the court.

On the bench between them, on top of his packet of Camels were three joints lined up like little logs. She sat back down. How had he known? How had he put them there without her seeing him move? He could be a cop. This could be a sting. She kept her eyes on the brightly lit court, then slowly looked around. No solitary men lurked in the shadows ready to take her down, no men in blue with guns drawn, no squad cars parked behind the bushes on the bordering street. The girls near the fountain giggled, the boys continued to play would have reacted. Polly was the only one on guard. From her pocket she pulled her money and slid it next to his cigarette packet.

"Is this enough?"

He made a deft move she didn't see, but her bill disappeared. He stood, his cigarette packet back in his pocket, and descended using his hands to lift his bad leg. He high-fived the boys courtside and slipped into the shadows. She placed her hand on the joints he'd left on the bench afraid to move, afraid of being caught, afraid of looking down and seeing that the joints were regular cigarettes, and she had been tricked. When she felt steady enough to walk, she made her way to the ground, fighting a grin. This was the first new thing she had done in a long time. She wished she could tell Bob, see his surprise.

● ● ●

The next morning, the summer intern filling in for vacationing Milly smirked at Polly when she arrived late and half-stoned. "Looks like you're still sick."

"I'm fine." She pushed up the too-big sunglasses that kept slipping, not wanting to give the girl a glance at her puffy eyes, then took the handful of While-You-Were-Out slips.

Wishing she'd taken off another day, wishing she hadn't smoked two joints, she walked to her cubicle. On her file cabinet, Bob in his aviator glasses and his rolled-up shirt sleeves grinned at her. Even here he had marked her space, like a dog, even in this miserable cubicle he had never entered. Had he? Had he ever bothered to visit her? She couldn't recall one time, even when he still worked at the *Trib* on the other side of the plaza. What she did held no interest for him. She shoved his photograph into the top drawer of the cabinet and slammed it shut. Later she'd figure out what to do with it, and the rest of his stuff.

She picked up the phone messages. Three from Mitch Klein, in one lousy day. Had he nothing better to do than pester someone he barely knew, who had no desire to talk to him? She rumpled the messages and dropped them into her wastebasket before reaching for her to-do list, wishing she could recapture how she had felt leaving the park, buoyant, confirmed, confident that what lay ahead was wide open and waiting for her.

In mid-afternoon when she returned with a coffee from downstairs, Janine stood outside her cubicle, like a sentinel. "I was worried when you didn't show up yesterday."

"I should have stopped by to thank you earlier. I got buried..." She had no excuse. "I did phone in. Food poisoning, I said."

"I heard." Janine followed her into her cubicle.

"Sorry about being a total jerk." She pictured her immaculate kitchen with washed glasses lined up neatly on a folded towel. "When did you leave?"

"Around two."

"I'm sorry I dumped my man-woes on you. I'm sorry I got smashed. I am sorry for you name it, I'm sorry for it. But thank you for coming over, the kitchen, for getting me out of my filthy clothes and into bed—I saw the state of my T-shirt—and for putting up with me."

"Want to go to dinner after work?"

"Not tonight."

"I understand."

What she didn't understand was that the other night hadn't made them friends. "Maybe the movies on Friday night?" Polly offered, immediately regretting it. Why couldn't she stand the ground she wanted to establish?

Making up for missing a day and coming in late, she stayed until the cleaning crew arrived. As she slipped on her heels and waved in the woman with the trash cart, she realized that she felt better than she had since she read Bob's letter. Not thinking about him or what would happen next helped. Completing simple tasks, writing letters, responding to queries, examining transparencies, this helped, too, giving her a sense of accomplishment. During her mother's stretch in rehab and in the months afterward, Polly had told her that she was getting better day-by-day, quoting from the saccharine poster in the physical therapy unit, and they both laughed. But it was true. Time passed, or was lost, and she wasn't reeling. She was less furious with Bob, and more disgusted with herself for being such a fool.

"Miss." The cleaning woman held out a rumpled While-You-Were-Out note and pointed to a spot beside the wastebasket. "You need…?"

Mitch's phone number. Polly shook her head, then reached for it. What did she have to lose?

· · ·

After dinner and a TV sitcom, after ironing an outfit for tomorrow and vacuuming her living room that didn't need it, when it was late enough that Mitch might have left his office, she dialed his number.

"Hello, Mitch. " She positioned her kitchen stool by her open back door, hoping for a breeze.

"So, you're doing all right for yourself. Encyclopaedia Britannica, not bad."

"I'm doing fine, Mitch. And you?"

"A touch of emphysema, but otherwise. And Wingspan is doing great."

"Eileen told me. She said you'd taken on a partner. How's that working?"

"Can you believe he thought he could do better elsewhere, as in the Big Apple, where he's currently making booze ads? Do you have any idea how much money there is to be made shooting liquor splashing over those fake ice cubes?"

"Trading St. Paul for New York, imagine that." She hadn't known that the ice cubes were fakes. That's why real drinks never looked as good as the ads. "But you're hanging in there."

"That I am, Miss Pollyanna."

"Don't call me that." Bob's beginning with Pollyanna was his final flourish. He knew she hated that name.

Mitch cleared his throat. "Eileen said you were away for a time, taking care of your mother. You're a good girl. Then this new job. So, life goes on."

"Life goes on and you phone." She heard the impatience in her voice as she reached for her iced tea glass and inspected its ordinary, clouded ice cubes.

"You in a hurry at ten o'clock at night? I leave message after message and you return my call when you're in hurry?"

"No hurry. Just curious why you got in touch. Not that I don't enjoy talking to you."

"I got a call." He coughed, a dry ratcheting smoker's cough.

"You sound terrible."

"Give me a minute." A muffled sound as if he'd wiped his mouth. "So, I got a call from Shelley's schmuck nephew."

She should have known this was connected to Shelley. "The lawsuit nephew?" The breakup between Mitch and Shelley came when Shelley sued Mitch for partial payment on a job that Shelley never completed.

"The same. He pretends we never talked before. Which is fine by me. So, he's cleaning out Kino's office." Mitch was chortling.

"What's taken so long? Shelley died four years ago. Someone's been paying for that space for more than four years?"

"Not my problem. So, he's found something addressed to Polly Wainwright, postmarked December 21, 1964."

Ten years ago? Two years after Shelley fired her? Kino's crowded front office, his footsteps echoing down the hallway, her standing by her desk, waiting for what had happened to reassemble into coherent reality. She took a slow breath waiting for the memory's pain to recede, then switched the handset to the other ear. "What's in it?"

"The nephew didn't say."

"Which would be very strange, his not opening it. And why did he get in touch with you, not Eileen? She's information central." She interrupted whatever he was saying. "Why didn't you just give him my number at EB?"

"I said I'd have you get in touch with him."

As if he were concerned about her privacy. What he wanted was an excuse to talk, and grouse about Shelley.

"Really, Mitch. You thought this was a better idea, me groveling to Shelley's idiot nephew, whom I don't know, for a letter moldering away for more than a decade? This is perfect Shelley, not to go to the trouble of forwarding a piece of mail. Isn't it a crime to interfere with the mail?"

"So Shelley's a fucking criminal. So what else is new?"

He was enjoying this. She tipped forward on her stool and smiled, forgiving him for being a windbag, she and he on the same side regarding Shelley. Although what did it matter now? That time was so long ago.

"What did you say, Mitch? I didn't get that."

"The return address is Starlight Lodge."

Starlight Lodge. Mailed three months after everything blew up? It had to be something she overlooked in her panicky packing with Ernie waiting outside Borus' cabin. Underpants under the bed resurfacing a dozen years later, that would be the perfect coda to her aborted filmmaking career.

"And whose name is on the return address?"

"He didn't say."

As Mitch went on about the nephew and the old lawsuit, she carried the phone onto the porch and looked down at the dark alley, her gaze fixing on the orange islands cast by the security lamps on the asphalt, seeing Ernie's headlights sweep through the trees as they approached the Lodge that first night, the lit trunks, the firelit folds of Watkins' ratty sweater, his whiskey tumbler on the carpet as his housekeeper led him away, him reaching for her as he fell and kept falling.

When Mitch stopped talking, she gave him not her home address but EB's, which he could have gotten from the phone book. She didn't want him to know anything about her he didn't already know.

● ● ●

Lashed by driving rain, she hurried up the back stairs from the basement laundry room eager to make her weekly call to Eugenia. She hadn't told her about Bob's dumping her, or about getting high with an overbearing woman from work with whom she was competing in an unacknowledged way for a continuing job at EB, or about her dismay about her life going nowhere. All that she wouldn't talk about felt like a breath held, held underwater, but even so, connecting with Eugenia was what she needed. She dried off, pulled her stool toward her open back door, and dialed her number. After asking if Eugenia was up to talking, she asked if she'd gotten the Neruda collection Polly had sent three weeks ago.

"Did I forget to tell you? It came a while ago."

"It's supposed to be a decent translation." Into English. Polly had worried this might insult Eugenia who read his French and Spanish work, but hoped that ultra-simple would be welcome.

The rain pounding on the porch roof drowned out Eugenia's words.

"What did you say?"

"I couldn't read it. I flipped through the poems and realized I've lost it. I can't write anymore."

"You're sick. It's temporary." Why had she not picked an Agatha Christie? Polly shut her back door.

"What just happened? Did the world end?"

"I shut my door. It's raining here, making a huge racket on my back porch. Do you want to talk about Crete for next summer? I found aerial photos of the Minoan site. It looks amazing."

"Mathias and I had planned to go this summer."

"Would you rather go with him?"

"Let's talk about your Bob? Is he still in Vietnam reporting from the tattering front line? Isn't the war over?"

"Let's have a Tell-a-Movie about an A-1 asshole."

"I've seen that movie." Eugenia exhaled a contempt-filled sigh. "My mother would say Bob was 'unsuitable.' I say, what took you so long? Can we not talk for a few minutes? I'm tired. But don't hang up."

Polly pressed her ear close to the phone. Eugenia's assumption that Polly had dumped Bob almost made it seem as if Polly had dumped him, which made her feel better, even though she wished she could tell Eugenia the truth. She couldn't, not if glancing at Neruda's poems she had to know by heart had defeated her. Polly couldn't unload what weighed on her—her shock at being dumped, the purposelessness that washed over her every morning when she woke to the question of what was ahead for her, how the now empty place Bob once occupied in her life emphasized the uncertainty of her future, how she'd lived thirty-four years and had nothing to show for it.

She walked to her refrigerator.

"What was that?" Eugenia said.

"I poured some iced tea. Did you know they use fake ice cubes in advertisements?"

"Next you're going to tell me there's no Santa Claus."

"Of course, there's a Santa Claus. You saw the movie. But here's something to test your credulity. I bought dope." She made it into a comedy downplaying her fear and her absurd sense of victory, dwelling on the uptight office worker buying a joint from a vet with a skull tattoo.

"Describe his arm with the tattoo. God, I love men's arms."

Polly described the swell of his bicep, guessing Eugenia was thinking about Mathias. Early on, Eugenia had said talking about him was too hard for her, and Polly hadn't asked again. Neither one of them was allowed to share what worried them. Hodgkin's had crushed the easy, intimate conversation they once had. But still, their breathing could align.

"One last thing, can I come for a visit sometime over the Labor Day weekend? Just for a few hours or one hour, short, simple. I'll be at my mother's for the weekend. It will be easy for me to make a quick run to see you, and a relief to get away from the Peoria festivities."

A muffled sound, then silence.

"Are you okay? Did I make you sick?"

"Wait." Eugenia breathed heavily. "There, I resettled this awkward device that holds the phone on my shoulder. My mother bought it. She thinks talking on the phone is too hard."

Holding the phone, talking to Polly was hard? "What I was saying was—"

"Not Labor Day weekend. That's only a month away. After Labor Day I have my last treatment. The doctors are pleased, I've said that, haven't I? They are positively jolly. After that and after I've recouped for a few weeks, then you come."

"You don't have to rest for me. You don't have to look like your old self. I won't stay more than fifteen minutes."

"At the end of September or early October, you bring dope, and we'll get high."

"I am marking that down in indelible ink," as they used to say, making fun of someone, she forgot who.

After they hung up, she looked around her kitchen, which no longer looked like it belonged to her, with her cereal boxes and peanut butter in the cabinet to the right of the stove and her glasses and plates above her toaster, but like a display kitchen from the fifties with empty cupboards and a fake refrigerator, or a test kitchen near an atomic test site after the blast, where everything was still unaccountably in place. Wanting evidence of something real, she opened the back door to a rush of damp air and inhaled a lungful, grateful for the mist wetting her face and the roar in her ears, but, blinking her eyes open, she saw that her village was hidden behind the silvery curtain of rain falling from the roof above her. The world beyond might have vanished and she was alone.

10

August, 1974

IN THE MIDDLE OF ANOTHER TENSE WEEK AT WORK, after takeout Thai dinner from the new place under the El, Polly carried the smelly containers down to the dumpster and something sharp bit into her heel, a glass chunk piercing her sandal. She twisted it out and dropped it into the dumpster, too. From Bob's blender, it had to be, though Mrs. Menendez had swept up the mess weeks ago.

After washing her feet and applying a Band-Aid, Polly stared at the door to the room that held his stuff. She'd gotten his letter three weeks ago. After retrieving it from the garbage, she'd read it to the end: all about setting up in Bangkok, his shared house on a river, motor bike hell, the differences with Saigon, nothing about them as a couple. Not a classic Dear John but a Fade to Black. He was spineless. She wanted him out of her house.

The door she hadn't opened since the night with Janine had swollen tight with humidity. She attacked it with her hip and half-stumbled, half-fell in, sliding on his stained letter that she'd shoved under the door. Trapped heat struck her like an ocean wave. She waited for something—a reprimand? from Bob?—but nothing happened. Outside in the alley the dumpster lid banged shut. She looked at his stacked boxes, the tacky plaid suitcase, the rocking chair, his old Olivetti, then pried open the cardboard boxes, one by one. All were stuffed with papers, notebooks, clippings, materials connected stories he had written, what he would need if he were to write a memoir, *after winning the Pulitzer,* he'd said one sleepy Sunday morning, after reading his front page story in the *Trib.* Was it his piece on the West Side after the riots? None of this mattered to her. She wasn't going to be the custodian of his archive. The boxes would go in the dumpster. But his personal things, his beloved typewriter, his rocking chair, the suitcase with his diplomas and childhood mementos she would keep, for now, in case a friend of his contacted her. She had room in the closet with her winter coats.

The sky to the north grew dark and heat lightning crackled in the distance as she made trips down and up the back stairs to the dumpster, pausing only to wash sweat from her face at the kitchen sink. The storm passed without breaking, and when the room was emptied of Bob's boxes, she sat on the floor in the half-dark and noticed the scratches she had made dragging them across the pretty, old oak floor. That's how she felt, scratched and emptied, too.

• • •

Going into the air-conditioned office was a relief, except for having to face Janine, who hovered. She popped into Polly's cubicle offering help with her assignments—"I'm doing fine, really"—and inviting her to lunch—"I brought mine from home"—and drinks after work—"I'm on the wagon for now." "No, nothing's wrong."

August vacations began and rumor had it that several of the picture editors would not return, which didn't change the calculus. It would be she, Janine, and Hank who would be in contention for the remaining job, and she was the least likely to be chosen. Whenever Polly thought this or about her future, she was overcome with lethargy. She hoped Vanessa would choose her, the way she had hoped in high school to get into Radcliffe, to which she hadn't even applied. She should have begun looking for a new job, but she hadn't, not seriously. The Women Wanted ads still listed nothing but Gal Friday and Typists jobs, which were too depressing to consider. Later, if she had to.

Returning from the copier station with the Amtrak timetable to plan her Labor Day weekend at her mother's, she found on her slide viewing table a messengered box from a LaSalle Street law firm, from Shelley's nephew. Inside was a dusty padded envelope smudged with what looked like a shoe print, addressed to Polly Wainscot, % Kino Films, postmarked December 21, 1964, the return address: *Agnes Borus, Starlight Lodge, Wisconsin*

Mrs. Borus, the disapproving housekeeper. Her elegant cursive was a surprise. A local who probably hadn't finished high school, Polly had assumed, but her handwriting said otherwise. Mrs. Borus had been educated, or at least had educated herself. She was at least sixty-years-old back then, maybe seventy. Now she could be dead. Polly squeezed the envelope, feeling pliable materials around something rectangular and hard. Reaching for her scissors, she heard a rustle behind her.

"Polly."

She turned to see Vanessa.

"Please come to my office."

When Polly tapped at Vanessa's open door, Vanessa was already seated at her massive desk, hands intertwined on her green blotter, as if she were holding playing cards. She nodded for Polly to sit.

"This summer you have done an outstanding job. You completed assignments I had assumed would never close, that would have had to run without illustrations, an unacceptable failure. A few weeks ago, I spoke to you about the possibility of finding a place for you after Plan B. Now we are in August and letters announcing the first round of layoffs will be issued in the next ten days. At this point, I need to know if you are sincerely interested in staying on at EB."

"Yes, I am interested, Vanessa." Realizing her fingers were locked in the same gesture as Vanessa's, Polly unlocked them.

"You are the least experienced picture editor, after all, and I would have to argue for someone with so little seniority."

Was praise laced with belittlement typically British, or personal to Vanessa? The film companies where Polly had worked were less hypocritical—they didn't bother with praise.

"Since I began," she said, "I have demonstrated my value to you and the company, not just this summer. You also know, I'm sure you can tell, that I enjoy working here. I would very much like to continue." Polly smiled brightly. "What job you are thinking about?"

Vanessa peered at Polly, a new calculation behind her eyes. "It's a bit too soon to get in front of ourselves." She disentwined her fingers and appeared to check her manicure, before looking up at Polly. "I will be able to speak with more precision, with details, after Labor Day. About this conversation, not a word to anyone, I don't have to say." She leaned back and placed her hands on her desk, meeting over.

Polly stood. "I'm grateful that you're still considering me."

Passing through the worktables on her way to her cubicle, she paused to pick up a ruler, Hank's, his initials were inked on the back, understanding that a shift had occurred in Vanessa's office. Her last direct look at Polly suggested respect that hadn't been there before, because Polly had learned to play the game, a lesson she should have learned long ago. Getting ahead required not ability, not energy and commitment, but the recognition that it was a game, a game with rules with its own language and strategy. After nearly two years at EB, she had learned the language. Use the word "you" often: what you want, you know, you, you, you. Incorporate phrases like "demonstrated value," "part of the team," "how would you like to handle this?" "enjoy working here," blah blah blah. She had expressed interest and withheld her misgivings, she could always say no later. She had pressed Vanessa for a few details, but expressed interest without saying definitely she did want the job. That was the game, too. Polly's being somewhat non-committable could suggest to Vanessa that the job would have to be enticing or Polly wouldn't take it, although almost any job at EB would be better than starting out again as the "new girl." She left the ruler on Hank's desk. He was her competition, he and Janine.

It was to Vanessa's advantage to string her along, her and Hank and Janine. Each of them would work diligently trying to outshine the others, while Vanessa's insistence on secrecy would prevent the competition from flaring into anything public and ugly. While Polly was the least likely, what was certain now was that she would not be among the first to be let go, which meant that she could delay her job search until after Labor Day.

At the entrance to her cubicle, Polly stared at the half-walls papered with her movie cards, to-do lists, production sheets, and

Mrs. Borus' envelope on her desk, which she shoved into her bag to look at later, at home. When Plan B wrapped, she would leave this cubicle, EB would vacate this floor, and whoever got Vanessa's job would get a new office, probably a real office.

She waited until Vanessa had left for the day before gathering her things. She didn't want to go home to her hot apartment with the empty back bedroom. If Bob or anyone were ever to approach her to claim what he'd left behind, dumping his papers would seem like a pathetic gesture of a scorned woman, while keeping his few personal things might seem, not considerate, but a tease to draw him into a negotiation. Why could she not get things right? What she wanted was him gone. What she wanted was for the space he had filled in her life to be taken over by a purpose she didn't have.

Outside on the plaza, she maneuvered around tourists who never knew where to go, crossed the bridge, and walked south toward the park where she turned east toward the harbor, the air immediately cooler. She couldn't remember the last time she had set out without a destination. At Lake Shore Drive, she waited in a mob at the traffic light. Four lanes of rushing cars separated the placid park and business side of the city from the harbor where a holiday-like atmosphere prevailed. On the harborside, cyclists zipped along the concrete embankment, and beyond, sail boats moored to cans bobbed beneath the bright blue sky. The signal changed and the crowd crossed in a mass, then dispersed. Polly perched on a concrete ledge to take off her heels and rub her feet watching a tan couple with a picnic hamper drag a dinghy from a locker and lower it into the water.

If she locked her vision straight ahead, the Lake met the sky without interruption in a wide arc from the Aquarium on the south to the lone dark high rise to the north, the water in between blue as a sapphire and sparkling, the sky above the same blue, but velvet. This was so beautiful. Why didn't she come more often? The only time this summer had been for Janine's Fourth of July party a month ago. Last summer she and Bob would walk from the golf course to the zoo, or swim at Fullerton beach after work. Long before him, after college, she and her girlfriends, Eugenia, Halley, Claire, others she'd lost track of, would hang out at Oak Street beach where there were plenty of guys. By their second summer, that scene was too frat party and they shifted to Fullerton beach where the already-coupled gathered with their fold-up picnic tables and wine glasses. She and her friends mocked them and spread out their blankets to sunbathe. She hadn't sunbathed in years. She burned, Eugenia too. This summer Eugenia lounged in her parents' garden, the sun was good for her, the doctors said, but she wore a hat. Her scalp looked like a plucked chicken, she said.

Polly held back her wind-blown hair. She didn't want to think about Eugenia or her bald head or her wig. She wanted to watch boats dip and sway in the harbor, and the ones beyond the seawall glide over the dimpled water, white sails up and taut, and the cyclists flashing by her in vivid shirts and tight shorts. The small boats beyond the seawall, maybe a sailing school, crisscrossed each other's paths, but when she looked again, they'd scattered, lost among all the other little boats, and the cyclone of gnats beside her suddenly vanished. Nothing stayed in place. Everything shifted. Everything altered its connection to everything else, but she kept missing the moment when everything changed. She focused on a two-masted sailboat. When a cycling club zoomed past her and she looked again, she wasn't sure she found the same one.

When the drone of traffic eased, rush hour over, she put on her shoes. She would do this more often. This weekend she would pack a picnic and take the bus to Montrose Harbor. The bra-burners were right. She could go where she wanted, do what she wanted, by herself. Buy dope to share with Eugenia, or for herself. She could stop in a bar and have a drink on her own, not to meet friends, not to pick up a guy, but to enjoy a quiet moment alone in a cool, dark bar before going home to her hot, oppressive apartment and Mrs. Borus' envelope that bulged in the bag by her feet. Not far away, a few blocks west, on the other side of the park, under the El was a low-down bar with a life-size Charlie Chaplin statue by its entrance. No one she knew would be in that grungy neighborhood.

The sign over the door read *Step-Hi*, and The Little Tramp with chipped cheeks and merry eyes beckoned her in. Except for the bartender serving a Black man in a janitor's uniform sitting at the far end of the bar, and three fat women in a booth, the place was empty, and safe-looking. Polly took a stool near the front and ordered a gin and tonic.

Someone behind her said, "Polly?"

She glanced in the mirror hanging above the bar and saw two men silhouetted in the open door to the street, one thin, the other muscular.

"That you, Polly Wainwright?" the thin one said, wiping a handkerchief over his sweaty forehead. Sid Dempsey, a former colleague of Bob's from the *Trib*.

There was no escape. "Hi, Sid. What are you doing in this seedy neighborhood? Isn't Riccardo's your hangout?"

"That it is. I'm steppin' low at the Step-Hi tonight. Working on a story. Over there on State." He jerked his shoulder toward the open door and settled on the stool beside her, the other man stood. "A woman fell down an elevator shaft. It's a flophouse, but it's a news story because of the elevator licensing scandal." He ordered a Michelob and introduced the other guy, Lorenzo something, who ordered the same, and stood silent as Sid talked about the scandal. Lorenzo was good-looking in an Italian mobster way with gold chains, open-neck black shirt, and shoulder-length hair, swept back, a union plumber, a source for Sid's elevator story. The building was crazy out of compliance, Lorenzo offered, the city inspectors on the take. He raised his palms—what can you do? Not her kind of guy, but his animal bulk felt like a counterbalance to Sid's windy bombast, and she was sorry when he left for the men's room.

Sid leaned close. "You're on your own tonight? Where's Big Guy?"

"If you mean Bob Kitchener, he's in Bangkok." She had braced for this. "He and Stu Holtz, you might know him, and another reporter have set up shop there. The war should keep them busy for a while."

He lifted an eyebrow and his glass to Bob's future, skeptical—of Bob's future or her cool disinterest, she couldn't tell—and asked what she was up to. She told him, adding that she was looking for a new job. Did he know of any openings for a picture editor? He didn't, and complained about things being tight at the *Trib*. Even if he had known of any jobs, he wouldn't tell her, newspaper men were clannish.

"If Kitchener's out of the picture, what are you doing for company?"

She made what she hoped was a face that said she was surprised by his question, and took a long sip of her drink, then said, "Keeping busy."

"Come keep busy at O'Brien's retirement party, at Riccardo's—where else?—this Saturday night."

Before she could beg off, Lorenzo rejoined them, putting his arm on the back of her stool, and waved to the bartender for another round.

Sid said, "This one's looking for a job."

"You could become a plumber." Lorenzo pressed his hip against hers. "Aren't you ladies pushing for that?"

"God, they're angling into the newsroom, too."

"Can't you imagine this one on her hands and knees under your kitchen sink?" Lorenzo said, winking at Sid. He touched her back. "Want me to check if they're letting ladies into the union?"

Polly slid sideways off her stool, fumbling in her purse for bills to pay for her drink. "I'll leave the dirty work for you. 'Night, Sid."

"Come on, Polly. We're just joking."

Outside night had fallen. She lifted her face to the El train rattling by overhead, blinking against the shower of cinders, feeling triumphant in a minor key, like the ordinary woman heroine in an early Godard evading the loutish moves of men.

• • •

A few days later, after dinner and a phone call with her mother to make plans for Labor Day weekend—her mother would pick her up at the train station and they would go straight to the farm stand to get salad-makings for the Lindstrom's party—Polly poured a second glass of wine and plopped Mrs. Borus' package on her kitchen table. Moths batted against the screen door, drawn by the kitchen light. She couldn't recall the woman's face, but remembered her dyed brown hair.

The old envelope shredded when she pulled it open. Inside was a letter written in Mrs. Borus' oddly elegant script on stationery bordered with pansies, a thick business-size envelope marked "Private," and a bundle of newspaper clippings and other papers secured with a book clip.

Dear Miss Wainscot,

It has been seven weeks since Mr. Watkins died, and I am at a loss about what to do with these papers, which he did not want his sons to see. He had his secrets from that pair. Mr. Watkins was sliding downhill when your film crew showed up. I'm not saying that all that fuss with your lot gave him the stroke, but it did. I blame Neil and Cyrus. That pair insisted Mr. Watkins make a film. As if he wanted publicity. That was them, not him. That is water under the bridge now. He's gone. They've kept me on these past months to keep house while they brought in their people to ship out or sell most everything. That's done now. I'm to close down the Lodge and be out of here by the end of the year.

Mr. Watkins showed you his personal box. He told me about that. He liked you. He didn't like the rest of your film crew. He wished you were making the film. He said you had the right attitude. I don't know what happened to the box, probably sold with everything else. Mr. Watkins trusted me with these papers. I am trusting you. From what I overheard, the film is off. That's fine by me. But these papers I can't destroy, so I'm sending them to you.

Best Regards,
Francine Borus

Mrs. Borus had it wrong—Watkins hadn't shown her a box. Not that night in the library, and the two other times she'd been near him, others were present: after Mongo kicked her out of the studio when Mr. Watkins was with his younger son; and that last time, when he reached out for her and everything crashed down. She pushed away from the table and walked to the screen door, pressing her forehead against the mesh as the moths fell silent.

That night in the library, he told her to start the fire, he poured drinks, he looked through her, and they talked. He asked her to get his diary, not a box, and she'd just spotted it when Borus yelled at her. Borus in her ratty robe, her scrawny legs rising out of heavy farm boots—Polly touched the woman's elegant signature. Had she been Mr. Watkins' lover? How little Polly had understood about anything in that house. What had absorbed her at Starlight Lodge was learning as much as she could about filmmaking and trying to prove herself to the Kino crew. Her future, that's what she had focused on. At the beginning she had been curious about the legendary Watkins; later she'd been drawn to the man who had seemed like an elemental force; but she had been more or less incurious about the real life of old man Watkins who was living as a recluse in the middle of nowhere tended by his ferocious housekeeper.

She set aside the envelope marked "Private" and unclipped the bundle of papers held together with a book clip. One paper she recognized, a half sheet torn from the film's logbook. Why had he saved this scrap with her name? And why had it ended up among these papers he hid from his sons? She touched her fingertip to the silly signature she had developed in high school, the crossbar of "t" in Wainwright a long, wavy swoop she'd seen as a banner floating above her name. Now her letters were jagged, not loopy, the "t" crossbar a dash, and she was no longer the girl who'd written her name on a scrap of paper torn from the logbook.

She unfolded a yellowing microfilm copy of a birth certificate for Wiley Coleman Jenks, born August 22, 1931. Seven pounds, three ounces. Mother: Maureen Jenks—Maureen, the woman Mr. Watkins had mistaken Polly for. Father: the space left blank. Attending Doctor: Otis Baumgarten, MD. Hurley, Iron County, Wisconsin. Polly flipped over the slick paper, hoping for more, and found only a chemical stain.

In 1931 when Maureen Jenks had the baby, Watkins had been a world-renowned photojournalist working from New York. In his clipping file at EB, Polly had seen a photograph of him perched on a ladder in his studio in the recently completed Empire State Building, his fancy sport car in the background. The Empire State Building had an elevator that took his car directly into his studio. All this a world away from Iron County, Wisconsin. When Maureen Jenks' baby was born, Watkins was married to Oona, and they had two sons, the middle-aged men she had met at the Lodge.

She teased apart two sharply-folded newspaper clippings, the first, a recipe for pickled green tomatoes, the other, an obit for Maureen Jenks Reed, died on November 19, 1940. She had died more than twenty years before Watkins.

...survived by her husband, Alvin Reed, and their nine-year-old son Wiley."

The obituary had been cut from a newspaper. The name of the paper and the date of publication were missing. She reached for the thick envelope marked "Private." Inside were five letters without envelopes, all signed, *Maureen.*

February 5, 1931
I am pregnant. Now is time for you to break
with Oona finally like you promised. I'll
come to New York. We'll live as a family.
Your boys will be welcome.

March 3, 1931
How can you think that I wood have an
operation? You had no business phoning
Francine. That snake!!! She came to the
house with her bag and everything and said
you had paid her. I kicked her out. That two
hundred and fifty dollar check you sent me
will buy a ticket to NYC. How about I show
up at your hoity-toity building and tell your
doorman to take me up!!

September 1, 1931
Our beautiful baby boy is one week old.
I named him Wiley Coleman, Wiley for
my dad, Coleman for you. Jenks is his last
name. We will change it when we get mar-
ried. Wiley Coleman Watkins. Don't that
have a nice ring! The three hundred dollars
covered everything. Thank you. When will
you come?

October 27, 1931

You are right. I do not want to live in NYC.
If your work means you must travel, so be
it. Me and Wiley will move to Milwaukee or
Minneapolis so you can be near an airport.
You must break with Oona!!!! When????
For now, seventy dollars on the first of the
month will cover things so I don't have to
work, but I need you and Wiley needs his
father.

The next was dated four years later, *February 2, 1935*

It has been a terrible time, worse than you
know. You in Germany at Christmastime—
don't that say just about everything—while
I'm here nursing our dying little boy. When
your secretary asked, "Wiley who?" I just
said someone you knew. I glad you noticed
that I kept my word, even in this terrible
time and me so sad. Don't bother coming.
You didn't bother about us when Wiley was
alive. It's too late now. But I need money
for a proper headstone. That will close us
out. Bet you're glad no more checks. At the
end Wiley was so thin from the nomonia.
An angel. Now he is in Heaven with his
Heavenly Father.

Polly turned back to Maureen's obit. In November 1940, Maureen had been survived by her nine-year-old son Wiley, but five years earlier, she had written to Watkins that Wiley had died. She had lied, scamming Watkins for Wiley's headstone—five hundred dollars, real money back then—and giving up child support. Why give up child support? Might this have been when she married Alvin Reed? Maybe she had not wanted checks from another man coming into their home. Maybe she had wanted to keep Watkins' identity secret from her husband. During those years, Watkins had been married to Oona with two sons growing up in New York, while he was mostly in Europe photographing Nazi events, the 1936 Olympics, the buildup to war in Europe and its outcomes. Polly had seen the photographs of hollow-eyed children who would have been the same age as his son Wiley. No wonder Watkins kept these letters secret from his other two sons.

Your boys will be welcome, Maureen had written in the first letter. Middle-aged men in dress shirts and khakis. Neil and Cyrus, Mrs. Borus called them. Big Fish and Little Fish the Kino crew nicknamed them, the elder being the driving force behind the film project— Mongo could barely hide his hostility to his interference—and the younger son was a blur. She re-read all the letters and found no sign Watkins had ever visited Maureen or seen Wiley. If there had been other letters, he hadn't saved them in this secret cache.

She swept the lint from envelope's padding into her palm and rolled it into a tight ball. That Shelley hadn't opened this envelope or thrown it away, that twelve years later his nephew went to the trouble to track her down, that Mrs. Borus decided to entrust Polly after what she had done, these facts created a chain of coincidence that made Polly the guardian of these papers. Improbable, absurd, yet Watkins had seen something in her he trusted, and he met Polly because Mitch brought to Kino a film project that Watkins agreed to in spite of having secrets he didn't want exposed. Why?

The stove clock said ten o'clock. Mitch worked late. He might still be in his office. When he answered, she said she had gotten the package forwarded by Shelley's nephew; it came from Watkins' housekeeper.

"The housekeeper? Oh, the battleaxe. Was something going on between those two, you think?"

"I have no idea." She pictured Mrs. Borus leading Watkins out of the library, his weight on her shoulder, her expression patient. His lover? Or his long-time fixer and abortionist, if Maureen was to be believed. "She sent papers he wanted me to have. But he obviously confused me with someone else."

"What kind of papers?"

"What old people keep—letters, some newspaper clippings, a recipe for pickled green tomatoes. Who eats pickled green tomatoes? No key to a safety box, no treasure map. It's bizarre that these came to me, but now I'm curious: what was behind the Watkins film in the first place? Do you remember anything about this, or do you have any paper work on the project?"

"Does Mitch Klein ever throw anything out? Noooo. Somewhere in this office, I don't know where, I must have whatever I had at the time, and, Jesus, the threatening letters that came afterward, when I tried to collect on expenses and the *per diem*. Jesus H Christ, it is all coming back on me, like a case of bad indigestion."

"Would you be able to pull out those files and tell me what you have?"

"Sugar, somewhere in this office doesn't mean I can put my hands on it."

The same old Mitch. "How hard would it be for you to check?"

"I'm busy. Did I tell you how business has been hopping?"

"You said kaput. The business was all but finished."

"Some days it's kaput, some days it's hopping."

"Will you check, Mitch?"

He said he would. After they hung up, she returned the papers to the large envelope and stared at her name written wrong by Francine Borus.

Mr. Watkins had asked Polly to write her name, so when he instructed Mrs. Borus to give Polly his secrets, he hadn't confused her with Maureen. He knew who she was. That night in his library, he had looked at her and seen more than anyone else ever had, more than her parents, who saw a version of themselves, and more than any lover, far more than Bob, who saw the compliant helpmate he wanted to see. Watkins had seen more than she ever had staring at herself in the mirror trying to figure out who she was. He had peered through the naïve, nervous girl to the true Polly. She had held his probing gaze. He, who had looked at thousands and photographed thousands, he, who was a legend for capturing the essence of the person, he regarded her as worthy.

11

August, 1974

SHE WAITED A FULL WEEK before calling Mitch again. He'd been too busy to dig into storage. "August, would you believe busy in August?" No, she didn't believe it, but Mitch promised he would get to it. She returned to Watkins' file in EB's library. Nothing had been added since she last looked, and nothing she'd seen before cast any light on her new questions: Why he'd dropped out of his career? Why he'd left New York and his family? Why he'd been willing to open his life to the scrutiny of a film when he had secrets?

A heat dome settled over the city. Vanessa took a week's vacation, which eased the tension in the office. Everyone came in late, left early, and those who went out to lunch, came back tipsy. Polly stayed at her desk. When she did what she could on her own picture assignments, she turned to the department's Closed-Incomplete files to see if she could succeed where others had failed. An expensive phone call to a picture agency in Delhi netted the promise of a photo of The Temple of the Tooth in Sri Lanka. Tina had failed, probably because she hadn't known the country changed its name from Ceylon. Polly's success would impress Vanessa. Twice a week she called Mitch who offered excuses each time, saying how he liked hearing her voice, and the weather, how's the weather in Chicago? The days blended together. On the Monday before the Labor Day weekend, she was surprised to hear Mitch's voice on the phone. He'd called her.

"The proposal, I got right here, Pollyanna, *Cole Watkins; A Life in Pictures*, and the contract signed by the sons."

She spun her chair to face away from her cubicle's entrance as Mitch explained how he could not believe how he'd lowballed his bid. "Me and Shelley, we both took a bath when the project went belly up. Split our losses amicably though. Those were the days. I'll send you a copy of the proposal. The contracts I'm not copying."

"Any odds and ends?"

"A couple draft proposals, the dates changing. Months it took to get them off their asses to commit. Nothing of interest."

"No margin notes, no hand-written scraps?"

A shuffling sound. "I'm telling you. I'm looking at nothing here, nada, zip, nyet. Like I said, I'll send you a copy of the proposal."

"Mitch, I have a thought. Why don't I come visit you and take a look?" She couldn't afford a round trip ticket, or a night in a motel, and Mitch might have nothing more than what he'd said, but she wanted to do this. "How about Saturday? I could come up on Saturday. I'd like to see your shop."

"Labor Day weekend? You got to be kidding. The wife's having a barbecue on Saturday."

"Mitch, if I'm willing to come to you, surely you can give me a couple of hours."

She could take the train. The Empire Builder ran from Union Train Station to St. Paul before heading west. Picturing the photograph from the clipping file of Cole Watkins in the then new Empire State Building, an aura of kismet shimmered over this hasty plan.

"I'll give you an hour," Mitch finally said.

As soon as they hung up, she called her mother to tell her a friend in St. Paul had invited her for the Labor Day weekend.

"The Lindstroms will be disappointed," her mother said, meaning she would be disappointed, but she didn't ask which friend.

"I'll come in a few weeks, late September or early October, when I can visit Eugenia, too. She wants me to wait until her treatments are over."

"How's she doing?"

"Well, she says, but she doesn't want me to see her now."

"You're right not to push. When I was in rehab, you were the only one I could bear to see me."

After they finished, Polly stared at the notes she'd taken while talking to Mitch and felt a surge of excitement and liberation. A trip on her own, something new. At a sound outside her cubicle, she turned and saw Janine, a mailroom tray balanced in her arms.

Polly waved her in. "I've got a new plan for the weekend. I'm going to St. Paul."

"Merry St. Paul?" Janine smiled. "Fun spot of the Midwest?"

"I'm going to see an old colleague."

"The boring old loser you knew way back?"

"He's not a loser. He's a blowhard. But he's got some documents I want to see. I'll take the Empire Builder, I've always wanted to take that, if the schedule works out. If not, the bus."

"Borrow my car." Janine shifted the mail tray to her other hip. "My Okie cousins are visiting for the weekend. They'll come in their van, and they'll do all the driving around town. My Thunderbird is too small. She'll be idle all weekend."

"I can't borrow your car."

"You'd do me a favor. Big Bird needs her gunk cleaned out."

Even with the price of gas, it would still be cheaper than a round-trip train ticket, and she wouldn't be tied to the train's schedule.

Seeing her soften, Janine said, "Saturday morning then, any time early."

If Polly weren't a hypocrite, she would turn down her offer. "Seven o'clock too early?" If she had any scruples, she would tell Janine about Vanessa's dangling the job offer. If they were friends, she would say they weren't really in competition, that Janine deserved the job, and that Polly was playing along so that she wouldn't be the first fired, so she had more time to search for a new job, but she didn't say any of this. They weren't friends, and besides, she wasn't sure any of this was true.

•   •   •

On Saturday morning, Janine was waiting under her building's portico, parked at the curb, her yellow Thunderbird sparkling with water drops. Wishing Janine hadn't gone to the trouble of getting her car washed, laying on more guilt, Polly said, "Aren't you worried that I won't bring it back?"

"Oh, come on, you're a friend." She pointed out some dings on the front fender. Polly wasn't to worry if she added a couple more, the gas pedal had lost its rubber pad, which made it slippery, but it was still safe, and the insurance card was in the glovebox. Opening the trunk, she let Polly wedge her duffle in beside the spare tire, then handed her the keys. "You are off on a Girl's Own Adventure."

"You sound like my grandfather."

"You liked your grandfather, right?"

Polly gave her an awkward hug and promised to bring the car back in one piece, then waved goodbye, and pulled away slowly. After rounding the corner, she sped up and relaxed into the luxury of the plush, well-worn leather seat, admiring the gleaming wooden dashboard. She had never driven such an expensive car.

So early on the holiday weekend, few cars were on the road. She merged easily onto the expressway, envisioning the route she'd memorized: north to Milwaukee, westward across lower Wisconsin to the Mississippi River, up to St. Paul. After fixing her route on the map spread out on her kitchen table, she located Iron County to the east, where Watkins had been born, near Lake Superior and bordering the Upper Peninsula of Michigan. In the green swath of forests, she found a red dot for the town of Hurley, where Watkins' son Wiley had been born and where Maureen died, and searched with no expectation of finding a tiny Notable Attractions triangle marking Starlight Lodge. It could be anywhere in the northern part of the state. She had forgotten the name of the village with the two-pump gas station where Ernie dropped her off to wait for the Trailways bus to take her back to Chicago, the memory as always, a fish hook twisting in her belly. She remembered nothing about how long the trip back to Chicago had taken, whether it was still daylight or night when she arrived back at the apartment she shared with Eugenia, remembering only Eugenia's concerned face.

The traffic grew dense around Milwaukee, then cleared. She had forgotten how much fun driving was, feeling the engine's power, hands on the wheel, windows down, wind whipping her hair, Top Ten blasting on the radio. She pressed on the gas pedal, ten above the speed limit, twenty, flying past pickups loaded with canoes and campers with flapping curtains, she unencumbered, soaring and wanting this never to end.

After a few hours, the flat soybean and corn fields gave way to hills dotted with black and white cows, like in a kid's picture book. At the Mississippi River she dropped down to the speed limit, crossed the bridge, and turned north. Before she reached the outskirts of St. Paul, she stopped at a gas station to ask for directions, suddenly flooded with trepidation. Soon she would see Mitch. On the phone it had been easy, she pretended to be on an equal footing, but on the phone, you can end it, as Eugenia said. You hang up.

• • •

In a low strip mall of mostly vacant store fronts, a dental supply company anchored the far end and an awning store on the other, with Wingspan in the middle. She was fifteen minutes early and the parking lot was empty. In the chain link fence separating the asphalt lot from the scrubby field beyond, someone had formed a peace symbol from shoved-in plastic cups.

She parked facing Wingspan's door wondering why she'd come. Did the origins of a film that never got made matter now? She was tired, she needed a shower, she would see what Mitch had, leave, get a motel room, and tomorrow either hang around St. Paul, or head south to that touristy-town people talked about. She had nothing better to do, a depressing thought.

At the sound of a car, she woke to see a black pimpmobile Caddie roll alongside her, the driver's window lowering.

"Hello, Pollyanna. Sweet wheels."

"It belongs to a friend."

He drove in a loop to park beside her, facing the same direction and climbed out. He was a shock—shoulder-length hair, fringed vest, bellbottoms embroidered at the hem, shirtsleeves rolled up to show off hairy forearms festooned with Indian bracelets. Aging Mitch was a wannabe dude, and he looked ludicrous.

"What happened to the coat and tie and slicked-back hair?" she asked, climbing out as he strolled around Janine's car, admiring.

"Gotta keep up with the times, Sugar. You, you're looking, I gotta say, like those nuns who don't wear habits but don't fool anyone."

She smoothed the front of her loose blue chemise, which she had chosen as an invisibility cloak, to prevent exactly the scrutiny Mitch was giving her. She did look like a nun. "It's comfortable for the long drive." She extended her hand.

He wrapped her in a hug. "Come on, Pollyanna. I don't have all day. I've got ice in the trunk for the barbecue."

Sun streamed through Wingspan's store front windows. It took her a few seconds to register the cartoonish daisy wallpaper and the screaming orange counter that separated the waiting area from where the receptionist must sit at the desk with the mug sprouting flower-topped pens. A kindergartener with a big budget would decorate an office like this.

Mitch spread his arms. "Cheery, no? You got to keep up with the times."

"Cheery, yes." On the wall hung a pair of enormous puffy wings made of sparkly white fabric.

He grinned. "Wingspan, get it?"

"Got it."

Mitch's getup and this goofy office made her feel as if she'd dropped acid and landed on the wrong side of the looking glass, but Wingspan wasn't a hippie shop but a successful film production house, and Mitch had kept up with the times. Had she? After twelve years, the country tearing apart, the war, demonstrations, drugs everywhere, women railing against the obvious, the president shot, and his brother, Martin Luther King Jr shot, too, cities burning, through all of this, had she not changed? And by not changing, had she become staid? Was this why Bob had dumped her? She touched her sad sack dress. Was it not a protective costume but an accurate expression of who she was?

"What do you think Shelley would say?" Mitch asked.

"Far out."

He chortled, surveying his reception area. This was why he had agreed to her coming, to show off. He was alive and Shelley was dead. He was a success and Shelley had died broke. Polly was his witness: Mitch had won.

"Come. Let me show you the layout." He started down the hall with track lights overhead trained on a row of large glossy photographs of puzzling closeups. A wasp's nest? And the next, a moth or an orchid? She stepped back to read the long line of calligraphy above, *What's My Secret?* That was hers, her title for the series she had brought to him, about changeling insects. He had shot it down, saying that there were a million bug shows.

"Mitch." He was gone.

His head appeared in a doorway ahead. "You like? That one's my favorite. It's a microscopic view of tree bark. Fooled you, right? Not a wasp nest. That's what everyone thinks." He beamed at the row of photos. "My top filmstrip. Nature centers, elementary schools in nearly every state, even international."

"Mitch, that was my idea. I urged you to do a series on camouflage and self-devouring and look-a-likes. I was going to—"

"Sugar, I been making these filmstrips since forever."

"But that was my idea."

"Your idea? Please. If I had a nickel…"

"But, Mitch, that's my title. We talked, at length, more than once. I showed you my friend's pictures, Camilla Meyer's, bugs she photographed in the Chicago parks. You really don't remember?" She silenced the furious squawking inside her as Mitch tilted his head to stare at her as if she were crazy.

"No, Sugar, I do not. It's not like *What's My Secret?* is copyright material."

Maybe her title wasn't exactly *To Kill A Mockingbird* but his *since forever* was a flat-out lie. He did not have a product with that title, or anything close to it, or the subject of changeling bugs, no, not in 1962. That she knew for certain. Before bringing him any of her ideas, she had made sure he had nothing like it in his entire catalogue, and he had shot down every single one of her proposals. Yet one of her ideas had been good enough to steal, and it hadn't even registered that he'd stolen it from her. That's how insignificant she was.

He made a face, genuinely not remembering, but considering that maybe he had made a mistake by welcoming her into his office. Not wanting him to usher her out, she wanted to see what he had on the Watkins' film, she smiled a fake smile and lifted her hands to say she was done protesting. "You're going to show me your Watkins' folder."

The tightness around his eyes eased. "First, let's get you something to drink."

In the breakroom, he kneed shut the dorm fridge and popped open two bottles of Coke. Kino hadn't had a breakroom and neither had the other production houses she'd worked at before she gave up. Mitch was doing very well. *My top filmstrip.* Throttling her anger, she clutched the cold bottle and fixed her eyes on a beige metal box the size and shape of a Kodak carousel box on the counter near Mitch. A lens on one side and a handgrip, it had to be a camera.

Noticing where she was looking, Mitch turned. "This baby's going to revolutionize the industry."

"Film or video?"

"Video, like I said, revolutionary. Sony's come up with this, calls it a Portapak. Easy to carry and you sling this over your shoulder." He pointed to a small tape recorder. "Go anywhere. No team necessary. Cheap magnetic tape. The quality is for shit, but someday."

"Show me." She put down her Coke.

"It's not a toy."

"You said it was easy."

"Okay, okay. Let me…" He handed her the camera—it was heavy as a box of rocks—and guided her fingers around the handle. Struggling for steadiness, she pressed the eyecup against her cheekbone. The file cabinet, the counter's edge, the refrigerator handle, everything had a crystalline reality that was so much brighter and more vivid than what she could see with her own eyes. She let the image of the fridge's chrome handle burn onto her retina, before pivoting to the stainless sink and a withered sponge. The magic of seeing the ordinary transformed into the remarkable delighted her. She tried not to tremble as she tracked over the confetti-patterned lunch table. This was what she'd imagined when she'd hoped to get into filmmaking, having the power to frame, to choose, to show through images what can't be described with words. This was how she'd felt in her early days at Kino, on the brink of something grand and full of possibilities.

"Like I said," Mitch's voice boomed too close, "I got ice melting in the trunk of my car." He lifted the camera from her shoulder.

Disoriented, disappointed, she watched him snuggle the cap onto the lens before setting the camera down. In the hall he pointed at doors to his editing suites, rattling off the names of the equipment inside, as she glanced at the last *What's My Secret* photograph of a white feathery explosion on a black field. After the experience looking through the camera, her anger was hazy and remote, and she felt vaguely unsteady.

Mitch's office looked like every other film production office: shelves with fraying catalogues, piles of papers, file cabinets topped with awards, even an old Pathé Films poster, just like Shelley's. They used to brag about meeting at Pathé in New York. Mitch moved an exploding three-ring binder from the visitor's chair and waved for her to sit. Sagging into the worn armchair, a tendril of sadness wound through her—how comforting this ordinary film office was. She reminded herself why she had come: for information about Watkins.

Mitch pulled a manila folder from his desk drawer. "What a fucking disaster. Looking at these papers brought it all back. One thing I got to say, what happened wasn't your fault. Mongo blamed you. He had to do something, someone had to take the fall, and you were the logical. He had to try to salvage…I don't know…the good will of the sons, the possibility that we could continue in some way. Not to be, but we didn't know that then. Truth, I should never have taken the damn project. I never met the old gent until the first day of shooting. At that point, I crossed my fingers—I knew it was dreck— and hoped to God we'd get through."

"Why didn't you say this to Shelley? He *fired* me."

"You weren't my concern. I had a project circling the drain. All along I told you Shelley shouldn't have canned you. God's honest."

"Last week on the phone, you didn't say this."

"I'm telling you now." He pushed the folder toward her. "What kills me is that we had some decent footage when they pulled the plug. The house, the grounds, his collections, his working prints, like that. What a waste."

Holding the file, her hand shook. She was the best available scape-goat? Why had she not understood this? Because she *had* broken the rules. Because she screwed up earlier, because Mongo kicked her out, and they all ganged up on her, and Ernie rigid with fury when he drove her to the bus stop, Shelley firing her.

She opened the file. *Cole Watkins; A Life in Pictures*, the final proposal, dated June 12, 1962: "documentary, biography," "35mm color film, running time, 75—80 minutes," "stills drawn from the archive of," "full consultation with Neil Watkins and Cyrus Watkins." The sons had signed the two-page agreement, but not Cole Watkins. Beneath was a photocopy of a doctor's letter, A. L. Hutton, MD, stating that Cole Watkins was "in health sufficient to the needs of the film. Interviews should be limited to less than one hour and monitored with consideration for Mr. Watkins' stamina and state of mind." A typed addendum stapled to the agreement read, "Upon Cole Watkins' death, any and all proceeds will revert to the Cole Watkins Trust registered at the Park Falls Union Bank," with a big question mark penciled in.

"What's this, Mitch?"

He blew out a weary sigh. "A big nothing. The old man phoned the office and spoke to Sally. She's been gone, what, eight years. That was before I moved here. When I asked the sons about this addendum, they said, the old gent was confused. I seem to recall I checked with Cole Watkins' lawyer. What I know for sure is that I followed his lawyer's instructions, and used his text, as written there. That's it, Pollyanna. You want to know more," he twisted loose some business cards from the back of his Rolodex. "Get in touch with these guys. Nope, not Cyrus, he's dead." He rumpled the card and threw it in his waste basket. "Here's the older asshole, Neil Watkins, and their lawyer back then." He waved the cards at her. "I don't need them anymore."

Cyrus, the younger one, was dead? He had been nice to her. The other one, the older brother, was the jackal driving the film whom Watkins hadn't trusted. "I won't need them either. Why, if the sons were driving this project without their father's total agreement, did he go along?"

"How about the usual—fame, glory, money. Listen to this, I got wind just the other day of an exhibition of his work that's coming together out east, so he'll get some posthumous glory. Big museum deal. Being dead can be a real career booster." He stuffed the cards back in the Rolodex.

"All along I thought I had scotched his legacy," Polly said.

"Jeesus Polly, you weren't that important. I'll make copies of these for you to take." He picked up the folder.

She didn't move as he walked past. She had never questioned that she was to blame, or spoken about it to anyone who might have corrected her. Eileen or Sid, whom she had run into a few times, they didn't bring up the subject. Why would they bother since it was obvious that she, the youngest, the inept, the last minute fill-in, would be the stooge? She followed Mitch down the hall to the front. She should feel relief, but what she felt was stupid. Was she being equally stupid to think she had a genuine reason to piece together the truth behind Watkins' secrets? What possible good to come of it?

Mitch stood by the copier waiting for it to warm up, his gaze on the glittery wings on the opposite wall. "This business it's not all… I got my share of projects that go bust. The Watkins' film, not that unusual, I'm sorry to say. Take a look." He pulled a clamshell box from a shelf and spread out some photographs of petroglyphs and a few hand-drawn maps. "I had a gal in Flagstaff working on this. A guy owns a ranch loaded with petroglyphs and pots that should be in museums. We're all set to make a film. We line up the backers, she, my Flagstaff producer, gets the talking heads lined up, and the guy, the rancher, he wants money suddenly. Money? My backers are financing for the cultural good, I'm pulling in my basic, nothing more, and he, the schmuck, sees Hollywood with Tonto on his pinto explaining about these things." He slapped the pictures. "I tell him it's for schools. He says he'll wait for a better offer, and my producer, she heads to LA."

"*She?*"

"Don't give me that look. I hired a woman. So what? I'm up with the times, but now I'm flying solo again." He shrugged. "I got to see what comes along. That baby I showed you, the Portapak, that'll change the industry. How? Who knows? I envy you, I really do. You get paid rain or shine, no hassles with the unions, no pain-in-the-ass constant hustling for the next job. You got a good position with a top-notch company, worldwide top-notch, you can't do better."

"That's what everyone says."

He locked Wingspan's door behind them and she wondered what she should do. Little more than a whim brought her here and the desire to not spend the weekend in her home town, but she did feel an obligation to Watkins because of how he'd made her feel that night in his library, and because he had trusted her with his personal papers. Why had he wanted her to understand a story that he wouldn't have exposed in the film? If she were to drive to Park Falls where Mr. Watkins had banked, she might be able to find some clues. Why not? This would be better than hanging around St. Paul or that touristy town her mother liked.

"Is Starlight Lodge near Park Falls?"

"In the general area. I don't remember exactly." Mitch nodded toward Janine's car. "You dig up anything, you let me know, right?"

"Will do."

She gunned out of the parking lot, and a few turns later, pulled to the curb in a residential neighborhood of cracked sidewalks and one-story frame houses with weedy flowerbeds and tiny American flags like Mrs. Menendez's. After cutting the engine, she rested her head on the steering wheel. How had she gotten so much wrong? Her failure was not in what she had done—the film was doomed from the start—but in who she was, so inexperienced she hadn't understood that she was the patsy. She was still so naïve Mitch's revelation shocked her. Sick with self-loathing, she reached for the map of Wisconsin. Park Falls, C4. She traced the grid lines to where they met, then looked at the mileage calculator. She would get there around seven o'clock, the bars would be open, and she could look in the phone book for Jenks and Borus. Some of the loose pieces around Watkins might fit together. A Girl's Own Adventure, if nothing else.

An engine backfired. In the rearview mirror, she watched a motorcycle roll down the driveway three houses back, two teenagers on board, a bare-chested boy and a girl behind clinging to him. When the cycle's front wheel met the street, the boy stood on the pedals, twisted the handlebars, and a roar erupted. They thundered past, wind whooshing through Polly's window. She watched the motorcycle grow smaller, wanting what they had—propulsive energy toward what was ahead. She didn't have that, but she did have a reason to head to Park Falls. She dropped the map, turned on the ignition, and made a hard U-turn.

12

August, 1974

AFTER SHE CROSSED INTO WISCONSIN, the road narrowed from four lanes to two. Gone were the rolling hills, no cows, no red barns, just scrabbly black-green forests, not the storybook woods she'd driven through that morning, or the overwhelming forests she'd driven through with Ernie twelve years ago when they had been aiming toward the same place, but from a different direction. The forests she'd driven through then seemed majestic. These on the western edge of the state were dense, too, but blighted with clear-cut hillsides and here and there a few farms, most of them failing, some nothing more than caved-in barns and broken-tooth foundations. On a winding stretch she passed several dead deer, one recently hit, not yet pulled to the shoulder, its chest puffed, one eye catching hers as she passed. Unnerved, she searched for a radio channel, one that wasn't staticky, but the he-done-me-wrong lyrics made her think about Bob, so she lowered the volume to a comforting hum. At each small town, she slowed to the twenty-mile-an-hour speed limit, but no one was out on this holiday weekend, except kids. In a church parking lot, a group of them stopped circling their hot wheels to stare at Janine's zippy car. Polly tooted the horn and a little girl with her arm in a cast waved back.

Ahead against the hem of the clouds, fireworks exploded and twilight came on slowly, like the gradual closing of a lens' aperture. At the first sign for Park Falls, she looked for a motel. After passing a string of No Vacancies, she pulled into Bill 'n Lu's No-Tell Motel, a retro A-frame office attached to a cedar-shingled strip with maybe fifteen numbered doors alongside curtained picture windows. Behind the motel, behind the forest pressing close, a lake twinkled through the trees.

The office screen door slammed shut behind her. The woman leaning on the counter stubbed out her cigarette, Lu of Bill 'n Lu's Polly guessed, and gave no sign of being surprised by a single woman asking for a room on a holiday Saturday night. She handed Polly a key and told her she could park anywhere except near the boat ramp, and if she wanted the best burger in the Northwoods, go right out of the motel lot, take the first left, and follow it to where it ended in a T. No way to miss it. Downtown Park Falls, if you could call it a downtown, was a half a mile on, to the east. Keep going, don't turn right. The fireworks would be tomorrow night at the ball fields in town. Would she be staying two nights? Polly had not thought that far. Tomorrow, the Sunday of Labor Day weekend, how much investigating could she do? And if she stayed on through Monday morning, everything would still be closed. What was she doing in Park Falls? She told Lu she'd let her know.

Entering her room, Polly wondered if she'd been here before. She had never spent a night in a Wisconsin motel or stayed in any motel anywhere on her own, but the double bed with a lumpy green bed-spread, the old TV, the plastic-covered armchair, battered ice bucket, all looked eerily familiar. She threw down her duffle and flicked on the bedside lamp, its fake rawhide shade painted with tiny cowboys and green smudges, sagebrush, springing to life with a warm glow. A tiny stab behind her ribs caught her breath. One like it had been in her bedroom in Mrs. Borus' cabin.

She pushed aside the curtains. Through the thicket of pines, twinkling from a shore she couldn't see streaked the lake. She could feel it, out there somewhere close was Starlight Lodge. Out there, twelve years ago, her life had jumped off track. In the months after Shelley fired her, she had relived those four days at the Lodge as if she might rewind and change the outcome. Eugenia said what she was doing was no better than picking at a scab, that it was past time to get on with her life, and Polly did, but ordinary things still reminded her, Claire's pine-paneled den, the heavy coffee mugs at Jerry's Diner, like those Mrs. Borus served coffee in, the echoing marble floor of Eugenia's family's church so like the Lodge's atrium. If she were to see the Lodge again, would the haunting end? This was why she'd come, not to learn what she could about Watkins' last years or why he agreed to participate in a film that might unravel his secrets, but to see Starlight Lodge again.

After her year in Paris, when she stopped by her old grade school with her mother—why had they gone?—she saw that the main hall was no longer the terrifying gauntlet she remembered where big boys stuffed you into the lockers you couldn't open from the inside, but only a wide corridor lined with short green lockers below crayon drawings and it smelled happily of wax. Without the Kino crew, without the interfering sons, without her own over anxious, eager-to-please, inexperienced self, with Mr. Watkins gone, the Lodge might simply be an odd house that had no special aura and held no power over her. She snapped the curtains shut. She had to get out of here. She slipped out of her blue sack nun dress, showered, and pulled on jeans and a T-shirt.

As Lu had said, the burger joint was impossible to miss. At the T a logjam of pickups and vans were parked around a low log building that was topped with a winking neon sign that spelled *The Woodcutters*. Polly found a spot along the weedy verge where the woods met the unpaved road and walked back toward the entrance. Something inside her knocked when she saw the wooden trolls with gigantic noses and hatchet chins guarding the door. She remembered these trolls. The neon sign she didn't remember, or the name, but she had been here before. The sky, it wasn't as dark as that night twelve years ago when she'd eaten dinner with the crew before the day everything fell apart. After a day of shooting, they wouldn't have bothered with a long drive. Starlight Lodge had to be close.

She waited until she could draw a full breath before pulling open the heavy door, and a roar washed over her. The din quieted as heads turned in her direction. She walked through the packed tables pretending she hadn't noticed, aiming toward the bar. Behind it ran a long picture window, thirty feet long easily, that overlooked the woods—this she remembered. The fading light from outside was bright enough to silhouette the customers seated on stools along the shining tin-topped bar. The room grew noisy again as she spotted an empty stool at the far end. Some heads followed her, not hostile, just interested, as if she'd crashed their party.

The heavy-set man next to the free stool nudged sideways to give her room, and she sat, trying to hide her nervousness. Outside in the clearing, a few spot-lit birches surrounded a circle of squat plaster gnomes with their red caps. A nearby toppled sign said, *The Seven Dwarfs*. She remembered the clearing, but not the dwarfs.

"What'll it be?" A bartender with weird pale eyes slapped down a coaster.

She ordered a Leinie and a burger, medium, no fries. Coyote was embroidered on the pocket of his gas station attendant shirt. The name fit his pale eyes.

The noise level rose, and the heavy guy on the stool next to her leaned close to ask if she'd like a cigarette, and held out a pack. His knuckles were so hairy she couldn't look away. He asked again. She said no, becoming a statue of disinterest, and he made a show of turning his back on her. The Hamm's Land of Sky Blue Waters clock above the picture window said twelve. It couldn't be that late.

The bartender set down an overflowing glass of beer then held up his forearm to show her his watch: 8:25. He nodded at the clock. "It's broken."

"Then I'm not in the Twilight Zone," she said to his retreating back, although it felt as if she were. As with the motel, the almost-familiarity of The Woodcutters was disconcerting, even though it confirmed that she had come to the right place to chase down ghosts. She took a deep swallow of beer and swiveled to survey the room.

This tavern was nothing like a Chicago bar, no characters like Sid and that lowlife creep—Lorenzo?—or the table of old floozies drinking green cocktails. Everyone here looked outdoorsy, especially the men, too wholesome, like TV characters of her youth. Even the men her age and younger were strangely old-fashioned, slimmer, more fit versions of the older men. If any of them had served in Vietnam, they were proud of this, not disillusioned or scarred. She turned back to the picture window, her knee knocking the stool of the hairy knuckle guy who was now talking to a sunburnt younger man with a heavily-bandaged hand. "From wrestling a stubborn Evinrude," she overheard him say. Wishing the bartender would hurry with her burger, she finished her beer, and tamped down her uneasiness at being where she didn't belong by watching a bunch of little girls dance in front of the juke box. The vibe was more community center than tavern, but not her community. No long-haired dope smokers, no braless women, no tattered combat jackets with ironic upside-down flags; this was a throwback to an earlier era. Why had a man as urbane as Cole Watkins chosen to live out his days where this was where people came on a Saturday night?

When she spun around to look for the bartender and her burger, the man with the hairy knuckles was gone, and the guy with the bandage had taken his place. He nodded to her, an inviting nod, and shouted over the din, "Not from around here, are you?"

"This is a public place, isn't it," she half-shouted, half-smiling. He was a little older than she, late thirties, brown hair, unusually shapely eyebrows. He'd shaved recently and nicked his Marlboro Man chin.

"Damn straight it is. I'm welcome and you are too." He waved his bandaged hand in a welcoming gesture, then lowered it, backing away from what she might take to be a claim of ownership of the place. "Name's Glen. You don't look like you're here for the fishing, and it's not hunting season. Not that you look like a hunter either."

"You are right, Glen. I'm not from around here, and I'm not here for the fishing. How could you tell?"

"See those gals over there." He pointed to a table with five broad-chested, big women, all with exhausted perms. "They fish. The one in green, she holds this year's muskie record. Pleased to meet you…?"

"Polly from Chicago, passing through." It was fun to talk with a new man.

"Glen from Green Bay, passing through too. I pass through regularly. I rep Carhartt. Can I get you another one?"

She glanced at her empty glass. "If you can get the bartender's attention." Customers were lined up three-deep near the taps where he was filling glasses as fast as possible. "I'm still waiting for my burger."

Glen gave up on catching the bartender's attention and stood on the rung of his stool to reach over the bar. He was taller than she'd noticed, moving with unexpected grace as he extracted a bowl of nuts from a hidden shelf with his un-bandaged hand. Setting the nuts in front of her, he asked what she was doing passing through, and she said she hoped to connect to some people she once knew. Had he heard about Starlight Lodge? He hadn't. He had taken over the territory last spring. He held up two fingers at the bartender who had eyed them and signaled for two beers. How long she was staying? Overnight, she said coolly, glad she hadn't quit taking birth control pills. Why mess with her hormones she had reasoned in February, since Bob would be back in five or six months. After his letter, stopping would have seemed like a further defeat, as if she expected never to have sex again. She dug some cashews out of the bowl. Glen talking about his cousin's boat might not be her kind of man, but she was far from home, had a motel room, and no one needed to know. No-strings. An X-rated Girl's Own Adventure.

When the bartender, Coyote, set down two beers, Glen said, "Wait up. You know about a place called Starlight Lodge?" He turned to Polly. "That's what you called it, right?"

She said, "It's near here somewhere," wishing he hadn't asked for her.

"Can't help you." Coyote grabbed their empties.

"Wait," Polly said. "Cole Watkins, he was a famous photographer from New York, he built it. It's the kind of place that stands out."

"Don't know anything—"

A whoop of laughter erupted. A scrum of men lurched between the tables, knocking over glasses, grunting and cursing as their boots skidded on the floor, scattering the little kids in front of the jukebox and emptying the nearby tables. The bartender raced from behind the bar to pull the men apart, and forced them into chairs, yanking them upright. The bystanders applauded as he righted the last overturned chair. Polly and Glen turned away to see a basket with a burger waiting. With his thigh promisingly close to hers, Glen hailed the retreating waitress to order one, too. Polly watched the bartender as old men slapped him on his back. Later she would press him about the Lodge, when he wasn't so busy. She would describe it to him. It might have a new name.

As they waited for the waitress to bring Glen's burger, he told her how he hurt his hand, on his brother-in-law's boat. His brother-in-law made a bundle custom-making lures, works of art, they were. Did she say the guy who built the Lodge she wanted to find was an artist? Not an artist, a photographer, who covered the big war, not Vietnam. Glen had dodged that bullet, had served a tour in Germany, but why he took the job in the Northwoods was the fishing. He explained about the ins and outs of lake fishing vs. stream, and she imagined unbuttoning his shirt and gently easing the left sleeve over his bandaged hand. The way he offered her a cigarette after the waitress cleared away their burger baskets said he was thinking the same thing as she was. Having a motel room to herself was a first. Sleeping with a man she'd just met would be a first too. He nudged his stool closer and ordered a couple more drafts.

The surrounding racket enclosed them as Glen talked about the changing season, who knew what tomorrow would bring, an unsubtle code, she was sure, for what lay ahead between them, which charmed her, then something shifted, the air became charged as though a torpedo were corkscrewing toward them. Before she could turn, she heard a sharp, "Glen," and he spun around. Two women stood a foot away, both blondes, hair piled high, the pretty one with furious red dots on her cheeks locked her eyes on Glen, the other woman stared at Polly.

"Charlene," Glen said, easing away from Polly. "I'm talking to Polly here." He held up his bandaged hand. "Hank's Evinrude got the best of me."

"He told me. Said I'd find you here. What the hell?"

"I had to eat, didn't I? After I got Dr. G to clean me up and check, nothing serious, I came here. You weren't around. Why aren't you two at your cousins'?"

Charlene flicked her eyes at Polly. "Does it matter? The kids were sick. It was going to be a drag. So I come home…to this?" She aimed bullet eyes at Polly.

"I'm Polly Wainwright." She slid forward on her stool, to suggest that she hadn't been planning to invite Glen to her motel room and have sex until dawn. "I'm passing through on my way to Chicago. Glen was just telling me about fishing."

"I bet he was."

"Would you like to join us?" She shifted again, as if offering her stool, but the woman sharpened her jaw, ignoring Polly and glaring at Glen.

"Let's go."

Without looking at Polly, he slid off his stool, tamped out his cigarette, and held his hand aloft, as if it were more vulnerable than he'd said, as if he'd been brave discounting his pain moments ago, and the three of them pushed through the nearby bunch of Germans, Charlene tucking her hand into the back of Glen's jeans. This gesture was for Polly.

She turned away, her face burning, blotchy, not adorably angry like Charlene's. Outside the long window behind the bar the spotlights were off and all was dark. After a time, the waitress cleared away the burger baskets and Glen's wadded napkins asking if Polly wanted another beer. She did. She needed a stiff drink but she ordered another beer.

She wished she could shrink into a dot and vanish. She was a fool. She had concocted a fantasy about no-strings sex with a simple man who fished, sold and serviced tools in the Northwoods, and had a brother-in-law with a balky boat. She should write a romance novel. Charlene could be his wife, and Polly might have invited a married man back to her motel. That would have been a disgusting first.

When the waitress brought her beer, Polly asked if she would send Coyote over. She watched the waitress whisper to him, but he stayed at the far end of the bar refilling the tubs of lemon wedges and polishing glasses. When she finally caught his eye, he walked toward her.

"Another?" He picked up her empty.

"That place I'm looking for, it was called Starlight Lodge, twelve years ago, but it might have a different name now. It's near here, and—"

"Like I said, I can't help you." He kept his too-light eyes on a spot behind her and asked if she wanted to settle up.

The tab included Glen's.

She dropped some bills beside her coaster and wended through the emptying tables toward the archway below the restroom arrow. What a fool she was. Between the Gents and Gals hung a pay phone, the shelf below holding a tattered directory. She had forgotten that she had hoped to find Mrs. Borus or any Jenks. The phone book was soft from handling and some of the pages were missing, but the S pages were intact. Starlight Lodge was not listed, why would it be? Neither was Watkins, Cole—dead for twelve years, why would he be?—but a Watkins, Mildred, in Fifield, an optometrist, was listed along with two Jenks, Rob and MM, both in Lac Du Flambeau, and no Borus. With the pencil stub dangling from a string, she copied the numbers onto a half-page she ripped from the front of the book. At least she'd found something.

13

August, 1974

WHEN SHE DROVE UP, THE motel's vacancy sign was off, the curtains drawn in every picture window, those inside sleeping the sleep of the just, anticipating a fun-filled day tomorrow, unlike Polly who wished she was anywhere else but here. She had walked into a bar in the backend of nowhere thinking it was filled with rubes and she had made a fool of herself with one of them.

Inside her room, she double-locked the bolt, latched the chain, and turned to see her blue nun dress on the floor beside the bed. The rube's long torso had stretched so appealingly when he reached over the bar, and his warm breath had loosened a knot low inside her. To be close to an anonymous man that's what she wanted, to taste his skin and feel his weight, to lose herself, a man she wouldn't have to see again. Sex with no repercussions. She hated missing Bob's lovely, heavy, teddy-bear body, the way it enwrapped hers and left her unbounded. She kicked aside her nun dress, wishing she weren't too old for the free love touted in the magazines, or wasn't revulsed by the idea.

She flopped on the bed, remembered the phone numbers in her pocket, and stood to wrestle out of her jeans. If she'd thought about it, she could have found the same information at Marshall Fields, in their gallery of phone books from everywhere in America and most of the rest of the world. None of this had she thought through. She tossed the rumpled paper beside the phone, wishing she had brought a bottle of booze. Piecing together the mysteries of Cole Watkins' secret life, finding Starlight Lodge, these were excuses for what she really wanted: an escape from her everyday eat-sleep-repeat life. She turned on TV, canned laughter erupted, she clicked it off. She was alone on Saturday night in a budget motel in the woods with no one to ask what the hell she was doing in Park Falls, Wisconsin. She couldn't call Eugenia. She had missed their usual Saturday afternoon call, and now it was far too late, but her mother was a night owl.

"Hi, Mom. How was the Lindstrom's party?"

"Thank God. How'm I supposed to reach you? You didn't give me the name of your friend in St. Paul. I called Claire but she—"

"Why did you call Claire?"

"I don't have anyone else's number. Your boyfriend is a world away."

Polly had meant to tell her when they were together in person, which should have been this weekend. Now nearly two months had gone by since his humiliating letter. "Mom, what's going on?"

"I've been trying to figure out how to get ahold...Mrs. Pappas called."

"What happened?"

"She said she'd tried your number several times. You really shouldn't leave town without—"

"Mom. Tell me."

"The treatment, Eugenia has a bad reaction. They don't know why."

"Don't know? What kind of a bad reaction?"

"Sit down, Polly."

"I *am* sitting down." Polly slid to the floor and pushed her back against the bed.

"She's in a coma."

Polly clamped shut her eyes. Tiny explosions sparked against the red-black. "The treatment is going fine. I talked to her last weekend. She's doing great. She said to come visit in a couple of weeks when this was over. I told you."

"Mrs. Pappas wanted you to know."

"That Eugenia's in a coma? What the hell does that mean? Give me their number." Why could she not remember their number? All summer long she had called their house every Saturday.

"You can't call them at this hour," her mother said before reciting their number.

"And the hospital?"

"I don't know what hospital. All I know is what Mrs. Pappas said. Your friend, so young. Call in the morning. I know it would mean a lot that you're concerned."

Concerned? The inadequacy cracked open inside Polly's chest, a fist pushing through her bones, through her lungs, not stopping. She could barely breathe.

She shouldn't have listened to Eugenia. She should have gone to Peoria for the weekend, instead of embarking on this pointless trip. She would have gotten Mrs. Pappas's call at her mother's house and at this moment she would be at Eugenia's side. Even if Eugenia was unconscious, asleep with tubes in her arms and a mask covering her face, she would feel Polly's fingers touching hers.

"I'm coming."

"Where are you?"

"In the middle of Wisconsin."

"I thought you said St. Paul."

"We were at a bar and my friend's husband flirted with some woman. They started arguing, and I decided I didn't want to stick around for a weekend of this." How far away was Peoria? Eight hours, ten? Her map was in the car, and it was too dark, the roads unlit, she was too jangled to drive. She could start before dawn, phone Mrs. Pappas along the way, arrive at her mother's in the middle of the day, shower and change, then drive to wherever Eugenia was. She told her mother her plan.

"I thought you took the train."

She explained about Janine's car, saying she was sorry she hadn't mentioned it, or her changed plans, not saying she was sorry she'd lied, sorry she hadn't told her about Bob, sorry about everything.

● ● ●

Car doors slamming woke her. Furious that she had slept while Eugenia was in danger, she dressed quickly and headed out, the sky gray and threatening until she reached the interstate when the clouds broke up, a good sign, as was the lack of traffic. The kid handing her coffee-to-go near Madison told her that the usual speed trap ahead was devoid of cops: another good sign. She needed good signs.

Pine forests gave way to rolling pastures, which flattened into fields of scorched corn and soybeans as Janine's car ate the miles. Polly recognized Illinois. She kept her eyes forward, ignoring the wind roaring through the car's open windows, not thinking about what was ahead. A pickup truck spilled ears of corn on the road, and she swerved. The time, eleven thirty, the Pappas would be at church. They never missed a Sunday, Eugenia had said. *One advantage of having cancer, it gives me a pass, but my parents are doubling down on their prayers to make up for me.*

Polly prayed.

At noon, she left the highway to find a pay phone. No one answered at Eugenia's parents' home. Every half hour after that, she pulled off at an exit, and tried again. When they still didn't answer after two o'clock, long after church would be over, she realized that they would be with Eugenia, and let the phone ring, hoping Eugenia would sense Polly was calling out to her.

● ● ●

Her mother lived in a condo in one of the four-story buildings that angled around a large patchy lawn that would be a courtyard if the buildings were connected. Polly parked in a visitor space and saw her mother on her third-floor balcony. If Polly couldn't reach the Pappas on the phone, she would call every hospital in St. Louis until she found Eugenia, then she would shower and change. She couldn't look like a panicky mess who had driven since dawn even if Eugenia was in a coma when she arrived. She lifted her bag from the trunk.

Her mother stood beside her open apartment door. "They called," then disappeared into the apartment.

Polly set her bag under the hall table, careful not to jar it, fearing any disturbance might set off a cascade of destruction, then followed her mother to the dining table, and sat where she always sat. Her mother's cheeks were crazed with faint lines. When had she become so old?

"Polly, it's not good." Her mother reached for her hands and squeezed. "I'm sorry. Eugenia died. Her heart stopped beating."

This wasn't possible.

"Mrs. Pappas said the doctors did all they could...she was so young...the doctors didn't...treatment...adverse effect...weakened by..."

They were going to get drunk together in a couple of weeks, buy new lipsticks, and for the rest of their lives they were going to report to each other everything that mattered. That first day freshman year in their dorm room, when Eugenia turned from fiddling with the crooked Venetian blinds to look at Polly in the doorway, she had known that this girl with the Greek name she couldn't pronounce, who smiled at her with a breakout grin and then went solemn, this girl would be her friend for life. She couldn't be dead.

"Last night, around eight."

When Polly was in the bar. If Eugenia had died, Polly would have felt it. At eight twenty-five the bartender with the too-pale eyes held up his wristwatch to prove she wasn't in the Twilight Zone.

Her mother pulled a slip of paper with the Pappas' phone number from the fruit basket, the same number she'd given Polly over the phone, and Polly shifted her gaze to the window. Outside branches swayed, and below a dog barked and a child laughed, while in the distance, traffic hummed on the road she'd turned off to enter the condo complex, cars carrying people where they wanted to go. How could that be if Eugenia was dead?

"Why am I here?" Polly said.

Her mother leaned too close. "You need to sleep."

Polly maneuvered her duffle from beneath the hall table she had refinished three years ago, when she was living with her mother after the accident, stupidly wasting hours of her life on this inanimate piece of furniture. It was still here.

• • •

She woke smelling something sweet and unfamiliar. She touched the headboard. She was in her mother's condo, her mother was making breakfast, and Polly had slept through the night. Eugenia was dead and she had slept.

She stood in the entryway to the kitchen watching her mother close the oven door and straighten, her twisted hand on her hip that still hurt from the accident, the accident that had almost killed her. Her limp had worsened.

"What time is it?" Polly asked.

Her mother smiled over her shoulder and put the oven mitt on the counter. "You're up. Eight-thirty. Mrs. Pappas called about twenty minutes ago."

Polly looked pointedly at the stove clock.

"She said not to disturb you."

"You not waking me, *that* disturbs me."

"I did what she said. The funeral will be tomorrow, Tuesday, because of the long weekend. It should be today, that's required, she said. She was angry they couldn't do that, and started talking in Greek. I didn't know Greeks bury their dead so quickly, like Jews."

Their dead, Eugenia had become one of the undifferentiated dead.

"She gave me directions. Go sit and I'll bring you coffee."

"I have to call Janine. It's her car I'm driving."

"I'll drive us to the funeral," her mother said, turning back to the stove. "Is this Janine a friend?"

"Not really. An office friend."

She located Janine's number in her notebook and apologized for not returning her car, explaining why. Janine said she was sorry. Polly cut her short, saying she would return the car on Wednesday evening.

• • •

St. Nicholas Greek Orthodox Church was a gold-domed building in a neighborhood that once must have been prosperous. Inside it was packed, the entire Greek community of St. Louis must have turned out. At the front of the central aisle, a cluster of people surrounded Eugenia's parents. Mr. Pappas, Polly remembered, was on the church board and Mrs. taught Sunday school. Polly's mother touched her arm, nodding toward them, but Polly resisted, stepping sideways into a pew searching for anyone from college or their Chicago days. There was no one. Had the Pappas contacted no one except Polly? Not Eugenia's married lover, that was certain. They didn't know he existed. *My parents know nothing about my real life.* Mathias wouldn't know she had died.

Near the crowd around Eugenia's parents was a pewter-gray casket, elaborately embellished, high on a bier and heaped with lilies, fit for a Victorian dowager. If Eugenia were here, she would write a poem about the absurdity of bank-vaulting the dead. For one wavering second Polly wondered if she and her mother had come to the wrong funeral. But there was Eugenia's mother near the casket patting the cheek of a skinny woman in a feathered, black sweater. Were those crow feathers?

"Thank God it's closed," her mother said, seeing where Polly was looking.

"Dad's was nice," Polly said. A simple coffin covered in the flag because he'd served in the Army during World War II. She'd been twelve and not allowed to go to the cemetery. Mrs. Laughlin took her home from church and set up the buffet for afterward.

She glanced down that the prayer card she held. Where had it come from? It featured a washed-out painting of a long-faced woman, the head draped in a blue shawl, a tiny white cross above the forehead. Not Eugenia. On the flip side:

Eugenia Nicoletta Pappas
January 21, 1940—August 31, 1974

Her life reduced to two dates, nothing about the woman was alive in each moment between the beginning and the end, whose molecules had hummed with life, who had plans, hopes, fears, desires, worries, memories, mundane thoughts, who sizzled with insights, liked word play, grew silent around fools, who loved deeply, loved Polly, her family, Mathias, poets Polly had never heard of, and the workings of her own mind. *I am my own best company.* She couldn't stand to handle wet clay or the smell of cornbread or the touch of velvet, and she'd plucked her eyebrows too thin her senior year, so she no longer looked Greek but startled. Where had all this gone?

Polly stared past the altar to the screen of black-eyed saints Eugenia couldn't abide. What good had they ever done, for anyone or Eugenia? Polly despised them, too. Her mother whispered to Polly as two priests in stiff robes and flashy toques appeared from behind the screen of saints. Iconostasis? That's what Eugenia called it, with a beautiful rolling growl that ended in a hiss.

People in the aisles quieted and sat, then altar boys marched from the sides swinging sensors. Fog filled the air as the priests spoke Greek. The congregation stood, then sat. Polly followed along, pulled up and down by puppet strings. Her mother held out the order of service for her to look at as words floated through the incense-clouded air.

*...give rest, O Christ, to the soul of Your servant, Eu-
genia Nicoletta Pappas, where there is no pain, nor
sorrow, nor suffering, but life everlasting."*

The service over, her mother led her into the crowd streaming
out of the sanctuary and into a corridor that smelled disgustingly
of cinnamon and braised lamb, the stench more intense as they
approached double doors to a vast banquet room. Polly pressed
her hands against her thighs holding herself steady and was startled by the unfamiliar fabric, the black dress her mother had lent
her. Inside the packed hall, the roar was deafening. The aggressive
fleshiness of smells, of over-filled plates, and everyone gesticulat-
ing with wild hands the way Eugenia would mimic assaulted her.
Right out of Brueghel. If she had Mitch's new camera, she would
pan across the old people seated along the wall beneath the crystal sconces, pause at the two arguing men with magnificent mus-
taches, move onto the row of dried-crabapple-faced women, and
close in for a tight shot of the woman with a bird-sharp eye on
her neighbor's plate. Cut to Eugenia's prayer card dropped on the
carpet beneath the chair holding the fat ass.

"Let's say a few words to her parents," her mother said, guiding
her through the throng toward a table where old women were trying
to force Mr. and Mrs. Pappas to sit.

Seeing Polly, Mrs. Pappas shoved them aside and grabbed Polly,
muttering in Greek then pushing her arm's length away to stare at
her, puzzled. Why was she still alive and her daughter wasn't? Polly
spoke useless words until she was interrupted by a jowly woman who
claimed Mrs. Pappas. Others came up, Polly stepped back while her
mother spoke to Mr. Pappas. Her mother knew what to say.

"Polly?" A pretty young Greek woman in a festive dress, white splashed with red flowers, a shock in this sea of black. "Melanie, remember me?"

Cousin Melanie. "I didn't recognize you," Polly said stupidly, as Melanie hugged her. Dim-wit Melanie? She looked polished and settled.

"I cannot believe." Melanie pulled away, keeping her grip on Polly's upper arms.

"One of us would die?"

Melanie shook her head. "That wasn't what I was going to say."

"Which was?"

"I cannot believe we grew up."

Still a dimwit. "We did. And Eugenia died."

"Truly, I believe Eugenia is gone."

Polly hid her fury. The clichés that filled this room were an insult. The words Polly had uttered to Mrs. Pappas were an insult, the laughter and the chatter, everyone gorging on food, all of this was an insult.

Melanie said, "She told me about your job with that British firm. This was after she came home. I saw her almost every week." Eugenia had kept Polly away, but not Melanie. Polly's stomach folded on itself. "And she told me about your war correspondent boyfriend in Vietnam."

"Thailand, now."

"So cool and you, a real career woman. Me, I've got two little ones, over there with my parents, and that's my husband." She waved at a handsome, big-bellied man struggling with a baby squirming in a high chair. "Come join us at our table. We'll pull up a chair."

"I'm here with my mother."

"Her too. That's fine." Melanie's face sobered. "That summer I pictured our lives going on forever, didn't you?"

"I didn't think that far ahead."

"What breaks my heart is that Eugenia died single and alone."

She shook off Melanie's grip. "She was happy. She lived the way she wanted."

"All I know is that she left nothing behind." Melanie glanced at her children.

"Children aren't the only thing, Melanie."

"I don't mean that." She reached for Polly's hand again. "Just that, for Eugenia the end came too soon. Look at my aunt and uncle, they are bereft." She nodded toward where they sat. "What is there, finally, but family?"

Polly's mother approached and Melanie smiled. "You must be Polly's mother. I'm Melanie George, Eugenia's cousin."

"We have to go," Polly said.

Polly's mother ignored her, chatting about remembering the "girls" the summer after Polly and Eugenia graduated and landed their first jobs, that apartment, so hot on the third floor, what the fun they'd had, young girls in the city, like a sitcom.

• • •

They got lost leaving St. Louis, Polly, the navigator, not paying attention, and it was almost four o'clock when her mother insisted, they stop for food.

"Why do they always give you a pickle?" Her mother lifted the limp slice from her plate and set in on a paper napkin. "Now, eat something. You haven't eaten anything all day."

Polly stared at her sandwich and potato chips, hungry and revolted.

"Melanie is your age? She looks older."

"A year younger. She's turned into her mother, that's why she looks older. Eugenia and I are the same age."

"I won't take that remark personally, but she does look like she's from an earlier era."

"Like her mother's era?"

"I suppose. What's happening with Bob? I haven't heard about him for a while."

Polly scrambled for words. "We broke up." Her mother's eyes winced. "We broke up several months ago in July. I should have told you. I wanted to wait until we were together, not on the phone. I wrote him a letter. It wasn't working between us."

She held her face steady, hiding her delight in her mother's distress. She was sick of her mother's equanimity. One pat line after another had poured from her mother's mouth at the funeral, as if Eugenia's death was *sad*, a sad part of life, but not catastrophic. "And then there were the prostitutes."

"Oh, my God. How did you find out?"

"A medic friend of his told me. Bob had VD."

"You could have told me, dear."

Never would she tell her mother that she had been dumped by the slime ball her mother thought was so *handsome*.

"I didn't want to disappoint you. I know what you want."

"I want you to be happy."

"I am happy to be rid of him."

Her mother produced her tight smile, holding back what she wanted to say, and waved for the check. "So tomorrow you'll head back to Chicago. Why don't you leave after the rush hour? There's no hurry, is there?"

She had to call Vanessa. She eased out of the funeral dress her mother had lent her, put on wrinkled jeans and her last clean shirt, then carried the hall phone into her bedroom, yanking the kinked cord around the doorjamb, and closed the door. Flopping on her bed, she dialed EB as she peeled a rainbow sticker off her headboard that was covered with others she'd stuck on in middle school. Eugenia had lived her entire life, beginning to end, and Polly was still sleeping in her childhood bed.

"It's good that you caught me," Vanessa said.

"Thank you for understanding about the funeral."

"Of course. You have my sympathy for the death of your cousin."

Cousin? Janine's doing, always looking out for Polly. "Thank you."

"Now you and I must talk. You'll be in the office tomorrow." A statement, not a question.

"I can't make it tomorrow. I'm at my mother's downstate." She needed at least one day at home alone before she could face the office. "On Friday."

"Friday will be too late. Last time you and I spoke, I said that I'd narrowed the field of candidates. While you have the least experience, I had decided to take a chance with you. But this past week…If you're vacillating, I have another candidate."

"I'm not vacillating. I hope I've shown you—"

"This isn't a conversation I would choose to have on the phone, but time is critical. If you're interested, and I mean sincerely interested, I am prepared to offer you a job as my assistant on a project that has yet to be announced. I can't say much more, but I need your firm answer. My decision and proposed budget for post-Plan

B must be in the courier's pouch and on its way to London by close tomorrow. HQ insists."

Had Vanessa offered her the job? Polly sat up and stretched her face, trying to wake up her synapses. "Yes, I would like to be your assistant. Sincerely. Honored. Pleased. Yes. Can you tell me something about this new project?" This was surreal. The job should go to Janine. Had she heard wrong?

"When you come in on Friday, we'll talk specifics, including salary. I'm quite sure you'll be pleased by the packet. This new position will start on January 1."

She hadn't heard wrong. "Thank you, Vanessa. I'm sorry about my not being there, but thank you."

"I'm pleased we'll be working together," and hung up.

Listening to the buzzing phone line, Polly felt a sudden physical compression, as if what had happened in the last few days, Eugenia, Park Falls, the miles driven, Mitch, exhaustion, the job offer, all of it was squeezing her from all sides. She closed her eyes and waited for what Vanessa had said to seem real.

When she returned the phone to the hall, her mother called from the kitchen, asking who she was talking to.

"My boss. I called to check in, and she offered me a job."

"Tea is ready. What did you say?"

On the breakfast table two cups of tea waited. Her mother waved for Polly to sit.

"She offered me a job after my current one ends at the end of the year. I told you how I dreaded having to enter the job market, but now I'm set. I can't quite believe it. Now I'll be her assistant. Increase in salary, how much I don't know. I'll probably be able to buy a car."

"A car? You can come visit me more often." She touched Polly's hand. "I'm teasing, dear. You having a secure future, I'm happy about that, especially with Bob out of the picture. I had no idea he was such a louse. He sure had me fooled. Do you want honey for your tea? I forgot the honey."

When she returned, she twirled the stick in the honey jar with such concentration that Polly knew she was preparing to say something. "Losing Eugenia, that's a blow. I know how close you were, friends of the heart. There's nothing to say except it's a tragedy. But you'll get through this. You will. Daily life, that's what will get you through. That's what made it possible for me to go on. Your granddad taking care of you, while I got up every day, got dressed, stockings, heels, makeup, put on a smile, went to work. Muddling through, that's what gets you through."

"You don't have to worry about me, Mom."

"I'm not worried." She patted Polly's hand. "I'm just sorry about all this." She raised her eyebrows, meaning Eugenia and Bob, too. "But you have a new job to look forward to, with a good company and a good future."

"I do. I'll have to say that a few times before I'll get used to it."

She pictured Vanessa's office, Vanessa not there, but outside the window men in blue jumpsuits wiped away swaths of bubbles, back and forth, until as if on cue, they released their squeegees, bent their knees, and leapt from the platform, their jumpsuits luffing as they float away toward the distant high-rises, smaller and smaller, until they disappear.

● ● ●

She woke in a sweat. The bedside clock read 1:17 and she was in her childhood bed. She shook off tendrils of a nightmare she couldn't remember and swung her feet to the floor. Eugenia was dead and Polly would never see her again. She couldn't believe this, like she hadn't believed she would never see her father again after he died. No more climbing in his lap, or riding on his shoulders, or sneaking quarters from his coin bowl for the ice cream man. "Gone to Heaven," her mother said. Polly would lie on the grass and stare at the clouds, hoping he was watching her. Her granddad took his place in the practical ways, but her dad's absence haunted her until her mother nearly died. When her mother's death seemed imminent, her dad's death receded. He had been fifty-two, old. Her granddad, Mr. Calhoun across the street, Mr. Tindale, they were all old; they had lived full lives. Not Eugenia.

Polly padded across the dark room and peered through the blinds at the courtyard. Would Eugenia have lived her life differently if she'd known it would be cut short? Was translating abstruse documents at the UN how she would have chosen to spend her days if she knew they would end too quickly? When she moved to New York, the center of the universe and the literary world, Polly imagined her at parties in book-lined apartments with interesting men in tweed jackets trying to impress her, but when she visited her that once, she found Eugenia's apartment was elegant, but cramped, the opposite of Polly's. Instead of talking about literary events or invitations, Eugenia talked about Mathias, but she hadn't introduced him. She and Polly hit the museums, Central Park, the Village, like tourists, and Eugenia took her to one poetry reading. "Derivative," Eugenia called the humorless guy in John Lennon glasses, and afterward, let Polly read her new poems. Polly liked the ones Eugenia called "too narrative." She said she was getting published in better journals. Polly didn't think to ask if she was satisfied. In the middle, you don't think to ask because you assume there is always more.

She turned from the window. She had to get out of here. She had a new job ahead—she would be envied by everyone in her department. While she didn't have anything like poetry, she would have a secure future, she would live well, get a real couch, buy a car. She could go where she wanted, Doc Films, explore new neighborhoods, weekend trips out of the city. First, she had to wrap up her Watkins' investigation. Her sense of self demanded she not abandon it halfway. This was her chance to make something whole out of that ruptured mess. If she left now, she could get to Park Falls by mid-day, spend the rest of the day and Thursday morning, piecing together what she could before heading home, return Janine's car—that would be awkward, given the job situation—and be in the office on Friday to nail down the details with Vanessa. A packet, she liked the sound of that. In the dark she moved quietly from closet to bathroom hoping not to wake her mother.

"What's going on?" her mother called.

Polly opened her mother's bedroom door. "I'm leaving now. I've got too many loose ends. I can't sleep anyway."

Protesting, her mother started to get out of bed, she would make Polly breakfast or something for the road, at least some coffee. Polly kissed her. "I'll stop when I get hungry and I promise to phone by the end of the day."

The hall to the elevator was dim. Outside the night air was soft with a hint of early autumn. The year was turning too quickly. If she didn't pay attention, time would slip away without her noticing, one day after another, and her time would be over. She drove quietly through the condo's parking lot, cruising through the stop sign, then picking up speed.

14

September, 1974

ON THE INTERSTATE she merged into a stream of semi-trailers. Against the black sky the tiny lights rimming their tops looked like parallel strands of diamonds leading her north. With her headlights bright on the back of the truck in front of her, she slowed when it slowed, picked up speed when it did, eased left when it eased left, right when it did, following, not thinking, the thrum of the road humming through her body. After a time, a headache clamped over her skull. She pulled off at the next exit and parked in front of a 24-hour gas station/diner where the toxic overhead flood lights broke the road's numbing spell. She waited until she was sure the road hum had drained from her legs before getting out of the car.

The diner was empty except for some truckers hunched at the counter who fell silent as she passed, their heads swiveling in her direction. Polly took a far booth by the window, nodding to the weary waitress who sauntered over offering a menu as she poured a mug of coffee.

The coffee was bitter and strong, what Polly needed. She ordered scrambled eggs. Ernie had said were the safest thing to order on the road.

She bent over her plate of cold toast and eggs when a new customer slung open the far door and walked toward her booth, ignoring the greetings from the men. She pretended not to notice.

"That your yellow T-Bird out there?"

"It is." Polly looked up. A sloppy guy with a flattened nose, from fights he'd lost, she guessed. "Is it parked in your way?" She knew it wasn't, she'd parked carefully, off to the side, but looked out the window at Janine's male-bait car as if checking to make sure.

He leaned close. "You one of those women-libbers?"

He smelled of sweat, not booze. If he kept this up, she could swing her leg out from under the table and kick him in the balls. She shifted to make this easier, and took a slow sip of coffee. "I'm one of those women who like to eat their breakfast in peace."

"A fucking waste, that's what it is, a woman having—"

"Clarence." The waitress hurried over swinging the coffee pot. "You quit bothering the lady, you hear?" She waved the pot at him. "You go sit and I'll bring you your coffee. Git, I said."

"Am I right or am I right?" he called out to the men at the counter, who turned away as the waitress glared at them.

"Sorry about that, Hon." She refilled Polly's mug.

"The check, please." Why was she and every other woman open for scrutiny wherever they went? Did you have to be as old and as thickly upholstered as this nice waitress to evade constant public commentary?

Leaving bills on the table next to her plate, she walked toward the door, her spine as rigid as a shield, making a point not to rush. After this, she would never stop at an all-night truck stop or return to Wisconsin.

• • •

At mid-morning, a mile beyond the Park Falls turnoff, she drove past a playground, an elementary school, a row of prim white-frame houses, before crossing a river and arriving at the downtown of two- and three-story buildings. No one was out walking. She passed a furniture emporium, a plumbing supply store, a café, a dentist, a lawyers' office, and on the corner, the Park Falls Union Trust Bank where Watkins had registered a trust, or hadn't. Bankers would tell her nothing. After another block, she came to the post office. Opposite was the public library. She parked in front and stared at the planter of dried up geraniums. Why was it she had come? For Watkins? To put distance between her and Eugenia's hellish funeral? To get away from her mother's stifling concern? After she found whatever she could, she would check into the motel, and head home in the morning. She might not bother phoning the numbers she'd found at The Woodcutter. She didn't want to hassle strangers about whether they knew Watkins. By this time tomorrow she'd be half way home.

The library's doors were propped open to let in a breeze, but it smelled of trapped heat and unread books. In the foyer a *Community News* bulletin board covered one wall, ahead was the reception counter with the stacks behind, to the right a reading area with a few lumpy armchairs and a table. From the stacks came a woman with mushroom-colored curls. June said her nametag.

"Can I help you?" Her voice was musical, her smile friendly.

Librarians, a wonderful breed. Polly smiled back. "Hi. I'm interested in Cole Watkins. He was a famous photographer who lived around here before he died, which was in 1962."

June shook her curls. "Never heard of him. Watkins, you say? I'll check the local files."

She led the way through the reading area to a battered file cabinet, and produced a key from her skirt pocket. "U...V...W...No Watkins." She banged shut the drawer and straightened. "Could check the card catalogue, but I know pretty much every book we have and I don't recall any."

"Maybe you have something on Starlight Lodge. It was the home Watkins built for himself."

"Oh, I know that place. Years back, when we moved here, that'd be in 1964, it was for sale. My husband and I went to take a look. Boy, it's a doozy. Far as I know, it didn't sell and was taken off the market. No one lives there now. Let's see. What do we have here? This is should be filed under Watkins."

She handed Polly a folder containing two yellowed newspaper clippings. No date on the one headlined "Watkins Returns Home." The other, "Proposed Lodge: Fab or Folly?" was dated October 12, 1948.

Watkins Returns Home

After a lifetime abroad, Cole Watkins, graduate of Hurley High School, 1911, returns home. Watkins, born in Iron County, in 1895, son of Casper and May Watkins, left the North Woods to make a name for himself as a high fashion photographer in New York City. Later, he photographed the runup to World War II in Italy before joining the war effort as a combat photographer in the North African Campaign in 1940—41. (Pictures, sect. B.)

That was it. No pictures, no sect. B. She picked up the other clipping.

Having seen the wide world, Cole Watkins, world
famous photographer, returns home, and intends to
build a home...

This she wanted to read carefully. She closed the folder and asked if the library had a copier. If she had come here first on Saturday, she wouldn't have had to waste her time driving north again, but the library would have been closed on Saturday night.

"I'll make you copies. Library policy. Staff only on the copier. Each page is a dime. Be right back. You look like you could use a drink." She pointed to the water fountain.

After splashing water on her face, Polly felt revived. She had found something. Wrapping up Watkins before returning to EB and Vanessa, that was something, at least.

In the distance a phone rang and the librarian answered. Polly strolled to the bulletin board, curious about what counted as interesting in this back-of-nowhere town: a postcard of the State Capitol in Madison, a list of local soldiers who'd served in Vietnam, a trifold flyer for Flambeau Rama Days, August 1—4, a month ago, and layer upon layer of notices for Farm Equipment Sale, Handyman Wanted, Free Kittens, Upholstery Lessons. If she lived here, she would have one of those white-frame houses she'd passed driving into town, raise chickens maybe, and die in her own bed, probably alone, under a quilt made by someone's grandmother for the Thanksgiving Quilt Sale. She would leave instructions about a plain pine box. A flyer fluttered to the floor, probably trying to get away from her self-pity.

Films-For-All. Free. All Are Welcome.

The third item down: *Cannibals of Nature* from *the award-winning series 'What's My Secret?'* November 12, 7 pm. Chequamegon High School. A small photo pictured what could be a gray fuzzball from a lint trap or a baby owl eating another baby owl.

"*What's My Secret?*" Mitch, the old blowhard, had taken her wisp of an idea and made it real. Her idea, but he had done the work. *Ideas are a dime a dozen,* he or Shelley said. And Eugenia, *Getting an idea isn't the hard part. It's the one word then another word, that's the work.*

Polly tacked the flyer back in place. She would tell Mitch that she'd found his work in the tiny town of Park Falls. She pictured him tapping two fingers on the brim of his imaginary fedora, like he did in the Kino days.

"Here you go." The librarian startled her. "That'll be forty cents."

Polly pulled the Films-For-All flyer from the board. "Could you make a copy of this too?"

When she returned, Polly handed her coins and asked about the local realtor. "I'd like to see if I can find Starlight Lodge."

"That's what you want, I can draw you a map."

● ● ●

No longer tired, she took the two-lane road that ran straight north out of Park Falls along rusted railroad tracks that petered out in a swampy pond rimmed with blackened tree stumps before the dense forest enclosed the road again. The librarian's map showed the train tracks, the pond, zigzags that meant woods, then a deer-crossing sign, a dip in the road, and on the right, a star for Starlight Lodge. In what looked like a solid wall of trees was a narrow gap. Polly turned in. The woods blazed green with sunlight piercing the overhead canopy to spill on the ferny, brushy understory. That first night with Ernie, their headlights had swept over ghostly webs of brush, white against the murky dark.

She put the car into low gear and inched forward. Could be vandals, the librarian warned. Bumping along the potholed track, branches whipping the T-Bird's sides—please no scratches on Janine's car—she emerged from the woods into a sun-blasted meadow of half-mown grasses and stopped. Starlight Lodge, its black siding faded to gray; the dome that had radiated a pale yellow haze against the night sky was covered with shiny blue plastic; stained plywood covered the entryway; the high windows of Watkins' studio were occluded like eyes blinded by cataracts. She killed the engine.

A monument to broken dreams, Eugenia would say, as she had of every abandoned motel and shuttered tourist trap with crumbling plaster dinosaurs they had seen on their trip out west.

The insects were deafening. Starlight Lodge's aura, had it all been her imagination? Borus' cabin was gone, and near the barn's open double doors was parked a battered pickup. Vandals? Beneath the insect roar she heard a sound she couldn't identify. She started up the car and swung it into a wide arc aiming it back toward the track, in case she needed to make a quick getaway. In the rearview mirror, a tractor appeared from behind the Lodge driven a man in a baseball cap, a mower behind.

She stepped from the car, leaving the door open, just in case, and waved. The man pulled to a stop near the Lodge's entrance and shifted sideways to face in her direction, one hand on the steering wheel, the other on his seat back, pointedly not waving back at her. Should she jump into the car and get out of here, or drive the seventy-some yards to where he sat on the tractor—this seemed both timid and aggressive—or should she walk the distance? She tucked in her sweaty shirt and strode clumsily through the unmown grass as if she were not scared to approach a stranger in the back end of nowhere, deep in the woods, far from civilization. But a caretaker wouldn't harm her. Why would he? He was a worker. He'd been hired to cut the grass.

"Hi, there," she called out. He looked normal enough: stained baseball cap, plaid shirt, jeans, worn boots—a regular good old country boy, except for his yellow, mirrored, insect-eye sunglasses. "This is Starlight Lodge, isn't it?" Between cap and sunglasses, she couldn't make out his face.

"It's private property."

"I visited here years ago."

He climbed down and dug into his shirt pocket for his cigarettes, checking her out from behind his creepy glasses. Something about him seemed familiar. He shook out a cigarette, lipped it, then held out the pack to Polly.

"No thanks. She nodded toward the Lodge. "I was here twelve years ago. It was September, too, September 1962. This place was beautiful then."

He pocketed his lighter and exhaled a plume of smoke. "You from New York?"

"Chicago."

"And you're here today because?"

"Passing through."

"Passing through? You were asking questions about this place on Saturday." He held up his hand and counted, holding up a finger for each day, little finger last. "Five days. I don't call that passing through."

The bartender at The Woodcutters, that's who he was. A flush of blood stung her cheeks. "I'm curious, that's it."

He straightened. "You'll understand why I don't believe you."

"I told you, twelve years ago, in September, I was part of the crew making a film about Mr. Watkins. He died a few months later, and the project went belly up. Over there used to be the cabin I slept in that belonged to a Mrs. Borus. She was Mr. Watkins' housekeeper. Mr. Watkins was kind to me, that's all. There, in his library, behind you, we talked and drank bourbon. It was an important time for me."

A cry broke out from the woods, and they both turned.

"Hawk got dinner," he said. He dropped his cigarette and crushed it with his boot, then hoisted himself onto the tractor's seat. "It's closed up now."

"Do you mind if I take a look around?"

"I do mind." He revved the engine. "I got work to do." He kicked a pedal, adjusted his cap, and steered the tractor in a wide, slow intimidating loop around her. When he reached the point where he began, he headed toward the barn, the tractor's putter mocking her the whole way.

What would it cost him to let her look around? She wasn't a threat. She didn't ask to go inside. She didn't require any of his time. She hated jerks who couldn't muster basic human courtesy. She could come back later after dark, but she wouldn't. It was probably legal to shoot trespassers in Wisconsin. She'd never done one risky thing in her life.

15

September, 1974

NOT KNOWING WHICH WAY TO GO EXCEPT BACK TO TOWN, Polly stopped at a crossroad farm stand to ask for directions to the motel she'd left four days ago. The pasty-faced girl stacking coins didn't bother to look up when she answered. North half a mile, then head west.

Why had Watkins chosen to live among such yokels in the back end of nowhere? And build Starlight Lodge where it was hidden from the world, and left to decay unappreciated? Pulling away, she hit the gas hard, spitting roadside gravel.

The parking lot in front of Bill 'n Lu's was empty. Polly brushed aside the wasps buzzing outside the office screen door, and dinged the desk. If that jerk had let her walk around the Lodge, maybe look inside, this would confirm what was obvious from what she'd seen, the aura she remembered had vanished, if it had ever been anything more than her imagination. She needed a shower and dinner, any-place except The Woodcutters—running into that jerk bartender or Glen would top off this fiasco—then sleep hard before her long drive home. She had to be fresh and focused for her negotiations with Vanessa.

The same red-haired woman, Lu, appeared with a stack of folded sheets. "I's expecting you. I got a call from June." She dropped the sheets on the counter. "June, from the library. June's a friend."

Had Polly told the librarian where she was staying?

"June says you forgot Bud Wagner's number. He's the realtor. He's gone fishing for the week, and his assistant, who's dumber than dirt, won't give you diddly, so June told me to give you Bud's number. You can phone him next week. I asked what this was all about. Turns out, my cousin's place backs up onto the Watkins' place. June says you wanted to know who owns it. I can tell you that—the crazy old coot left it to one of the bartenders at The Woodcutters."

The bartender who'd sent her away owned Starlight Lodge?

"Of course, the family out east is kicking up a fuss and the whole mess is tied up in court." She handed Polly a piece of motel stationery. "Here's Bud's number."

Had Watkins been so unhinged he made a cat-hospital bequest? No wonder the ownership was being challenged. She folded the note trying to recall the details of her two conversations with the jerk bartender, on Saturday night when he said he didn't know the place, and half an hour ago when he asked if she was from New York. "New York" she'd assumed was his way of saying "outsider," but he was accusing her of being connected to Watkins' family. Her saying she had been at the Lodge before, he'd taken as a ruse. But why hadn't he told her the place belonged to him? Because he couldn't be bothered. Coyote, that was the asshole's name. Was this asshole a con man, or had Watkins been demented?

"I'd like a room for the night."

It was identical to the one she had on Saturday, same cowboy lamp, same chemical-blue Naugahyde chair, credenza, TV, black phone, as if the last four days hadn't happened, she hadn't driven hundreds of miles south and north, Eugenia hadn't died, as if Polly hadn't wasted all this time, only to find Starlight Lodge, and it was a bust. She pressed her forehead against the cold varnished door and slipped the security chain in place. She turned. It wasn't identical to the last room. When she heard that Eugenia was in a coma, she'd been on the floor next to the bed which was on the right side of the room, not the left.

Polly wished she could have told her that she hadn't been the friend she should have been. She hadn't asked enough questions, hadn't probed, had taken things for granted, had assumed that everything would work out, that Eugenia would get well, and they would go on. If Eugenia hadn't died, Polly would tell her that in her own life she had lost her way—this wasn't an excuse for how she'd let Eugenia down—but she'd overblown everything about Watkins and his Lodge. Twelve years ago, when they were setting out on their grown-up lives, Polly had felt that she was exactly where she was supposed to be when Shelley put her on the Watkins' project. She, the least significant member of the crew, had schlepped equipment for a company that no longer existed, shooting a film that fizzled, on a subject who died, and out of this, she had constructed an entire phantasm of beckoning promise. If only, she had thought, if only she could return to Starlight Lodge; if only she could piece together the clues to the mystery Watkins had left her; if only, if only—what? What had she expected? To reclaim her youthful certainty and drive? Find her groove? Grab the brass ring? Come down in the place just right? It sickened her. Eugenia would understand. She would smile her enigmatic smile making Polly not less foolish, but less alone. But Eugenia was dead at thirty-four, her life over, and Polly was thirty-four and she'd never gotten any traction in her life. Now she was in a budget motel with a worn path on the dingy carpet between the bathroom and the bed that smelled of cigarettes, and she wanted to cry.

She stripped off her clothes and turned on the shower. What she could do now, which Eugenia would urge, was act like a sensible woman. Finish up here, make whatever sense she could of the facts she'd gathered about Watkins' life, and share what little she had with whoever was writing Watkins' retrospective catalogue for the exhibition Mitch had mentioned. Mitch would connect her.

• • •

Clean, dry, dressed, and fortified by her plan, she spread out the clippings from the library, the photocopies Mitch had given her, the Watkins' papers she'd brought from home, and on a legal pad laid out a timeline.

Cole Watkins

77 years

1885   Born May 18, Iron County, WI (north of Park Falls)
1917   Covers WW I for *New York Tribune*
        (?)Fashion and celebrity portraits, NYC
1920   Marries Oona
1927   son Cyrus b.
1929   son Neil b.
            AND

seems to have bought property in Park Falls

    AND

began affair with Maureen Jenks

1931   Opens studio in new Empire State Building. Much news coverage.

    AND

1931   Maureen gives birth to Cole's son, Wiley Coleman Jenks (birth certificate and letter dated 2/5/31)

    AND

    Maureen blackmails Watkins 2/5/31 through 2/2/35 (letters), when she claims son died. (Why?)

1930   Maureen marries Alvin Reed. Date unknown. Did the blackmail stop because of Alvin? Did he adopt boy? photographs in Europe, esp. Sicily, Italy, Germany

1940   Maureen died. Nov. 19 (obit)

1942   Works for the US Army, propaganda photography, North Africa, *Life* magazine (57 years old)

1945/48 No published work. (A breakdown?)

1948   Park Falls, builds Starlight Lodge (see clippings) (63 years old)

1952/53 Photographs Japan during Korean War (in his late sixties)

1955   Last published series, coal miners Kentucky, *Life* magazine (where did he live in the fifties, WI or NY?)

1962   Sons commission Mitch/Kino to make a doc Sons, Cyrus (now dead, according to Mitch) and Neil

1963   Dies, January 15, stroke, 77 years old

Better than Eugenia's prayer card, but almost as irrelevant to the life as lived. It explained nothing about what had hooked her, which was his ability to see within his subjects, even within her. This was the source of his genius. This made him one of the most important photographers of his time. But he gave all that up to move here and build a remarkable home, like nothing else she'd ever seen. Starlight Lodge was the last expression of his creativity, and it was lost to the world, falling apart, and no one would ever know of it. That jerk-bartender-groundskeeper could do with it whatever he wanted. Once the law suit was settled with the New York family, which had to be Neil, he could move in, with kids if he had them, who'd write on the walls and roller skate in the atrium, or he might turn it into a vacation lodge, rent it to beer-swilling louts who would shoot out the glass dome. Before she left, she had to try to persuade him to let her have one look inside.

The sun was setting behind the trees to the west when she arrived at The Woodcutters and unlike on Saturday night, few cars and pickups were parked nearby. Girding herself, she pulled open the heavy door. Softball players crowded around two tables pulled together and some stragglers sat at the bar tended by a heavy-set, gray-haired and -mustached man, not Coyote. Torn between relief and disappointment, she took a stool near the far end of the bar, same as last time.

The bartender slapped down a coaster. "What'll it be?"

"Will Coyote be in later?"

"He works weekends. What can I get you?"

"Do you have his phone number?"

He flicked his bored eyes toward the picture window behind him. Outside Coyote sat on a bench smoking a cigarette. A plumb weight plunged through her. She slipped from her stool and walked toward to the archway that led to the kitchen and the bar's back door.

He had to hear the door bang open and her thrashing through the ferns, but he didn't turn in her direction, not even when she stood four feet away at the opposite end of the bench. He had showered but not shaved. His ugly mirrored sunglasses perched above his forehead held back his wet hair and winked at her with iridescent disdain.

"Mind if I sit?"

Not looking at her, he took a drag on his cigarette. She sat outside the range of his smoke and studied him. Damp dark hair with a dot of pure white above the ear facing her, forehead pale from habitually wearing a baseball cap, creased, heavy flesh on his cheeks. On Saturday night she'd thought he looked weathered in a not-unappealing backwoods way, but in this near-dusk, his features seemed blunted from booze or a hard life. He didn't look like a con man. She broke off a wand of grass that tickled her ankle. A con man wouldn't stick around after a big score. Or continue to work as a weekend bartender. Or bother to mow the meadow surrounding the Lodge. Or engage in a legal fight with Watkins' son he was sure to lose.

"You own the Lodge."

He shrugged and drew a beer bottle from beneath the bench and popped off its cap with a church key attached to a string.

"I'm from Chicago, not New York. Here's my driver's license." She pulled the evidence of her sincerity from her shirt pocket.

Without looking at it he took a swig of beer. "So?"

"I told you I met Mr. Watkins twelve years ago. I stayed at the Lodge. It struck me, how unusual it was. I was curious about what happened to it."

His lips turned sour. "Ever hear 'curiosity killed the cat'?"

She glanced at the window where she would be in plain sight of anyone sitting at the bar. She was probably safe. "I'm wondering why Mr. Watkins left you Starlight Lodge."

"What's your name Ms. Curiosity? Ms.—that right, isn't it? You're one of those."

She wouldn't admit it to him if she was. "Ms." belonged to the angry young and "Miss" sounded pathetic for a woman of her age. "I'm Polly Wainwright."

"I don't recall a Ms. Wainwright's name on any of the fucking documents I've received."

"I've got nothing to do with your legal fight." She hoped someone was watching. "And I am speaking to...?

A dismissive snort. "Coyote Reed, jack-of-all."

"Coyote, is that your real name?"

"To the government, I'm Wiley Reed."

Wiley? How many Wiley's could there be around here? Fixing her eyes on the sagging flesh along his jaw, she tried to quiet the flutter in her chest while calculating the age of Maureen and Watkins' baby. Born in 1931, he would be forty-three now. Was this beaten-down loser Watkins' son? Wiley Reed? She'd forgotten Maureen's husband's name. She said, "I'm not connected with the New Yorkers who're fighting you. I have no financial interest whatsoever."

"No financial interest." He saluted her with his bottle looking directly at her, his eyes a shock, blue like freezer blocks, blue like Watkins'. "Turns out," he said, "I should have been curious. I should have been curious as hell. Shit. I did odd jobs there before Watkins died. That's it. I do odd jobs at lots of places." He flung his bottle across the clearing, stood, and wiped his hands on his jeans.

"But you knew him."

"I did *not* know him. It was his woman who hired me and told me what to do. We never so much as spoke. I've said this a thousand fucking times." He strode toward the door to the bar.

Could he not know he was Watkins' son?

She hurried after him and grabbed the open door, a wave of noise crashing around her. The room had filled with men in sweaty jerseys, and a bunch of gray-haired women who had claimed the center by clumping together the tables. Coyote lifted the bar's hinged counter to slip into the narrow galley.

Over the din, she shouted, "Mrs. Borus sent me papers that belonged to him, papers you'll want to see."

He glared at her, then raised an eyebrow toward the mustached bartender, who pulled him a couple of beers. Coyote grabbed them and Polly followed him to a far table. He sat, she took the chair opposite, and he slid a stein to her. In the dim light, his eyes weren't even readable as blue, and they had none of Mr. Watkins' intelligence or his power. They were almost lifeless. Was she wrong? He lit a cigarette, and pulled the ashtray close, waiting for her to speak. She imagined Watkins spying on him from inside the Lodge, the old man watching his unacknowledged son.

"I have some letters that Maureen Jenks wrote to Cole Watkins in the nineteen thirties."

Coyote stared at the ashtray, then moved it sideways and back before saying, "Maureen Jenks was my mother's maiden name."

"And a copy of your birth certificate.

"Why would he have that?"

"He also had your mother's obituary."

Behind his locked-down face, she could see whirring confusion and calculation. She sipped her beer as the guys at the next table tussled over the check. Coyote inched his chair out of their range and surveyed the room.

After a time, she said, "Cole Watkins was your father."

"My father was Alvin Reed."

"Adoptive father?"

"What the fuck are you saying?"

"I'll show you the papers. You decide."

He set down his empty stein. "Okay, show me."

She hadn't thought this far. She didn't know what she wanted. She averted her eyes to the beefy guy behind Coyote who'd grabbed the check and was now waving it and some bills over the others' heads. "I don't have the papers on me. Tomorrow."

He crushed out his half-smoked cigarette, suspecting a ploy. Before she could explain about her long drive and being up for twenty hours straight. "Here, right here, noon."

She needed to think, but her brain stalled. "Okay."

He stood, dropped some bills on the table, enough to cover them both with a hefty tip, and walked away, stopping to say something to a couple of guys who were joke-arm wrestling.

The waitress appeared, blocking Polly's view. "That it then?"

"I'll have a club soda." When she turned back to where Coyote had been, he was gone. What had she done? Meeting him at noon, and after that, driving home, she wouldn't get there much before midnight, and the next morning she had her appointment with Vanessa, *nine sharp*. For this she needed a good night's sleep. Exhibiting her enthusiasm and asking the right questions to demonstrate the rightness of Vanessa's unorthodox decision to settle on her, this would take a bright face and a crisp mind, as would negotiating on the details in "the package."

When the waitress returned, Polly carried her drink to the bar, wanting to face something other than Coyote's empty chair. Why was she bothering with him? When she started this Watkins' quest, she had wanted to change her own life. Now she was about to change this stranger's. He had been born to a wheedling, conniving mother, who died young and left him to be raised by his stepfather or shunted from one relative to another, probably no schooling after high school, maybe a stint in the Army, knocking around, now a bitter, odd jobs handyman loser at the age of forty-plus. He meant nothing to her. Why expose Watkins' secrets? Cole Watkins had been a great man. To him she felt an attachment, not his son. Watkins' deceits, his arrogance, his personal failures, broken relationships, had nothing to do with her. If he could speak now, Polly might see his side. What she knew was that he had returned to this remote land to be near his unacknowledged son. He may have built the Lodge as a lodestar to draw him close. Bequeathing the Lodge to him had been a gesture of kindness and generosity, his silence might have been kind and wise too. She didn't know. She didn't have all the facts. Even if she did, what seemed like facts shifted meanings depending on how you looked at them. Like with Bob. She had known him intimately, planned to build a new life with him, until he faded to black and became a total shit. But had he really changed? Having run through two wives he never mentioned said he was who he'd always been. Eugenia had seen through him, but she was too discreet or too good a friend to say so.

A good friend who had changed. A friend of her heart, as her mother said, the person Polly knew the best in the world and who knew her best, but after Eugenia moved to New York, she withheld what was most important to her. Polly didn't know the basics: if she was content to do her job well, publish the occasional poem, have a distant, married lover. Was that enough? Was her relationship with the distant Mathias what she wanted? Had he deserted her when she became ill, or had she pushed him away too?

Polly left a few bills on the bar and slid from the stool.

• • •

In her motel room, she returned her driver's license to her wallet, then dropped onto the bed. She felt not the tiniest ping of satisfaction at having accomplished what she set out to do: find the Lodge and figure out why Watkins had returned here. Tomorrow she could leave without meeting his rude loser son and let him wonder what game she'd been playing.

A breeze ruffled the curtain at the window overlooking the lake behind the motel that she'd forgotten to close. She stood to peer at the boat ramp, the water, the forest beyond barely visible without the moon. Somewhere not far away to the northeast was Starlight Lodge. She tried to picture it as it must be, its sprawling form indistinguishable from the surrounding forest, but that image slid beneath the one from twelve years ago that first night, the Lodge's silhouette an angled black slab overlaid on the murky charcoal of the woods behind, its entryway a yellow rectangle casting a faint fan onto the grass, the dome above radiating what looked like glowing pollen into the night sky. That first moment she had experienced a kind of seeing deeper than seeing, a vision beyond what her eyes provided, a vision she felt with her entire body, something so beautiful it stilled her then, even as it excited her. Cole Watkin had created this wondrous apparition. What remained was the deteriorating shell. Starlight Lodge was Cole Watkins' last work of art, personal, grandly beautiful, forsaken.

This could be the subject of a film. A swooping aerial camera could glide over the dense forest before reaching the wide open space of the meadow, then zoom in on the Lodge's entrance boarded up with plywood as it was today, that image dissolving into the interior as it had been, footage Mitch had in his vault. An electric charge sizzled throughout her.

The bedside clock read 9:37, not too late to call Wingspan. Mitch picked up on the third ring.

"You said if I found something interesting, I should let you know. I did." His chair squeaked. "I found Watkins' Lodge, I met the man who inherited it, and he's Watkins' unacknowledged son."

"Okay, so that's interesting. I'm on my way out the door, an hour later than I promised the wife. Call me tomorrow, after lunch."

"Remember that Watkins called me Maureen before he fell. Maureen is this man's mother. I've got her letters. They prove the link. This guy, I don't think he knows he's Watkins's son."

"So, sell this to the gossip rags, but, sorry to tell you this, Pollyanna, they won't want dirt on a dead photographer, no matter how famous. Now if you were talking Dali or Picasso, you'd have a prize."

"Mitch, give me five minutes."

His chair squeaked again and he grunted.

"There's a film here, not a biopic, but a film on Watkins' last big project, Starlight Lodge. A short, fifteen to twenty-two minutes. The story would be the arc of ambition, from inception to decline—the last work of a 20th Century Chronicler. The footage you have from twelve years ago when it was beautiful, we'll need this, and I'll dig up the old permits and plans, find folks around here who either remember it going up or who took part in the construction, and new footage, as it is today, falling apart. And I'll get the talking heads." She could do this at the office, where she had all the research tools she'd need. "You said there's a big retrospective being planned out east."

"New York. Even if, no way a museum exhibition is going to front this kind of money."

"Mitch, the latest thing in museums is videos to accompany their big exhibitions. If this upcoming Watkins' show is big, they're going to want this. Tomorrow I'm going to show Watkins' son the papers I have. Did I mention that he's in a court fight with Watkins' other son?"

"The putz."

"I'll share these documents with Watkins' son *if* he gives me access to the Lodge and permission to make a film."

"And if he says no?"

"If he says no, no film. Before I talk to him, I want to know if you're on board. This is a good idea, Mitch."

"It's an *idea*, good, bad, I don't know, but if you get the son's cooperation, call me."

She fought a yelp of excitement. "Get ready to move on this, Mitch. I'm going to make this happen." She hung up, shaking.

16

September, 1974

SHE SLEPT FITFULLY, troubled by questions. Were building permits required up here? Issued by the township or the county? Did they need to be signed off by an architect or an engineer? The land—when had Watkins bought it and from whom? Transfer of title, probably of no interest. The construction? Local builders might know or the Lodge's neighbors. Searching through land titles to find out who owned what would take forever. Lu's information-central cousin might help. The rest she could handle from Chicago. She'd call the numbers she'd found in the phone book, one was a Watkins—an optometrist?—and the two Jenks. Making phone calls from her desk at EB would save her money, but she'd have to be careful. Any hint of divided loyalty and Vanessa would yank her job offer, and Polly needed the job. Even these extra nights in a motel were draining her bank account.

In the morning, bleary-eyed, she turned in her key and asked about Lu's cousin.

"Name's pronounced Bet," Lu jotted down her number, "but spelled Bette, but don't call her that." The county seat where all the permits and other legal documents were filed was in Phillips, about half an hour south on Route 13. Polly wouldn't have time for that today.

From the pay phone in the café in downtown Park Falls, she called Mitch who'd already phoned his contact at the museum. "First thing, Eastern time. Just putting out feelers. I talked them up. A film? Yes, they're interested. Very much interested. But they want a real proposal and budget by yesterday. I said we'd get them one by October 1."

He'd said we. She couldn't believe it. But three weeks didn't leave much time. She said, "Did you check your archive?"

"As it happens, I got all the footage we shot back then, all processed, much of it never looked at. So who's to say what it's worth? I own the rights to every foot of it after all this time. Turns out my lawyer wasn't useless."

"Then this is a go?"

"Depends on what you come up with and pronto, Pollyanna."

Beneath his usual hesitation to commit, she heard barely concealed excitement. Suddenly scared—what if she came up with nothing?—she glared at the waitress at the nearby water station who was eavesdropping on her conversation.

"I'll call you back in a few hours."

Returning to her table, she dawdled over her coffee. Mitch had taken stock and realized that if this worked out, he could salvage what he'd sunk into a lost cause, and he would best Shelley who had fumbled the job Mitch had brought in. She watched customers at the counter banter with the waitresses, not letting herself think about what would happen with Coyote, and waited for the library to open.

June was glad her map had led Polly to the Lodge—"what's going on out there?"—and happy to make photocopies of her documents.

• • •

At The Woodcutters the same red pickup Polly had seen at the Lodge was parked by the side. She drove past it, pulled in front by the entrance trolls, turned off the engine, and listened to the T-Bird's engine ping as it cooled, waiting for her jittery tangle of dread and excitement to quiet. A loaded logging truck rumbled past and slowed to make the turn at the T. She tucked the envelope stuffed with the photocopies into her bag and climbed out.

Inside, the long window behind the bar was as bright as a movie screen, its reflection on the recently-mopped floor glistening between the islands of tables stacked with chairs. From the back came the sound of dishes rattling. It stopped and Coyote appeared wearing the same clothes as last night and his unshaven face looked spongy. Either he'd drunk all night or he hadn't slept any better than she.

"You came," he said.

"I said I would."

After righting a couple of chairs, he motioned for her to sit.

"You're saying that Cole Watkins was my father, and you've got the papers to prove it?"

"That's right."

She opened her bag. He scraped back his chair and walked away. Was this already over? She watched him disappear down the back hall that led to the kitchen, willing her ears to tune in to what was going on in the kitchen, inside his head. No matter what Mitch had, without Coyote, this was over. She counted the seconds, her hope draining away.

He reappeared with two mugs of coffee.

"Show me what you've got."

Trying not to tremble, she placed the envelope on the table, keeping her hand on top. "I want something from you."

He made a face. "Now we're getting to the point. Now you hear me, lady, I've got no money. I can't afford to keep the place up, can't pay the taxes, can't pay my lawyer, my debts are piling up, and I can't fucking sell it because—"

"What I have here will make your legal problems go away. They prove why Watkins left the Lodge to you."

"Right." He rocked his chair onto its back legs, his eyes narrowing. "And what's in it for you?"

"What I want is your cooperation to make a documentary film about Starlight Lodge." She told him what she'd told Mitch: Starlight Lodge as Cole Watkins' last great project, how it represented a vision, not a simply a dwelling. From Coyote she needed permission to film the Lodge as it was today, inside and out.

He slid his coffee mug in circles on the table top. "One, why would I agree to this? Two, who the fuck would want to see this movie? Three, who the fuck will pay for this?"

"As for paying for it, my partner, Mitch Klein…" Partner? She inhaled dry ice. "Wingspan Productions has already approached some museum people who are interested in a movie to accompany a big exhibition on Mr. Watkins' photographs. The money will follow from granting agencies and rich people who fund the arts."

"I get it. There's money to be made?"

"*Nobody* will make any money on this, including me. The money will cover the expenses of making the film." She slid the envelope toward him.

"You giving this to me?"

"They're copies of the originals."

He carried the envelope to the bar and spilled out the photocopies.

Had she just proven how naïve she was by giving him everything she had? Should she have given only one thing, maybe his mother's obit? But photocopies wouldn't be sufficient for his legal purposes. Too nervous to watch him delve into what she'd given him, she walked to the back door.

At the edge of the clearing, the bench where they'd sat last night was spattered with sunlight. Unwilling to let herself think about what might come next if he did agree, she thought about him reading his mother's wheedling letters and probably making a timeline about what he remembered against what was revealed. Everything he understood was being upended, and she'd delivered the blow. Why would he let her make a film about the man who wouldn't acknowledge him as his son? Or let her, the bearer of this news, anywhere near the Lodge? Maybe he would think that Watkins' releasing these papers to her was a sign that he wanted this secret to be revealed. Coyote might even think that had Watkins not died suddenly, he would have reached out to him. If considered from a certain angle, maybe. But Coyote would never know the answers to any of the questions raised by the papers he was looking at. Death left behind a blighted field stubbled with facts that scavengers could pick over to construct any interpretation they might want.

Why had Eugenia kept her secrets from Polly? Was her pulling away a condition of her fighting cancer, or had her withdrawal begun even before she became ill, when she moved to New York? Not introducing Polly to Mathias had that signaled a change in their connection Polly hadn't recognized? Not probing, skimming along on the surface, wrapped up in her own life, Polly had assumed their friendship was as it always had been, deep and solid. She must have missed the signs that things had changed. Eugenia had slipped away without giving any notice that she was going. Had she lived, would the gap between them have widened or shrunk? Polly missed Eugenia. Polly wanted to ask her questions. She wanted answers. Above, a squirrel leapt across an expanse of sky, landed on another tree's swaying branch, scrambled down, and disappeared into the brush. No matter what those answers were, she wanted to apologize.

A pine cone dropped nearby.

Mathias, the man Eugenia loved, might not know she was dead. What he had was silence, no explanation. The letters he had sent, disguised in embassy envelopes, would have been read by Eugenia's parents, but Polly couldn't imagine them writing to him, not to Eugenia's secret and foreign lover. Not the Pappases, not their unmarried daughter. A colleague at the UN would have told him, but Eugenia had said their affair was secret. Her silence had to consume him now. Why silence? The question Polly had. The question that Coyote had. Soon, in the week ahead, no matter how pressed she was, Polly would find a way to contact Mathias. He needed to understand that Eugenia's silence wasn't rejection, but a tragedy.

She lifted her face to the warmth. The sun was in a different position, almost directly overhead. She tugged at the bar's back door and went inside, her eyes taking a few seconds to adjust to the dark. Coyote had returned to the table, the envelope lay squarely in front of him. How long had he been waiting for her? She sat.

"No way am I going to have this shit in a movie." He shoved the envelope toward her.

"It will be exclusively about Starlight Lodge. It will not mention your mother. It will not touch on Watkins' personal life, except to say he returned to Wisconsin where he was born. The originals of what's in that envelope will end your legal problems. Ask your lawyer. The place will be yours. Sell it all, sell off some parcels to pay the taxes."

He glared at her.

She went on. "I told you this film will be about Cole Watkins' last project, that alone."

"Why should I trust you?"

"I can give you right of refusal on the script. You can be present while we shoot. Would that do it?" Mitch wouldn't like this.

"What's to stop you from changing up, after you finish up here?"

"I won't. I will give you the originals of your mother's letters after you open the Lodge to the film crew, the day we begin shooting." Mitch might walk away when he found out what she'd negotiated without him. Given away the store, that's how he would put it. "The film will be about Starlight Lodge as it represents your...as it tells the story of Mr. Watkins' creativity at the end of his life. I have a basic framework, but the story will grow from what I discover in my research, from whatever paperwork exists, and from talking to people who knew him. Is Mrs. Borus still around?"

"Borus is dead." He patted his shirt pocket, found it empty, pushed away from the table, strode to the cigarette machine, slammed its side, and retrieved the dropped packet. "Cancer took her. She'd moved to the Cities."

He lit a cigarette, not offering her one, and sat, inhaling deeply and slowly exhaling two long plumes.

"I get the call, November 3, '71. A lawyer saying I'm named in Watkins' will. I should come to his office to discuss. Not a local, his office is in Eau Claire. I tried to get hold of Borus, that's when I find out she's dead." He stared at the envelope as he explained he had been caretaking the place when Watkins was alive, then let go when he died. Someone else took care, then three years ago, he was brought back by Bud Wagner, who managed property for out-of-towners. The place had gone to hell. When he went to see the lawyer in Eau Claire, the guy had nothing to say about why Coyote was in the will, or why he hadn't found out sooner. Hadn't the will been read out years ago? It had, but it was tied up, no explanation. After that visit with the lawyer in Eau Claire, he got challenging letters from New York saying the will was illegitimate. Made sense, but none of it made sense. What was he supposed to do? Surveyors came snooping around, the taxes were piling up, he had to hire a lawyer, Bud Wagner's brother, but now he couldn't pay him, much less pay the taxes. Why him? That's what had crazed him. Why did the old geezer who'd never said a word leave him the place? Had to be a mistake. He stubbed out his cigarette, then tapped the envelope. "This is going to cost me what?"

Beyond his whole life unraveling? But he meant money. "Nothing. It will cost you some time. How much time will depend, but the shooting will have to be completed in the next few months. I'll want free access."

"And you give me the original letters?"

"Like I said, on the first day of shooting, I hand over the originals. This needs to be clear—no money will change hands. I give you Maureen's letters, you give me and Wingspan shooting rights, complete access to the property, inside and out, and your agreement and cooperation with this project, and your agreement not to sell any of it before we finish shooting. My partner will send you a contract." Again, partner. "Your lawyer—"

"I've had it with fucking lawyers. Write what you said on this." He tapped the envelope. "Originals of the letters, and no copies elsewhere. Sign and date."

Hiding her disbelief, she reached in her bag for a pen, swallowing her excitement. She'd written dozens of contracts for EB, buying or commissioning pictures, she knew the lingo and the order of logic, but as she spelled out what she'd told Coyote, her words felt momentous and life-altering. She wrote slowly, careful not to leave out anything, block-printing "producer" under the line on which she signed her name. Mitch would not fob her off with a credit at the end—no "Special Thanks To."

Her signature was a spiky jumble, nothing like her exuberant childish autograph on the scrap from the old logbook in her bag in the trunk of Janine's car. She spun the envelope to Coyote and passed him the pen. He read what she'd written slowly, as if reading was difficult, then scrawled his name below.

"That's it then," he said, handing back her pen. He pushed away from the table carrying the envelope to the bar and placed it underneath where she couldn't see.

She had to get a photocopy of the contract on that envelope before she left for home, but first, she wanted to make sure he would make good on what he'd promised.

"Can we go to the Lodge now?"

"Nope. Bar opens in twenty." He walked away to the far end of the bar and flipped up the hinged section.

"I need to get on the road soon."

He rolled out an aluminum keg. "I work the afternoon shift today. Randy comes in at five. Be here then, I'll take you."

"I can't wait that long. I have to be in Chicago." In Vanessa's office at 9 AM, ready to hold her own. He ignored her continuing to roll the keg toward the back door. She felt pinned to the wall, the floor dropping away, like on a sickening carnival ride. "Okay. I'll be here at five."

A quick look inside the Lodge, then she'd drive through the night, maybe grab an hour of sleep before she had to dress, get to the office, ready to put on a good show as pliant and worthy of Vanessa's confidence and eager to serve.

Coyote wedged open the door with his foot and wiped his forehead with his sleeve. "I got some stuff you might could use—blueprints, receipts, pictures someone took of the construction. Found them in the shed." He waved and disappeared as the delivery truck bleated into reverse.

Had he just offered her a treasure trove? She stared at the long window behind the bar, the tree trunks in the clearing, the dense forest beyond, the floor no steadier than it had been a moment ago. Then she was outside standing between the trolls. Amazement shimmered through her, imagining what Coyote might have found, maybe evidence of the Lodge's genesis. This was beyond anything she could have hoped for. She needed to think and she needed to call Mitch. Not from the pay phone inside, not from the too public one in the café with the noisy waitress. Her room at the motel. She climbed into the T-Bird, turned on the ignition, and pulled a U-turn.

How would this work? She would have to travel from home to here and from home to St. Paul to review Mitch's old footage. Then there would be scripting, and later editing. The only way was weekends. She couldn't let Vanessa know about this. How would she manage without a car? She had kept Janine's way too long, and she couldn't afford to rent one or buy one. That would come later, when her new job began. Bus or train were the options, but she'd arrive late on Saturday and have to leave by mid-day Sunday to be at work on Monday, which would give her too little time. And how would she sift through documents in the County's files on that schedule? She couldn't. With limits on her time, Mitch might try to wrestle this away from her. No. Coyote trusted, if that was the word, her, and he didn't know Mitch. Watkins' original papers were her insurance policy. She wouldn't even let Mitch see them until this was underway. She was rushing ahead. First, she had to persuade him.

In front of her a shadow exploded from the woods. She swerved, her body thrown sideways, the car skidded, tires squealing, her hands welded to the steering wheel, around and around spinning, then slowing into a careen, bumping over the asphalt's edge and jamming to stop. A high-pitched whine rose and quit. She wrenched her hands from the steering wheel, then pounded it with her fists. She could have killed something. She could have totaled Janine's car. She could have killed herself. She shoved open the door, climbed out, legs buckling, caught the handle, straightened cautiously, and turned to see the car's rear end hanging over a weedy trench alongside the road. Twenty feet beyond the skid marks, a deer stood still, head turned toward Polly, then ambled across the road. Another deer appeared on the woods opposite and leapt across. Thrumming with adrenaline, she kept her hand on the car's roof and worked her way toward the rear. The right back wheel hung over empty space.

She inched back to the driver's side door, climbed in, and pressed her forehead against her knuckles on the steering wheel. Stupid, speeding, unknown road, thoughts elsewhere—she was lucky. She wasn't hurt, no mangled animal, no damage to Janine's car. When her jitters subsided and the gas fumes thinned, she drove slowly to the motel.

● ● ●

The door to the room she had vacated a few hours ago was open. Inside the bed was torn apart, sheets on the floor next to used towels, faucet drip in the bathroom, smoke drifting up from a cigarette in the ashtray by the phone.

"Lu." Her voice was too loud.

Lu peeked around the bathroom door.

"Can I rent the room again for a few hours? I need to make some phone calls." Her voice sounded echo-y and artificial.

"I'm not through." Lu flung her rag into a bucket. "I'm going to have to charge you a full day's rate plus any long distance calls." She left with the vacuum cleaner.

Polly watched her cigarette burn, waiting for her to return. The clock ticked and her shaking quieted. She turned to look at the parking lot, empty except for Janine's car, and the woods across the way, and saw nothing frightening. She shut the door, stubbed out the cigarette, and sat on the unmade bed. She could have died.

Her head ached with thinking. After a time, she pulled the telephone close. "Mitch, Watkins' son is in. He agreed. He'll give us full access. We signed a contract."

"Who 'we'? You signed a contract? What the hell?"

After what she'd just been through, his tone was offensive, but she spoke calmly. "Listen, Mitch, this is going to happen. This is how." She shut her eyes to the room's disarray. "No fees, no money either way, full access and rights of reproduction. Coyote's payment will be the original letters from Maureen, which I am hanging on to for now. He'll need the originals to prove his right to his inheritance. He says he's got papers he's willing to share, and maybe some photos. That's what I've done. Now you do your part. If the Watkins' exhibition is as big as you say, they are going to want this. If not, we can sell this film to Pegasus Inc. or Critical Mass, both produce art and biographical videos."

"How do you know them?"

"And I can bring in a backer with front money—"

"Oh, so you got a backer now?"

"Old friend with money who'd love to get a credit." Maybe Vaughn would come through. "This is for later. Financing is your business, I know that. You're the expert."

"Got that right, Pollyanna. I am not going to take one more step until I see this so-called contract of yours."

"If you have a fax machine, you'll have it by the end of tomorrow." Getting a copy made—she had known she had to, but she hadn't factored the time in.

He gave her his fax number.

"The guy's going to take me to the Lodge before I leave for home. I'll see what's there, then dig into research once I'm home. This weekend I'll write a draft proposal to give you something to work with. Soon, we'll review your old footage together." She paused for him to interrupt with objections, but he only breathed heavily. "But you'll write the treatment, you'll run the show."

"Got that right, Pollyanna. First, I got to see what you—not me—signed on for, but if it's what you say, I'm inclined to say maybe."

Maybe was Mitch's *yes*. Incredulity corkscrewed through her. The museum must have been enthusiastic. She kept her voice steady. "And you'll pay me the fee or the percentage you paid your Santa Fe producer?"

He snorted. "*If* we sign. I got one question, there's a hell of a lot of work to be done quickly, front end. What about your job?"

"I can handle it and do my job. I know how to get things done."

His chair creaked, then he cleared his throat. "If you put your shoulder into this, what the hell have I got to lose?"

She smelt gas and burnt rubber. "Mitch, you have nothing to lose."

"Listen, Pollyanna. I got a call on the other line. Fax me the contract and we'll talk after that."

She listened to the severed line. Exhausted, she pushed up from the unmade bed and walked to the back window. The lake she'd seen only at night winked sunlight from ripples in the middle. Near the boat ramp, a boy in white overalls, shoulder length blond hair, scraped the hull of an overturned dinghy. On a tree stump, a portable radio played barely audible rock music. Urban music, not Detroit, not California, probably British. Where it came from probably didn't matter to him. It came from the radio. He might spend his life around here, like Coyote, with no interest in what went on anywhere else, content to grow up, get a job, a woman, a family, Saturday night at The Woodcutters, fish, hunt, grow old, die, a stone recording his birth and death dates. Who was to say that being content with what came easily wasn't the best way to live?

She lay on the bed, listening to the faucet drip and the kid's faint scraping, metal on wood, that almost sounded like her own heart. She jerked awake to a knock and the door opening.

"Thought you might could use some towels," Lu said. Seeing Polly stretched out on the bed, she muttered an apology and dropped the towels next to the TV before gathering the sheets and damp towels.

When she was gone, Polly chain-locked the door, and looked around the dismal room. The numbers on the bedside clock clicked, another minute gone. She had caught Mitch at the right moment. Going forward, she would have to fight for every inch of involvement with this film, and when it was over, where would she be? Where she was before she'd gotten Watkins' papers. She would have a job at EB, make more money, buy a car, and become someone like Janine, she'd work the ropes, do her job, curry favor, the boss's desires would be her desires, and in a few years, if she was lucky, she'd become a Vanessa. Polly had been ambitious once. Each time she landed a job at a film production office, she had expected her eagerness, energy, and smarts to lead her into actual production, but she had been stuck as the cute, nice-to-have-around office girl. Sure, things were stacked against women, but she could have pushed harder. Some women got ahead. She'd remained a good girl, playing by good girl rules. She had been timid. Leaving the field when her mother needed her had been a perfect excuse to quit trying. Returning to her own life, she hadn't even tried, grabbing the job at EB, grateful to find something safe and secure. Bob, too, was her safe, secure bet. She had accomplished nothing that mattered to her. The scraping of the dingy had stopped. The faucet had quit dripping. She had settled, just like Claire, just like most of her friends, but not Eugenia, she had at least published some poems, not enough, but she hadn't settled. Polly had. Settling was easy, accepting what was, what is, what will be. She turned over her hands and stared at her palms. This moment, this flexing of her fingers, she might not have had if she had hit something on the road. She was still alive.

She pulled the phone close to dial Mitch's number.

"Jeesus, Pollyanna, what's it been, a couple hours? What's up?"

"You said what did you have to lose. I'll tell you what you have to gain *after* this project is me, my skills, my ideas, my contacts. I can expand your business in ways you can't even imagine. In the past couple of years at EB, I've gotten an insider's view of a developing field, which is high end A-V materials in the humanities for colleges and universities. Not archival material for their library collections, that's old, but for A-V for classroom instruction: film strips, boxed slide sets, often with audio tapes, and documentary films. Think of how many colleges and universities there are in this country. Not your market, right? Don't you want a piece of that?"

He made a sound of unwilling acknowledgment. She stared at his fax number. "What you have to lose, Mitch, is losing out on this expanding and vast market. Now's the time, not later. What you need is someone who can generate the right ideas. You've saturated the natural sciences for kids' market for what, fifteen, twenty years? New salamanders will have to evolve if you're to grow your business there. What you need is an idea machine for the college market. That's me. I know who's acquiring, I know the market, and I've got ideas, dozens of ideas. American roadhouses, a phenomenon of American culture that I've witnessed up here, not been documented anywhere for Sociology, Cultural Anthropology, Contemporary American culture. We call it "Drink Your Way Across the USA." Mitch barked a laugh. "And how about 'Designing Death,' the history of cemeteries with monuments produced by famous artists and weirdos. Did you know Lincoln—"

"If this is leading to you working for me, I don't have a job for you, sweetheart, or anyone else."

"I meant to tell you, in the Park Falls Library, I saw an announcement for "What's My Secret?" to be shown at the high school here."

"That series is a cash cow. I…" He stopped, remembering, she guessed, her insistence that the idea came from her.

"I took it as an auspicious sign. You and I will go places, Mitch."

"I'm stretched to the wire as it is."

"Your business has been on a deathwatch since I've known you. But I've seen your setup. That camera Sony loaned you, they don't loan cutting-edge equipment to outfits on the ropes. You had a Santa Fe producer. No longer. I'll be your Chicago producer."

"Sweetheart, you don't know the first thing about film."

"You won't be able to say that to me in three months, after we get this Starlight Lodge project off the ground."

"You get me the contract first. Later, we'll see."

We'll see wasn't *no*. "You will see, I'm sure," but she wasn't sure.

He hung up.

She'd brought him a gold-plated opportunity, but even if Starlight Lodge went well, he might not take her on. If he didn't, she would figure out what to do next, but what it wouldn't be was working for Vanessa. She put Janine's car keys on the table next to the phone and dialed her number.

"Polly, where are you? I thought you were coming in today."

"I'm still in Wisconsin."

"Still in Wisconsin? Have you gone off the rails?"

"I'll be in tomorrow. Vanessa and I have an appointment to talk about the details of the post-Plan B job that's she's offered to me."

Silence.

"As her personal assistant, that's the job. I'm not going to take it."

"*You?* She offered *you* the job?"

Janine's contempt stunned her. "She'll offer the job to you when I pull out."

"I can't believe you didn't tell me that this was going on."

"You knew Vanessa was—"

"You didn't tell me. This didn't come out of the blue. Vanessa had to have talked to you, over weeks, if not months. Am I right? I am right. I know I am. You could have…I can't believe you did this to me."

"She'll give the job to you. You are the most experienced and the best choice. Better than me."

"That's true."

Her contempt stung. "She'll choose you. Hank's a waste."

"Hank turned in his notice a couple of days ago. He'll be gone by Friday, tomorrow. But how would you know? You haven't been here."

"I'm telling you now that I'm not taking the job. I haven't told Vanessa yet. If she doesn't say box up your personal things and get out, I hope to work until I'm laid off. Hank's leaving means that my chance of not getting fired just improved. I need this job for the next few months. After that, I'm going to try something else."

"What something else?"

"Filmmaking." She had stepped off a cliff and couldn't tell if she was falling or flying.

"Have you gone crazy?"

"I'm working on a film about Watkins, with Mitch, that I hope will be an opening. I don't want to end up in ten years wishing—"

"You don't want to end up like me?"

"That's not what—"

"Mitch, the sad old man whose phone calls you didn't return? You're throwing your lot in with him? When are you going to return my car?"

"Janine, I'm sorry."

"I taught you everything, and Vanessa turns around and offers *you* the job. I cannot believe…"

"I'll return your car late tonight. I'll phone from the road to let you know when."

"Don't bother. Park it where you picked it up."

"I'm sorry."

"I'm sorry. I thought you were my friend."

17

September, 1974

AT FIVE O'CLOCK SHE PULLED UP AT THE WOODCUTTERS and found Coyote slouched against his pickup looking more haggard than when she had left him five hours ago. She, too, felt as if she'd lived years since then. Before she could shift into park, he twirled his hand—follow me—opened the door to his truck, climbed in, and peeled out, skittering gravel. She floored Janine's car wishing he would slow down as he swerved south on a narrower, twisting road, the forest on both sides churning with wind and pressing close. She was afraid of losing him, afraid of what might leap out, afraid of going so fast, losing control. Rounding a bend, she saw him brake sharply and turn left into the woods. She slowed, bumped from asphalt to rutted track, hearing his muffler ahead, but unable to see him through the murky blur of wind-tossed branches and brush. Following the twisting, pot-holed path, she burst into the meadow. Under the gray sky, the Lodge looked not just decrepit, but forlorn, as if its faded gray-black wings were cowering around its core covered with flapping blue plastic.

Was the inside as grim as the outside? What if there was nothing here worth making a film of? What if all signs of Watkins were gone? Her hope to make an interesting and important film would dissolve, and with it her plan to jumpstart her own creative life.

Coyote's pickup was parked by the courtyard that separated the library and kitchen wings. She pulled alongside. He wasn't in sight. She climbed out, the wind roaring, and closed the car door gently, anxious, now that she was here, that she might inadvertently upset some part of their agreement that hadn't been spelled out.

That first night twelve years ago, light from the kitchen window had glossed the cobblestones, but she hadn't known it was the kitchen window, hadn't paused to see the Kino crew inside, being intent on following Ernie to the back door. Then it was intensely blue, now grunge-beige, its bottom stained algae-green, and the cobblestones were choked with weeds. Inside the facing windows of kitchen and library hung washed-out flowered bedsheets. At the library window, she touched the glass, remembering Watkins in his saggy sweater and pajamas, the fire, her first taste of bourbon, and how she had felt—seen, discovered, understood.

"Storm's coming."

She leapt back.

Coyote stood behind her, studying the scuttling clouds.

Up close, he looked worse than haggard. The flesh of his face had loosened from the bones, as if it, and he, had become unmoored. He took a long drag on his cigarette and she listened to the plastic sheeting snap in the wind.

"That window," he lifted a shoulder toward the kitchen. "Borus'd lean out, tell me what to do. When I checked back, she'd offer me a beer, cup of coffee, pie. Made a fine pie. Never once did I see the old man. His bedroom has two windows, the wing opposite where we're standing. Can't see it from here. Whenever I was back there clearing brush—you don't cut back the woods a couple three times a season, it'll take over—I thought I was being surveilled. Never did the blinds move, not that I saw. Back there, out of sight. Never saw him." He dropped his cigarette and ground it into the cobblestones. "Was he an asshole or a coward?"

Both, she guessed. Coyote had agreed to their filming so he could to get his hands on papers that made sense of Watkins' will and would get him out of his debts and legal limbos, but he must want to learn about the eminence who had refused to acknowledge him as his son. Maybe he wanted to watch the film being made. Maybe he wanted to be part of something that wasn't bartending or odd jobs. Maybe in the weeks ahead, he would regret that he had agreed.

He glanced at the back door. "Go inside? The electricity's off but I've hooked up a generator. Got to get tools from the truck."

She watched him walk away, slowly, as if his body hurt, as if he were almost too weary to take another step, but when he reached his pickup and unlatched the back panel, he leapt up, his expression, not that of a hired hand but of a man full of authority. Maybe because of what he'd learned, what she'd revealed. Finding out why he'd been given the Lodge had given him what he needed, even if it had pummeled him.

With his tool box, he lumbered past her to unlock the back door. "Careful where you step. It'll take me a couple minutes to get the lights on." He disappeared inside.

She stepped over the threshold. The door blew shut behind her, leaving her in a dark underwater cave with a cone of faint aqueous blue filtering through the tarp-covered skylight and falling on the floor that seemed to undulate. Disoriented, she shuffled toward the spiral staircase until her shoe nudged the bottom riser, then grabbed the bannister, and inhaled air thick with dust and abandonment. Nothing was left of what she remembered. Beneath the stairs where Kino had stacked its equipment were lengths of galvanized pipe and rumpled packing paper, and across the way, a sawhorse blocked the Lodge's entryway. On all sides the doors were closed: entrance, studio, store room, darkroom, kitchen, back door, the library. Too many times she had relived what had happened here: the ordinary interactions with the crew, hauling the equipment in and out, boxing it up, her fearful, bumbling eagerness, the men's harsh laughter, the dramatis personae entering and exiting, Mongo, the sons, Watkins himself, Mitch that last day, and she had spun other outcomes, vengeful, fantastic, triumphant, some simply not shaming. No trace of all that busyness, all that life remained here or in her. She waited for something to happen. Overhead the tarp ruffled.

She walked to the library and opened the double doors. Streaky light drifted through the bedsheet stretched across the one window. The ceiling-to-floor bookshelves were empty, the fireplace sealed with plywood, no furniture, except for the long table that once had held books and photographs, now shrouded with a canvas drop cloth. She picked up a corner hoping to glimpse something of Watkins', a scrap of paper with his scrawl, a darkroom test strip used as a bookmark, a lost button, nothing but the smell of something musty and stinging.

Do you drink bourbon?

A sensation like a knifepoint skimmed along her spine. She

dropped the cloth and straightened to shake off the feeling and survey the shadowy room. A vaulted ceiling, empty bookshelves, a boarded-up fireplace, dust and mouse droppings, nothing echoed of what she remembered. The questions she'd had then—What do you see in me? Am I worthy? Will you guide me into a glorified realm?—no longer meant anything. She had become who she was. She had lost more times than she had succeeded, but she had figured out how things worked, how to solve problems, and how to make do. She knew nothing about the mechanics of film, but she did know how to get things done. From what she would find in the Lodge and among Coyote's papers, she would form questions that would drive the film. They would center on how Watkins' creativity intersected with the practical demands of building a home and workspace in this unforgiving, northern environment. Was there a correlation between how he represented the world in his photographs and how he designed the Lodge? His ways of working with natural light, his unique sense of what to include and what to exclude in a picture, were these evident in the choices he made in the Lodge? Underlying these questions and others she would formulate as she dug in would be: had he sought to embed the ineffable here, in his last home?

She paused in the doorway to the atrium to look back over her shoulder at the empty library, feeling freed, not disappointed, but aware of her body, herself, alive and surging with life. The throbbing of her heart struck her, and her lungs' slow pulse, and deep within, excitement bubbling, like champagne.

She turned to see Coyote pass through the currents of blue light, and vanish into the kitchen. She closed the library doors behind her, impressed by the quiet of the latch's click. Well-designed, well-built, Watkins' work, but Coyote had taken care.

It was almost six o'clock. She needed to see the papers he had discovered and the entire interior before she left, and she had to leave soon. In front of her on the floor, she noticed a trail from Coyote's boots prints that revealed the shining white marble below the grime. Wishing she had her camera, wanting to make a note, she dug into her bag just as crackling exploded. Light flooded the room from a constellation of now lit, bare bulbs strung below the skylight exposing water stains on the dome and a gaping hole where a sconce had been torn out. The plywood over the entrance, the litter, the debris in what she remembered as a glowing, chapel-like antechamber came as a shock, and yet she felt a rush of possibilities. This was the start. The film she would make would come from this reality. From what she experienced now, and what was to come next, she would make what she could, but whatever happened, if the film came together or not, this moment was her beginning.

Coyote emerged from the storage room below the staircase. "I got what I found here. Want to take a look?"

"And I need a copy of our contract. There's a lot to be done, and quickly."

About the Author

Lynn Sloan is a writer and photographer. She is the author of the story collection *This Far Isn't Far Enough* and the novel *Principles of Navigation*, which was chosen for *Chicago Book Review*'s Best Books of 2015. *Fortune Cookies*, an art book featuring her flash fiction, was produced by Sky Lark Press in 2022. Her short fiction has appeared in *Ploughshares, Shenandoah, American Literary Fiction*, and included in NPR's *Selected Shorts*. She graduated from Northwestern University, earned a master's degree in photography at The Institute of Design, formerly the New Bauhaus, and exhibited her work nationally and internationally. For many years she taught photography in the MFA program of Columbia College Chicago, where she founded *Occasional Readings in Photography* and contributed to *Afterimage, Art Week*, and *Exposure* before turning to fiction writing. She lives near Chicago and serves on the Board of Directors of the Society of Midland Authors.